THE SEA RAVEN

A Novel

by
Laine Stambaugh

Book III: The Heart Stone Trilogy

Other books in *The Heart Stone Trilogy:*

Raven Wakes the Dawn (Book I), 2023
Raven in the Runes (Book II), 2023
The Sea Raven (Book III), 2025

THE SEA RAVEN is a work of fiction. Names, characters, places, and incidents are either products of the author's imagination or are used fictitiously. Any resemblance to actual persons living or dead, events or locales is purely coincidental.

Copyright 2025 by Joan Elaine Stambaugh
All rights reserved.

No part of this book may be reproduced, or stored in a retrieval system or transmitted in any form or by any means, electronic mechanical, photocopying, recording, or otherwise, without express written permission from the author.

Write: lainestambaugh@gmail.com

Published by Ingram Spark
1 Ingram Blvd.
La Vergne, TN 37086

ISBN: 979-8-9878612-4-0
ISBN E-Book: 979-8-9878612-5-7

Cover design by: Daria Selezneva @ ustya978978
Interior design by: Nadine (PurpleHug.com)

Printed in the United States of America

From over the hills and in the glen,
On the rim of the sparkling sea,
Deep within the darkness
Magic protects thee.

Prologue

To My Daughters,

    As I, Saraid of Clan Macafie of the Western Isles, sit here in this dank prison cell, I await my fate. Eight months have passed since my false guilty sentence. My husband, Murchadh of Clan Maccoinneach, abandoned me while he awaits a live heir to his fortune. I will shortly give birth to twin girls, whom I will name Marsaili and Davina. These girls will grow into independent, strong women, and though they will be raised in separate locations, they will make a team that is difficult to vanquish when the time comes. I won't go into details, but my dear daughters, know in your heart I am no witch, but a seer into the future. Since I will have passed on to the Otherworld in a few short days, these are my thoughts and instructions for my female descendants in the clan bloodline. Marsaili will marry into Clan MacAoidh.

Although not raised a Druid, I had the honor of studying with a high priestess on the Isle of Skye the summer after my thirteenth winter. The experience forever changed me, and provided the understanding for what the Goddess had planned for me. I developed a deep respect for Druid knowledge and wisdom. The Goddess has decreed that the time is at hand to share the Druid legacy with the world. Following is how we shall accomplish that. She calls this "The Goddess Prophecy."

Each first-born daughter in our bloodline will receive a charge from the Goddess at the appropriate time, typically around the time of marriage. This charge must be completed within a given time frame. The accomplishment of every task brings us one step closer to fulfilling The Prophecy, so remember, if called to serve, your timely participation is critical. If you choose not to complete your task, The Prophecy will end in sorrow for all who follow.

A designated descendant will be appointed as "Keeper of the Wisdom" to collect and protect materials that have been gathered from the beginning of the project to the present day, so it may be accessible to later participants, if necessary. The Goddess has asked that my first-born, Marsaili, now of

Clan MacAoidh, serve as the initial Keeper of Wisdom. She will name a successor at the appropriate time.

My time on this green earth is limited, therefore, I must work quickly. I, Saraid, was given the first "charge" – to prepare a foundation that will guide you for what is to come. My charge is now complete with the creation of the accompanying document. For those of you "chosen" to participate, it will be your obligation to pass along these guidelines to your first-born daughter, so that she may expect to serve the Goddess.

The second charge, restoring *The Book of Delsiran*, was created for females only. The purpose for using Delsiran was to provide security and safety for those participating in this project who may experience closer observation than others. Delsiran is meant for women to communicate more freely, and to preserve and protect the work we are doing. It does not mean to imply subterfuge or to practice revenge. We may not yet live in a society that allows women the freedom to make their own choices in things such as marriage and bearing children, let alone access to education. But that can be the goal we work toward for future generations.

Be it known: If the above restoration project is not completed within twelve months, what currently exists will vanish into dust. In that case, we must start the whole process over again.

The Goddess of the Moon indicated her hope that this project would result in significant improvements to the plight of women throughout Alba and beyond. Documenting the Druid legacy using Delsiran should be considered a unique opportunity to provide accessible educational opportunities for women. The benefits of educating women will provide a safe place to bring together the females of this world, instilling in each other the will and determination to accomplish whatever we may aspire to do for ourselves and our families.

Guard this document carefully from those who would try to oppose or corrupt this most positive of prophecies. In other words, anyone judged cruel or vindictive would not be allowed into this inner world of women.

Wisdom comes from knowledge. How we gain that knowledge is up to us.

(signed)
Saraid of Clan Macafie
27th of October, 1086 AD

Chapter 1

1171 AD, Late March
Orkney Islands

It didn't require a seer to predict this would be a bad day.

Vor's elder sister, Aila, who was normally her mother's calm, logical daughter, rarely caused trouble. So when Aila burst into Vor's bedchamber, sank onto a chair and cradled her face in her hands, on the verge of a fresh wave of tears, Vor turned from her spot at the window.

"What am I going to do?" Aila wailed.

Through her bedchamber window, Vor had been admiring the gorgeous spring day and the sparkling jewel that was the Atlantic Ocean. She never tired of the sea birds that soared in the sky and followed her on shore, demanding crumbs whenever she made an appearance. Today was no different as she watched the yellow-headed gannets from a distance. They flew straight up to the top of the sandstone cliffs, then folded their wings and plunged head-first into the water, barely making a ripple. Such was their daily quest to find food for their chicks.

At Aila's abrupt entrance, Vor turned from the window and started to protest the lack of privacy when she noticed Aila's blotchy red face and swollen eyes. Vor rushed to her and held her by the shoulders.

"What's wrong? Did something happen?"

"I . . . I don't know what to do."

Vor knelt down in front of her and pulled her hands from her face. "About what? Which husband to choose?"

Aila's blue-green eyes grew huge. "About the ... charge I'm to fulfill. The Goddess Prophecy."

Vor had heard rumblings about a charge behind closed doors and had wondered if she might someday be given a charge from the Celtic Goddess of the Moon, but then she'd heard that only first-born daughters in the MacAoidh bloodline were allowed such opportunities, and her heart fell to know that she would never have one.

"What about the charge?" Vor pried.

Aila shook her head. "I can't tell you. I can't tell anyone. I've been sworn to secrecy because it's ..."

"It's what? Surely you can tell *me*, Aila." Vor squeezed her sister's hands. Although they hadn't been as close as they could have been as sisters—only two winters apart—as Vor got older, she found herself seeking advice from Aila more and more, too embarrassed to ask her mother.

Aila shook her head vehemently, refusing to look into Vor's eyes. "Mother would have my hide if I told you."

Vor sensed a crack in Aila's armor, so she pressed on. "Look, Aila, we've always been honest with each other. I would never do anything to betray your trust."

Aila paused, her mouth set in a pout and her thin reddish-blonde brows framing her pale face. "Alright," she said at last. "You've heard the story about Saraid and the twins, yes?"

Vor had never been told outright about them, but she'd heard enough to spark her interest. "I know that she was tried as a witch and hanged."

Aila bit her lip as if deciding whether to say more. Finally, she dipped her chin as if she'd come to a decision. "Well, before she died, she wrote a book—"

"A book?"

"*The Book of Delsiran.* The Druids used this book."

Vor gasped. It wasn't all that long ago that her mother, when a young girl, had followed Grandmother Marsaili everywhere, wanting to learn all her Druid healing and midwifery spells and potions. She'd even learned to wield a sword in self-defense. For thousands of years Druids had advised kings on war and spiritual matters, but when kings all over Europe embraced Christianity, they expected their loyal subjects to do the same. Druid power was stripped, and those who continued to worship the Goddess did well to take their activities inside or behind closed doors to avoid persecution. Druids faded into the woodwork similar to the Picts, integrating with the larger population.

Vor shook her head, certain her immediate family would never have continued such practices. "But I thought Saraid wasn't a Druid. Yet to own a book like that in Christian times would be considered at the very least ... controversial. What is the book about?"

"It's a grammar book that contains ... hidden messages. Women chosen by the MacAoidh bloodline teach other women and girls to read and write, which empowers them to gain knowledge that will someday lead to women gaining equal status alongside the men and allow them to speak up about what concerns them."

Vor plopped down on the bed, a whoosh of air filling her chest. Normally, only the elite were allowed to read and write. Vor had her own thoughts on the matter. She hadn't had much time to learn from her great-grandmother, Marsaili, but she saw herself in how her ancestor's mind worked.

"It's why she remained a Druid all her life," Vor said.

"Who remained a Druid all her life?" Aila asked.

Vor covered her mouth with her hand. "Oops. I shouldn't have said that out loud."

"Are you talking about Great-Grandmother Marsaili?"

"Mother says she was quite intimidating. And brilliant. And a perfect example of why the Christian priests didn't want a woman to be educated."

"What about the Druid priests?"

Vor poured herself a glass of water and checked outside her door before she continued. "I need to be more careful about what I say. I think the lesson learned is that the Druids were more progressive in sharing their knowledge with males *or* females. Whoever came to them."

Aila frowned. "What did they have to gain by sharing their knowledge?"

"Knowledge is power. Haven't you heard?" Vor emptied her water glass and poured another. "Since the beginning of Christianity, powerful men of the Church decided how the Church would function and who would be in charge. And it sure wasn't going to be women."

Aila sank into a chair and sighed. "That explains a lot. But can one book make that much of a difference?"

Vor glanced at her sister from over her shoulder, a sense of sadness enveloping her. "We may never know, if this book isn't allowed to circulate in the open. With it, our daughters and granddaughters could have amazing opportunities to learn. I hear the University of Paris, as well as universities all over the world are considering allowing female students in the not-too-distant future."

"You are so positive, Vor. And intelligent."

"I'll take that as a compliment. For now, the rest of the populace is kept in the dark. Powerless. The very idea that our mother has such a book is dangerous. She needs to be careful." She tied back her long hair. "What will you do?"

"We should get her to take a good, long walk with us and go somewhere where we can talk freely."

"You're running out of time, Aila."

"Don't you think I know that?" Aila rubbed the back of her neck beneath her strawberry-blonde locks. "I already told her I want nothing to do with it. I was raised a Christian, like all of our family. And I'm to marry a Christian." She stood to glance out the window. A look of alarm returned and her mouth dropped open.

"What? What's wrong now?"

"Oh, no! This is bad."

Vor nudged her sister away from her bedchamber window. "What? What's bad?"

"Father and Armand are talking."

Vor's brows arched upwards. "Isn't he the one from Frankia? I would think the fact that Father is conversing with him is good. Very good."

Aila stood behind her younger sister and peeked through the window to where the two men spoke using hand gestures.

"I won't be able to understand Armand if he speaks Frankish."

"Who cares? Look at him! He's gorgeous." Vor sighed dramatically.

"He does have the prettiest green eyes."

"And is that ... is that a dimple in his chin?"

"I know! I'm dying to run my hands through his wavy black hair." Aila fanned her face.

"Oh my. You're going to be beating off those Frankish ladies who chase after him."

"Oh, don't say that."

Vor held up a finger and waggled it. "You'll need to be firm that he can't have dalliances on the side. No mistresses."

"You say that like I'll be able to control him."

"You *will* be his wife, Aila. If he wants you, he will behave himself. I like the way he dresses, too. Lots of leather. Dark colors. I'll bet he reads."

"And how do you know that?" Aila ducked her head, her cheeks red. "Oh! He must have seen us. I'm so embarrassed."

"As for communication, just nod your head a lot and say *oui*."

Aila plopped on the floor and laughed. "I never thought I'd hear you say that."

"You can teach him words in Scots-Gaelic and Norse. It might be fun."

Aila rose on unsteady feet and peeked out the window, her eyes suddenly brimming with unshed tears. "What if *you* took the Goddess charge?"

"Me? Why me?" Deep down, Vor had always wanted a charge. But this one came with a dangerous price. No, the whole thing was out of the question. She had only to look at what had happened to Saraid to know that. "I can't, Aila. I'm sorry. I have big plans for my future."

"Fine, but I won't take it. I'm not strong like you."

Vor paused. "You think I'm strong?"

"Everyone does."

Vor gazed out the window and pondered that news. *People think I'm strong?* She felt a tingle in her center and heard a distant voice, as though the Goddess was calling her from down through the ages, pleading for her to be the one. More likely, it was just her own wishful thinking. She picked up her needlework, needing something to do with her hands, but just as quickly dropped it back into the basket. Maybe she *could* be the one. She loved books.

She always had her head in one, and she was unconventional, like her father, Torleik, who ran a horse farm. She loved working with animals and had become a skilled horsewoman, already well-respected for her horsemanship in her community. Maybe, just maybe ... no, how could she even think it? She was only fifteen, not yet an adult.

"What if Armand won't marry me because of ... the book?" Aila sniffled and blew into her kerchief.

"Then he's not a man of strong character. We all have our family legacies to deal with, good or bad. Because he's a man, he never needs to know anything about the book."

Aila bowed her head and poured a mug of cool water. "He's the last one on Mother's list of eligible bachelors. I suppose ..."

"At least he's young and handsome. I imagine you and Armand will have beautiful, healthy children. What more could you ask for?"

Aila started to sip her water, then paused. "How do you do it?"

"Do what?"

"Always stay so positive." Aila shook her head in admiration. "You're really something. Even Atli says so."

The sisters adored their twenty-two-year-old stepbrother, so Vor found this high praise indeed. Atli had taught her almost everything Vor knew about riding horses.

"Well, then, there you go. If I were you, I'd talk to our parents right away. Armand might get snapped up by some other maiden if you don't move quickly."

Aila laughed, and Vor noted her cheeks were no longer quite so red or blotchy.

"And as for the book, you're probably right," Vor said after a long pause. "If it's really that dangerous, Mother would never have it in the first place, don't you think? She wouldn't endanger any of our lives by connecting us to ... Druids. Still, I wonder where she hid the book?"

From out of nowhere, a poem started playing like a children's rhyme in Vor's head, over and over. She couldn't stop it.

> "From over the hills and in the glen,
> On the rim of the sparkling sea,
> Deep within the darkness
> Magic protects thee."

After the third repetition, Vor knew where to find the *Book of Delsiran*. And Raven, her spirit guide since birth, was going to help her.

The Caves.

As Vor set out for the caves, she thought of all the admonitions her parents had given her about going near the sea caves, but that made it only more exciting now to be headed to them. She just hoped the warnings weren't as dire as her family made them out to be. She pulled her cloak tighter against the chill and turned her attention to Aila.

Her sister had been born with the spiral birthmark, like their mother and great-grandmother Marsaili, which identified their chosen status to serve the Goddess. Whereas Vor would never have access to the book because she wasn't a first daughter—a chosen one.

As she started out along the shoreline, Vor gazed up at the tall sandstone cliffs and watched the spring activity amongst the seabirds. The kittiwakes and gannets were particularly vocal on this day, staying close to the high cliffs. The new season of spring chicks filled many of the nests, which the birds would spruce up and use again. By early summer, those chicks would be testing their feathers and learning the art of flying from their parents. Vor looked forward to this natural cycle repeating each year.

Every now and then, she'd stop and lean down to pick up an interesting shell or stone. The Druids called them heart stones, and she had two that had been given to her, the light pink rhodochrosite crystal from Great-Grandmother Marsaili, and her mother's red jasper. She recalled hearing her mother's stories of talismans and amulets, and how their properties could be enhanced using the power of three. Vor wanted a third stone so she could do more to protect her family. She'd set her heart on green aventurine, a crystal that was said to bring good luck, prosperity, and well-being. But more than that, this particular combination of three would grant her the gift of seeing the future. With that power, Vor would be able to look ahead and see where danger may be lurking rather than walking right into it.

As she continued to inspect seashells, she heard her three younger brothers playing "warrior" with wooden swords around the bend in the cove, yelling at the top of their lungs. At twelve, ten, and seven, the three complemented each other with their personalities and styles. Erik was good at taking responsibility for the two younger boys and in leading their latest adventure. Every day, he looked more and more like his older half-brother, Atli, now 22. Fionne was all boy—loud and attracted dirt wherever he went. And Graham, the youngest, liked to imitate his older brothers a bit too much at times. He was the quiet dreamer, and often found a reason to be near Vor, which she loved, though his brothers teased him terribly.

She smiled, then turned her attention to Aila's predicament as she rejected one shell after another. Was she being too hard on her? Even more important, was Vor being selfish in her wants and wishes?

Her head had stopped pounding and her muscles relaxed, when suddenly, she heard her youngest brother's scream of pain that echoed in the little cove. The sound bounced off the sandstone pillars that provided protection from the Atlantic wind. Vor raced up the beach, pulling her cloak tight against the brisk breeze.

Graham.

By the time she arrived at the scene, the screaming had stopped. This wouldn't be the first time she'd had to rescue one or more of her brothers. The boys played rough, and injuries were bound to happen. Still, she wasn't comfortable being the one in charge. She removed her shoes and hastened her steps in the dry sand. Erik and Fionne were standing in front of Graham, so she couldn't tell how badly he was injured. At seven, she thought him small for his age, but he tried harder for that very reason, and it didn't always end well.

She was out of breath by the time she knelt in front of her baby brother. Tears made dirt tracks down his cheeks, but he was smiling now.

"Look what I found!" He held something in his grubby hand.

"Are you hurt?"

"I'm fine."

"No, you're not. I heard you scream. Twice. What happened?"

Graham continued to study the thing in his hands that he held close so no one else could see. Vor looked to Erik instead.

"You're the eldest, Erik. You should be taking better care of the boys." She glanced at Fionne, but he was skimming rocks across the waves, his back to her. At ten, he was probably the most physical, and had numerous scars to prove it. Vor didn't mind mending hurt fingers or toes, but she didn't have the healing experience of her mother or great-grandmother. There'd never been any time to learn, with Eilidh devoting almost all of her spare time identifying logical candidates among the upper and middle classes, then finding locations to secretly teach the girls and women, according to Aila. Her sister revealed that her mother regretted that latter necessity, but Eilidh had learned the hard way that some men felt threatened to live beside an educated woman.

"He stepped on something, a rock, I think," Erik finally offered, bringing her mind back to the present.

"Let me have a look." Vor sighed, envisioning sand and blood mixed into the wound. She really should wash it off first. She held out her hand and Graham took it readily enough, still eyeing the object in his other hand as she led him toward the water.

"Wash off the wound and I'll wrap it for you. Try not to get more sand in it."

While Graham took his time, mumbling to himself, Vor tore off a piece of her petticoat, knowing her mother would chide her for being hard on her clothes, almost as hard as the boys. She kept the cloth dry and rolled it in one hand as Graham approached, hopping on one foot.

"What's that in your hand?"

"A rock."

"The one you stepped on?"

Graham kept his eyes down shyly. "Not sure."

"Let me see it," she said, gently prying his hand open.

Graham wore a worried look as he relinquished the smooth green stone. The freckles across his nose stood out on his pale face in contrast.

The stone was warm against Vor's palm. A sense of wonder filled her as she recognized the smooth contours of green aventurine—just what she'd been looking for earlier. As she clutched it, the stone sent a slash of energy pulsing throughout her body.

"Where did you find this? I've been looking everywhere for a stone like this." She turned it over in her palm several times, unable to contain her glee. "I'll hold onto this for now so you don't lose it on the way back. In the meantime, let's take care of that foot."

Graham's eyes were the same blue-green as his great-great-grandfather Niall MacAoidh. He followed the motion as she pocketed the stone, a furrow appearing between his sandy brows.

"I'll clean the rock up and give it back to you later. Alright?"

He nodded slowly, finally giving in. He then plopped on the sand and allowed her to inspect the wound and wrap the cloth around it.

"It looks like the wound's not too deep. When we get back, ask Modir to clean and wrap it. She probably has a soothing salve to make it heal faster. How's that?"

Vor reached out and tweaked a lock of sandy-blond hair. "It's a pretty green stone isn't it? You found it here in the wet sand?"

"*Ja*! It came right to me."

"That's pretty special."

"*Ja*!"

She gave him a hug, suddenly wishing he could remain that age ... before he turned into an emotionless wall of stone, like other adult Norsemen she knew. He wiggled out of her arms, and would have taken off if she hadn't grabbed him.

Every now and then, she recalled that night Graham had been born. Eilidh had gone into labor early, and eight-year-old Vor had thought her mother would die, like too many young mothers without trained physicians or enough competent midwives. But eventually, with help from Hallkel's wife, Astrid, they coaxed the tiny baby into this world, and he decided to stay.

Vor smiled at the memory, then sobered quickly so the boys would take her seriously. "Erik, Fionne, come here, please. I want you to help carry Graham up the path and back home without putting that injured foot down."

"Why?" whined Fionne. "I'm not done here."

"You were playing pirates. You *are* done. Do what I say and help your little brother, or I'll tell Cook you stole that whole blueberry pie last week. No more playing pirates."

Fionne's face turned white.

"Warriors. We were play-acting as warriors."

Clearly, the boys were afraid of the new cook, Klaus, a giant of a man from Nord Vegr, who had found a way to shame them into eating all their vegetables before they left the table. Vor liked having leverage. She'd remember that.

Erik heaved a loud sigh as he bent down to give Graham a piggyback ride up to the house. Watching the brothers united for at least a few minutes, Vor put her hands in her pockets and immediately felt the green stone.

It had been right there in the sand all along. How could she possibly take it away from her baby brother for her own selfish purposes?

The sun was fast approaching its midsummer mark in the blue sky, so Vor decided now was the perfect time to explore the caves without her brothers there to tag along. She figured her parents couldn't discipline her about looking for the *Book of Delsiran* if she'd never discussed it with them.

She followed an outside path to the bottom of the cliff, where the large underground entrance gaped open like a lion's jaw. She took her time, careful as she scrambled over rocks and boulders washed smooth. At the entrance to a tunnel, she found a torch. She had nothing to light it with, but she carried it with her nonetheless. When she arrived at a fork in the tunnel, she paused and held up the torch.

"Alright, Mr. Raven, this is Vor. It's been a long time since I last called on you, spirit guide of MacAoidh females, so listen carefully. This is important. I haven't asked for much of your time, but I've been told you can help me with just about anything. Can you please appear and light my torch? Then, I'll need your help finding the *Book of Delsiran*. She repeated the poem or song three times, just to be sure.

"From over the hills and in the glen,
On the rim of the sparkling sea,
Deep within the darkness
Magic protects thee."

She waited several moments and was rewarded when a cracked voice sang along with the poem. Raven repeated it three times, then hop-stepped from a boulder to her shoulder.

"That was a very civilized summoning, Miss Vor. Such a nice voice. I am happy to assist you in your quest."

"Good afternoon, Mr. Raven. You are most welcome. Can we start with some light?"

Raven cocked his head. "*You can do that yourself, you know.*"

"Wh-what?"

"*Repeat after me. Darkness be gone, light be bright!*"

She repeated his words, and the torch lit up. With the help of the light, she saw that the tunnel continued to the left then branched off to the right where a strange-looking door appeared with a sign written in Norse, Scots-Gaelic, and French.

"I did that? How? I have no special powers."

Raven chuckled, but it sounded like an old man coughing. "*Ah, yet you do have special powers, Miss Vor. That's just the beginning. Now, what is your quest?*"

"What does this sign say? It appears quite intimidating."

"*Well, you see, over time, many people unknowingly chose to follow the right path—which leads to a hidden cave with an entrance that goes directly to the sea. In high tide, anyone can be swept away. Hence, the warning. Never go down the right tunnel.*"

Vor eyed the rusty lock on the door handle. "I understand."

"*Now, your quest?*"

"The *Book of Delsiran*."

She left out the part about it being meant for only the oldest daughter. Raven showed interest, beady eyes alert and blinking, but then his attention waned as he stood on one leg, then the other, over and over until Vor's head began to swim.

"*What do you plan to do with this book, considering it's not blessed by the Goddess for you, but rather your sister?*" Raven asked in a stern voice.

So, he knew it was Aila's charge, not hers. Vor swallowed, not sure of her answer. She had no desire to betray her sister's trust, nor to antagonize her mother, who wouldn't have told her much anyway, since this was not Vor's charge. "Do I have to get the blessing of the Goddess to use the book?"

"Of course you do! You do." Raven stood on one foot and scratched his head.

"Let me ask this. Do you know where this book is hidden? Can you help me find it? Then, later, I can decide what to do with it."

Raven hemmed and hawed, clearly thinking this over. He coughed and cleared his throat. *"You must ask the keeper of the book where she hid it. Without permission, you may be punished for touching such a thing."*

"I won't take it. I just want to look at it." Vor waved a hand toward the tunnel on the right. "It's probably too big to carry, anyhow. Will you go with me and make sure I'm not harmed?"

"I will not help you defy the rules of the Goddess. You must go by yourself." Raven hop-stepped to the left tunnel entrance. *"Here you must go. Stay to the left. What you seek is fifty steps into the tunnel. You will find a shelf close to the ceiling. Therein lies the book. Beware."*

Disappointed her spirit guide would not accompany her, Vor straightened her shoulders. She'd get her hands on that manuscript one way or another. "Thank you, anyway, Raven. I understand your hesitation. You've been a tremendous help."

"I like you, Vor. You are very polite. That is why I must warn you to be careful."

"Thank you. I will. Here we go," Vor whispered to the darkness as she gripped the torch. "I will find that book today, if my name isn't Vor MacAoidh Torleiksdottir."

She immediately began counting to fifty using measured steps matching in length. When she reached fifty, she stopped and looked toward the ceiling. The ceiling was higher than she had expected, so she had to roll a giant piece of driftwood against the wall to the left. She stood on tiptoes, but the driftwood kept moving, so she kept having to start over.

When she finally got the driftwood to stay in place, she stood taller on her tiptoes and felt around the shelf surface. Twice, she thought she'd found it, only to come up empty.

"It has to be here."

She refused to accept anything else. She inhaled a deep breath and stretched her hand as far back as possible on the rough wooden plank of the shelf. She sucked in her breath when she caught her hand on something sharp. As she retracted her hand to inspect the wound, tiny white balls rolled off the shelf and onto the floor of the cave. She'd heard the legend of rare cave pearls, but had no time to explore at the moment. She swished her palm to the left, then the right. On her third attempt, she came into contact with something at the back in the center, that felt like a book. She used both hands to pull the book toward her and let out a brief cry when she saw what it was.

The Book of Delsiran!

"Ah, at last!"

She lifted the large vellum manuscript off of the shelf. The pages were loose, and it had clearly been used often. As she yanked it free, two things happened. First, she lost her balance on the piece of driftwood, ending up on her backside with the book in her lap. That indignity was followed quickly by a surprised yelp of pain when her hands lit up, as though she'd touched a strike of lightning. A current traveled up her arms and down her torso—all the way to her toes. Her fingertips turned red, and she couldn't pull them away from the edges of the cover.

How do I get loose?

She stood very still and breathed deeply. After a while, her muscles relaxed, and the book let go of her fingers. It floated slowly back to its place on the shelf.

"That's odd. A protection spell of some sort," she murmured to herself. "Mother must have placed that spell ... which means she knows how to remove it."

Disappointed that she hadn't had a chance to read it, Vor cleaned up everything that might be considered evidence, then picked up the torch to make her way back to where she started. She had to admit she was pleased with herself. Twice today, her sister had called her strong. Still, that's not how she felt. Especially after she'd summoned Raven, then lifted a book of secrets, only to have her fingertips nearly burned off in the process. Now, she'd have to have a serious conversation with her mother...and be prepared for her ire.

She had just reached the open "lion's jaw" portion of the cave when she stopped to take a final look. Surely, if she couldn't get the book, no one else would be able to take the book either. So for now, it should be safe.

She turned to face the opening to the sea when she noticed something in the sand beneath her and gasped. There, on a slick wet piece of sandstone at her feet was a woman's face. Her features appeared African, and her eyes fought back tears as her gaze turned to Vor. Another face appeared next to hers of a young girl, also of African descent. Both stared unseeingly at something or someone, anguish clearly written across their faces. Who were they and what did they want with her? Vor shivered and put her hands inside the pockets of her cloak, where she kept the green stone wrapped in a piece of linen.

Were the two Mother and child? She took a tentative step, believing the stone to be a mirror of something yet to come. But what? She glanced around in all directions quickly, then pocketed the piece of sandstone so she could study it in better light. It could be another magical clue, and she wouldn't want to miss it.

Vor hurried out of the cave and headed for the path up to the house. When she got to the top, the path straightened out. Vor looked over both shoulders before glancing down at the swirling waters. She shuddered as she turned tail and ran back to the house, no longer feeling like the intrepid explorer.

To her surprise, when she finally took the time to inspect her hands, she discovered no burn marks. None at all.

Chapter 2

It had been a long time since Gabriel had walked this shoreline in the Orkney Isles, although he had to admit his fondness for the location was more of a love-hate relationship. Nature could be harsh and cantankerous, if one wasn't paying attention. Also, he sometimes found the people superstitious and too willing to believe stories of magic and dark faeries or trows. On the other hand, it served his purposes.

I have big plans for Meginland.

Shoving his hands into the pockets of his old, threadbare priest's robe, he squinted and took in the view of the sun meeting the horizon. Half-hidden behind a small grove of birch and aspen trees, he could feel the ancient life humming and vibrating from the caves that carried their own mythology.

As he hummed his favorite church song from an early Irish Christian poet, a calm enveloped him, and he smiled. But as soon as he added the next verse, the smile faltered.

"Be Thou my breastplate, my sword for the fight ... "

He regarded the plot of ground around him. The man who legally owned this land had become Gabriel's nemesis without even knowing it. In fact, he was considered a savior by many of the people he'd helped in this community over the twenty-some years he'd been here.

"Be Thou my whole armor, be Thou my true might ... "

Instead of selling the land on which the caves were located, Torleik had acquired more and more land, until it seemed he owned the majority of the Meginland west coastline.

"Be Thou my soul's shelter, be Thou my strong tower ... "

Torleik Sorensson was known for his honesty. The stubborn Norseman had settled in with his wife and brood of half-Norse, half-Gaelic children. His horse breeding business, Valhalla Farms, must be doing well, because he'd built a larger longhouse closer to the cliff edge. It was a busy home, with people coming and going all day, and sometimes all night, when one of his prized mares was giving birth. Gabriel figured Torleik's thoroughbreds, when giving birth, must get more attention than the womenfolk on this island.

"O raise Thou me heavenward, great power of my power."

He was momentarily distracted when out of the corner of his eye, he saw someone leave the longhouse. A woman headed down the path that led to the caves. She was dressed like an Orcadian in that silly apron-gown they all wore here. She also wore a cloak with a hood, as the wind had picked up. She walked with purpose, but stepped carefully. As she drew closer to the shoreline, the hood flew back to reveal a very dark complexion. He couldn't tell if she was a slave, but she had a striking face with large brown eyes and a natural smile. *And* she was headed toward the path that would take her down to the shoreline and caves where Gabriel now conducted his business.

Should he stop her? Why had she been to see Torleik?

The path divided, one to the south and the other to the north. A man was waiting for her, and they greeted each other briefly. Gabriel couldn't make out the man's face, but he had wild wavy dark hair that needed taming. Something familiar niggled at Gabriel, as though he should know the man in the long black cape, but he didn't have time to figure things out now. The two took the north path and entered the cave by crossing a huge rock boulder that functioned nicely as a bridge.

Once he was sure no one was leaving the caves any time soon, Gabriel made his way down the path to the huge opening, stopping to listen every few feet. He was getting old and shouldn't be getting himself into these situations when his physical body was no longer as strong nor as agile as it used to be. Bah! He wasn't an old man. Not really.

He watched the entrance until his hands began to twitch from clutching the wall on the side. How could this be happening? Had someone else gotten wind of his new business plan to transport slaves around Frankia during this current underground crisis? The Frankish liked to keep a steady stream of slaves coming and going, but local politics had closed off that route temporarily. Gabriel had twelve ladies and young girls from gentle families in England, Spain and Portugal, to place in harams and brothels on the shores of the Mediterranean Sea. The Crusades meant business was booming, if one took the time to figure out the pitfalls along the way. And what a great deal of money the soldiers were willing to pay for lovely, cultured ladies far from home and with no way to return. But this woman he followed ... she wasn't one of his.

The woman had disappeared, and when she returned several moments later from one of the many tunnels, she carried what appeared to be a huge book with many loose pages. Setting it on a boulder, she showed it to another woman—a nun by the looks of it. Both seemed excited over something, and the dark woman pointed out several pages.

Gabriel took a few steps closer. He didn't want to miss a word of what she said.

"This book is of historic value," said the dark-skinned woman. "It should be kept somewhere where it won't deteriorate."

"You're right, Izora. But we don't have a lot of time. Gabriel's guard will wake up soon. Put the book back. You'll have to send someone for it when things calm down."

With those words, Gabriel glanced around and noticed the man he'd hired to guard the women in his absence was nowhere to be found. He debated if now was the time to act. Or should he wait...set a trap?

Chapter 3

Come suppertime, Vor's stomach rumbled and she felt famished. She was the first to sit at the dining table and wait impatiently for her brothers and sister to appear. Her mother fussed over each dish to be served, but that was her usual state. Whomever she served, the food had to be perfect. As Vor waited to dig in, her hand kept going to the stone in her pocket with the faces of two women on them. The sandstone had dried out, so the texture of the stone was no longer quite so smooth. The grooves that formed the faces of the woman and child made her shiver. Who were they and why did they look so forlorn? She didn't know, but she was sure to find out.

Then her hand touched a second stone, this one the aventurine that Graham had let her hold. Each time she felt it, an unpleasant knot formed in her stomach. Graham had found the green stone. She should have given it back and been done with it, but she hadn't. Instead, she'd kept it. Why did she feel the need to somehow fool her little brother into letting her keep it? She couldn't remember experiencing such a dilemma before—and she didn't like the duplicitous feeling. For the life of her, Vor couldn't let go of Graham's green stone. She kept turning the smooth crystal over and over in her pocket, as if waiting to see what it would do next.

What a peculiar feeling!

On a hunch, Vor placed the two stones in her other pocket, hesitant to put them all in one just yet. They vibrated enough on their own as is. She'd figure out why later. She realized she may need a guide if she wished to use these stones safely. After all, she didn't want to risk anyone's safety.

Hmm. She tapped her lip, thinking. Was Raven the one who knew how to summon the power of three to see into the future? Vor intentionally brought her breathing under control, as she sat and listened to her brothers squabble. It was impossible not to hear their volume rising in pitch until finally, Vor noticed her mother's pinched and tired face.

"Boys, settle down," said Torleik. "Now, Aila, what further questions do you have before we announce your engagement to Armand LaVelle?"

Vor glanced at her sister, wondering if her mood had improved with the day's activities. Normally Aila was the calm, centered child. One rarely saw Aila upset or her voice raised. But Vor could see the frustration on her sister's face mounting as she tried to figure things out. At least they had *that* in common. With this new addition of the green stone, Vor's life had become far more complicated as well. And now she had yet another stone, one with the faces of two very frightened women on it.

"Why must I live in Frankia?" Aila pouted. "After all, Armand has business in Alba, as well. Why not have a base here for trade and export?"

"It's not that simple," her father responded.

Aila set down her fork. "Then explain it to me. Please."

Skillfully changing the topic, Vor's mother turned to Vor. "How are your Frankish lessons coming along? You could help Aila with her studies."

"Fine," Vor mumbled. She didn't want to be dragged into tonight's discussion any more than she already had been.

"I just need to use my Frankish more. I'm sure once I get to Frankia, it will come." Aila glanced at Vor and raised a dark brow. "I wish I could take Vor with me. She learns languages so much easier than me."

Vor laughed and pulled apart a piece of bread. "I'm not going anywhere until I have a husband to carry my travel luggage."

Aila pursed her lips. "That's not all a man is good for."

Erik and Fionne whispered and burst out laughing.

"That's enough of that. You're making your sister nervous. Aila, surely you can hire someone to teach you once you arrive. Someone your own age perhaps?" Although Vor's mother was trying her best to be helpful, Aila seemed unable to focus.

Vor jumped in. "Mother's right. That's a good way to make a friend. Find someone who knows the etiquette and customs."

"Oh stop it, Vor. You're always so optimistic. It makes me sick." Aila pushed her chair away from the table. "Just wait until it's your turn to go through all this."

"At least you'll get your wish to travel when you marry Armand. He travels a lot." Erik shrugged.

Aila covered her face with her hands. "I'm getting married to a man I barely know. Furthermore, I won't even be able to speak to him. In fact, Armand wants me to pick our wedding day because he's too busy."

Torleik smiled as he buttered his bread. "We can help with that. You could have the wedding in Frankia on the 13th of June. Right after the wedding, you and Armand could move into his home, Château La Belle Rose, and have almost ten days to relax before the race."

"What race is that?" Vor asked.

"It's a horse race scheduled for the twenty-third of June," Torleik said, pausing to take a bite of his bread. "Armand's father is co-owner of Ivor, the Frankish horse, so Armand is assisting with some of the logistics for people coming from outside of Frankia. He will need time for that."

Eilidh hustled around the table, the boys attacking the platters of food as soon as they left her hands. "Your father learned this morning that there's going to be a horse race around the time of the wedding. He says you've been invited to ride in it, Vor. You and Fillian would go up against another female rider and her horse."

Vor fell back in her seat, shocked. How had she not been told about this before now? She felt a mass of butterflies in her stomach, and they all seemed to take flight at the same time. She'd grown up on horses, and had always felt they were an extension of herself. There wasn't a feeling in the world that duplicated the power of the beast's muscles cooperating with her body's subtle commands. She'd trained with her brothers, and she'd accepted challenges from prideful men who didn't know better. She rarely lost. But this race would be different—and with a female competitor she knew nothing about.

Eilidh passed the bread basket to Torleik. "How soon would we need to begin our journey to *Frankia*?"

Torleik ate the rest of his chunk of bread in one bite. "I'll go into *Kirkjuvagr* tomorrow and see what ship is available for the month of June. It could take up to a week, depending on the weather. Some ships are faster than others. We'd want a good start to ensure no delays."

"Can I come with you to *Kirkjuvagr*?" Erik practically squirmed with excitement.

"We'll see."

"What about me?" Fionne demanded.

"And me?" Graham piped up.

Vor's mother sighed. "Settle down, boys. Even though we'll host the wedding sooner than I'd planned, I confess I'd love to see the guests leave quickly so that they don't drag out the week and we could return sooner." She set a mug of tea near Aila's right hand and turned to Vor, offering her an encouraging smile.

"This is the first I've heard of this race. What are the details?" Vor maintained her calm on the outside, not wanting to draw attention, and yet, her hands began to shake beneath the table.

Torleik took a piece of vellum from his pocket and set it beside his plate. "Apparently, the race was originally set to take place in *Alba* in mid-October. But Louis, the King of France, has taken a keen interest in this event, and has found free time in June. With two female riders and a considerable purse rivaling any male riders' prize money, we are talking about making history here. He's calling it The King's Race."

"So, all this rearranging is for the King of *Frankia*?" Vor set down her spoon and straightened her shoulders, not liking the sound of that. "That means they get the advantage? We'd have to travel a long way with a horse that gets seasick."

"Fillian recovers quickly." Atli stuffed grilled squash in his mouth.

Torleik gave a quick nod. "I met with Jarl Harald this morning, and here is what he had to say. A man named Gabriel de Maci owns half of Ivor, and Armand's father, Xavier LaVelle, owns the other half. Xavier wants us to use two females to keep the riders' weight distribution close. A male and female rider adds too much disparity." He looked up, his blond brow furrowed. "I suggested you ride for Orkney, of course. It sounds like the competition will be canceled if we don't supply a female rider."

Vor wrapped her hands around her tea, grateful for the warmth. "Who is this other woman rider? Where did she come from?"

Torleik held the porridge bowl up to his mouth and hesitated. "Her name is Vivienne le Clerc, and she's the ward of Gabriel De Maci. They live and work just south of Paris. He's anxious to publicize the race and build up a good-size audience and purse beforehand. From the sound of it, he wants to make money so that he can begin buying and breeding champions. That would mean competition for us, but we can handle it. Vor, it's your choice, but think about it tonight and I'll have your response by tomorrow evening?"

Vor nodded, head down. She wished she knew more about this other female rider. She'd never heard of Vivienne le Clerc. But then, Orkney wasn't exactly the racing hub of Europe.

Vor's mother rose and kissed Aila on the forehead. "Now that we have the wedding date set for June 13, and The King's Race for June 23, we can inform Armand of the news. June is right around the corner. Aila, if you want people to remember your wedding, then the horse race on the twenty-third should do it, for those who are so inclined. They'll be talking about it for years to come." Eilidh frowned at the three boys. "Since you boys ate your food like ravenous wolves with no manners, it's time to get ready for bed. Off with you, now."

Vor sat up and stretched her arm and neck muscles as the boys yawned and grumbled on their way up the stairs. As she lowered her arms, she heard a buzzing sound coming from both pockets. She cupped the green stone in her left palm, noting the warmth that wasn't quite noticeable earlier. She wished she could "read" the stones better.

Once the boys were out of earshot, Torleik poured a mug of ale and passed the pitcher to Atli. "Gabriel de Maci has heard about your success, Vor. That's why he wants to pit Vivienne against you, and Fillian opposite Ivor."

Once again, Vor caressed the contours of the green heart stone. As soon as she wrapped her fingers around it, the buzzing subsided, and an unnamed fear settled in her stomach. What if the stones were telling her something terrible would come to pass if she rode in this race? She'd had a sixth sense about these things, and she was feeling it now as her stomach suddenly made a loud, grinding noise. A vision flashed briefly. Vor closed her eyes and saw water everywhere. Where was she? Was she drowning? She found it hard to breathe, to make any progress at all.

"Vor, is something wrong? You look ill." Her mother frowned.

The vision cleared and Vor looked down so they wouldn't see the complete terror in her eyes. "No. I've seen ... something disturbing. I'm sorry, Father, but I can't."

"What did you see? Was it a vision?" Her mother almost dropped an empty platter.

Vor shrugged. How could she explain it to her parents when she could barely talk? After everything that had happened today, the risk felt too high. "If Atli wants to ride in my place, let him. If that's unacceptable to Monsieur de Maci, then we must cancel."

"I don't understand," her father said. "You've always wanted to race."

It was true. She loved the thrill of riding. Sometimes, she thought she was born to it. But the low buzzing in her pocket reminded her that her fate was no longer her own. She had duties, responsibilities to her family and her community. Sweat crept into the edges of her hairline as her father stared in wonder to see her so adamant. She was relieved when Aila spoke up.

"It makes me tired just listening to all of you. But I'm glad I don't need to share my day with anyone else, let alone a horse."

Typically, Aila was neither a pouter nor stingy, but Vor could tell something more was going on than just finding a wedding date. Besides, Alia needed a distraction. "Let's go for a short walk and check out what's in bloom in Mother's flower garden. We can talk all about the wedding ... or not."

Vor beamed her prettiest smile and put a hand through her sister's arm. "Maybe we'll find inspiration there for your wedding bouquet."

"Has anyone told you your optimism is annoying?" Aila groused.

"No, but I'll keep my optimism, thank you very much."

"That's what I was afraid of."

As they stepped outside into their mother's special flower garden Eilidh had named Saraid's Garden, Vor stopped to admire a deep pink rose bud a rose bush that would feature deep pink rose buds come June. "These roses should be at their peak for a stunning June bouquet. Let's hope Armand's mother has a nice rose garden at that fancy house of hers."

Aila paused and placed a hand on Vor's arm and spoke in a somber tone. "I want to ask you something."

"What did you want to ask?" To quiet her restless thoughts, they ambled through the garden and stopped where bright spring blossoms caught their attention. The cheerful yellow of Celandine, the pale, delicate yellow of primrose, and perfect purple of violets, all heralded the advent of summer on the island.

"Graham says you found the third stone and won't give it back to him. If you do keep the green stone, that means you now have the gift of a seer, am I correct? That's what Mother's legend says." Aila paused, as though afraid to ask the question that clearly bothered her, then plunged ahead. "What do you see for my marriage with Armand? Will it be one of love rather than convenience? I couldn't bear it if it were the latter."

The green heart stone pulsed as if it were alive. With Aila's question, the stone suddenly made it possible to see inside her own head. For a moment, she felt breathless, and had to pause to gather herself together. She put her hands on each side of her face, to help her focus. "Bear with me. This is all very strange."

"Where are you? What do you see?" Aila's voice rose in anticipation.

"The caves. I'm following Armand into the caves."

Aila shuddered. "Isn't that where people used to smuggle things? Or ... humans?"

Vor cocked her head, suddenly recalling the anguished women in the wet sandstone. The stone that now vibrated in her pocket. She'd heard rumors of smuggling, as well. But she trusted her father. Everyone knew what an honorable man Torleik Sorensson was. He would never be involved in something as controversial as slavery. Nor would he allow for something like that to take place on his property. And his waking hours were spent with the horses. She shook her head. "I don't see anything related to your wedding that you need to know."

Aila snorted inelegantly, her exasperation showing. "What is that green stone good for, if not for telling me how my marriage will go?"

"Lucky for you, the stone, by itself, inspires a feeling of humor, which can then stimulate a renewed sense of optimism, joy, and hope. It's considered the luckiest of all crystals, especially in manifesting wealth and prosperity, or for increasing favor in competitions or games of chance."

"Games of chance? Are you telling me I'm to marry a gambler ... *and* a smuggler?" Aila said, only half in jest.

Vor pondered a neutral response as she plopped down on a bench. "I don't want to lead you astray, but despite what the stone hinted at, I think Armand is a thoughtful man. You could do much worse. That's the best I can tell you at the moment. You must ask him any other questions, yourself."

Aila nodded and sat next to her on the bench.

"Now, I have a question for you."

Aila crossed her legs at the ankles and leaned back. "What did you wish to ask?"

"You've barely spoken to Armand since he arrived on Meginland. How are you ever going to get to know him better if you don't spend time with him?"

"All we've done is exchange a good morning and good night." Aila looked away and began chewing the tip of her index fingernail. "I thought we'd have plenty of time to get to know each other, but it's the exact opposite. He rarely even looks at me." She examined her nails. "And don't say it's because he's Frankish. I don't accept that as an excuse."

Vor considered her words and was glad Aila felt close enough to her to say what was on her mind. She'd always valued her older sister's calm ways, but from her experience when attending other peoples' weddings, the occasion was seldom the most relaxing day.

"Maybe he's scared, like you. He's only human."

"Armand, scared? Now, here's where I can say he's Frankish, which means he's afraid of nothing." Aila gazed at something in the distance and narrowed her eyes. "That man has an overabundance of confidence." She turned to listen to something over her shoulder.

"Also not a bad thing." Vor noticed the movement and went on alert. "What's caught your attention?"

Two people walked down one of the adjoining garden paths toward the cliff path. They spoke in low tones, so only a word or two was snagged on the wind for Vor and Aila to hear. But Vor was certain the person on the left was Armand, as he wore the same brown leather vest, tunic, and black pants he almost always wore. She didn't recognize the cloaked figure beside him, but she thought the voice was that of a woman. Vor just caught the words floating on the early evening air. " ... meet me at the cross-path that leads to the cave opening as soon as possible. I'll go inside first, as I have something important to show you."

Aila looked pale, her mouth agape. "Isn't that Armand? And that person he's leading—all bundled up. Is that a woman? Why does he want her to meet him at the caves?" She jumped up and straightened her gown. "Come on. I'm going to follow them."

"Oooo, not a good idea."

"Where's that optimism now?"

"Aila, I'll go check out the caves because let's face it, you hate small spaces ... and spiders and snakes."

Aila pulled up short. "Snakes?" She paused. "You're right, I am afraid of them. But *you're* not afraid of creepy crawlies, right? Follow him and find out what he's doing there. And it better not be meeting up with another woman right under my nose, or smuggling, or anything else illegal for that matter. Or the wedding's off."

"It's dark in those caves. I won't have a light, so I won't be able to see what he's doing."

"Scared of the dark?"

"Of course not." Vor's back stiffened, even though she knew it was a juvenile response to a dare. Aila was long past taunting her as the younger sister. Or so Vor thought. "I'll make a deal with you if you do one thing for Mother."

Aila shrugged. "Okay, what?"

"While I'm likely getting lost in the dark, you promise to tell Armand tonight about the wedding date and start writing invitations. Let Mother know right away. I'll tell you later what I saw or didn't see in the caves. Do you agree to that?"

"I do!"

The sisters shook hands on it.

Despite what she told her sister, Vor wasn't simply snooping on Aila's behalf. She was determined to ensure that *she* was the only person who touched *The Book of Delsiran*.

Chapter 4

Gabriel wore a huge smile as he hurried toward the caves. He might not be as agile as he'd been in his youth, but he wasn't going to trip and fall on this crude path to the shore, if he could help it. As much as he enjoyed life at the Frankish court, he appreciated getting out and taking these little side trips he'd managed these past few weeks.

Just then, a goose-like cackle drew his attention, and he looked up to see six red-throated divers land in the shallows below. Their slender up-tilted bills gave them an almost regal profile. Yes, his alternate personality, Father Alceste, birdman, had come in handy once again. People never suspected he was up to something when he started going on and on about local birds. He should have thought of that as a cover years ago.

He'd been so busy watching the birds that he stumbled on a loose rock and swore as he regained his balance. He had the good grace to glance over his shoulder, but fortunately, he was alone. It reminded him of another stumble—the day he'd trusted Jacques le Clerc, Vivi's father. Gabriel stepped onto the sand and squinted in the bright sunlight at the rocks ahead, thinking back to that dark day thirteen years ago. Vivi's father had been an apothecary and her mother a seamstress for the queen. When Vivi was five, her father was given an important assignment by King Louis. And not the kind he could turn down. But the fool had made a lethal potion for the wrong person. King Louis had been livid, and had taken out his frustration on Father Gabriel, the king's go-between. After all, who would suspect a man of the cloth of being a liaison between the king and his executioner?

He snorted and rubbed his shoulder. King Louis had asked Gabriel to shoot archery with him later that same day and missed, hitting Gabriel. He still felt that deep ache in the spot between his shoulder joint and muscle where an arrow had lodged.

The king swore it had been unintentional, so, of course, that's what people believed. But Gabriel knew the truth. Although the arrowhead had been removed, a cool breeze increased the ache, and he couldn't stop the shiver that followed. He'd been extra careful after that.

His thoughts turned to Vivi, who had become an orphan following that incident—her father killed for his mistake, while her mother committed suicide. Father Gabriel had taken Vivi in. Raised her as his own. Sometimes she came on these short jaunts, but not this time. It was just as well, as she'd been in a bad mood for weeks. Gabriel was looking forward to catching up with his newest horsewoman, Trinette, or Trini, as Izora called her. She was the typical fourteen year-old girl, full of adolescent aspirations, but, unlike Vivi, she kept to herself and rarely complained. That might have had something to do with her being half-African and half-European. Not that it mattered to him. To Gabriel, when she rode Ivor, she looked like a dark angel taking wings, brows furrowed in concentration.

Gabriel climbed up on the boulder bridge that led inside the caves, his thoughts returning to Jacques le Clerc. He was to poison one of the king's top advisors who was standing in the way of funds targeted for the architectural projects that would someday astonish the world—the cathedral of Notre Dame de Paris, and the University of Paris.

The advisor, Valère LeCorbusier, insisted that money be funneled into war funds. The French and English were forever finding reasons to declare war on each other, which tended to get in the way of good business. Unfortunately for Jacques le Clerc, he'd never seen Monsieur LeCorbusier, so he ended up poisoning the wrong man.

Gabriel ran a hand over his mustache, the gloom of the day matching the one all those years ago. The king had demanded le Clerc's execution. That one experience changed Gabriel's outlook on everything. He could smell the possibilities. Power was everything, and he aspired to the highest position he could, using that knowledge ... especially after what had happened to his father.

Gabriel shoved any memories of his father aside as he continued walking toward the caves, his thoughts returning to the King. When the King had somehow gotten wind that the new priest had once killed a man, Gabriel had gone from being a simple priest to advising the King of France. Soon, he worked his magic. *He* became the King's Executioner, using the priesthood as cover, and Jacques le Clerc was his first assignment. A week after Jacque's death, his wife, an ambitious woman named Veronique, took her own life by swallowing one of her husband's potions. That left a small, active little girl with an uncensored mouth and no parents. He'd had his eye on her. If he could teach her to race, perhaps she could win him enough money for the down payment on a stud horse, one to rival the ones at Torleik's farm. Begin a breeding program and he knew just the person to help him. *If* he could somehow get Torleik out of the way with the help of Torleik's rival, he could build his business up. But first he had to deal with Vivi.

Gabriel sighed.

Vivienne, or Vivi, as he called his ward, had started out strong, taking to horseback riding by the time she was six. The riding instructor Gabriel had hired claimed she was fearless. But at eighteen, she wasn't shining quite so brightly on the racetrack anymore. She'd won fewer and fewer races over the past six months.

"I can't have that," Gabriel growled as he set out for the last part of the trek to the caves.

He'd learned of a big race coming later that year to take place in *Alba*, known as a challenge for non-experienced riders. It was filled with hills and glens, and very few straightaways, similar to the track outside Paris. Gabriel studied everything he could get his hands on. Ultimately, a cancellation on the king's summer tour of the kingdom left King Louis with some free time for a bit of entertainment. Gabriel stepped in and told the king about the potential income for the King's Race between two amazing horses, and two determined women riding them. The king owed him a favor, so eventually, he gave in and put up more prize money.

The first thing they did was announce a change of venue so the race would take place on Frankish soil in the Bois de Boulogne, a beautiful park-like setting that would attract every Frenchman in the country. Even those who couldn't attend the King's Race would be betting on one or the other. Gabriel watched Vivi each day, and could tell she was not her determined, focused self. A week before the race, she wasn't eating much, but she was drinking, so he slipped something into her nighttime wine to make her sleep.

"You were a wonder girl, my dear," he whispered to no one.

The more Vivi slept, the more she started remembering thoughts and experiences she had suppressed. One night, she and Gabriel got into a shouting match, and she'd stared at him in shock, her eyes huge, her body cringing. It was almost as if she'd seen him lift that ax and chop off her father's head.

She knew he was a monster, and exactly what he'd done.

And that was not acceptable.

His heart thundered in his chest. Underneath her bravado, she was weak, and one of these days she was going to talk. When she did, she was going to tell the authorities an ugly story. And they just might believe those stories when they saw the bruises on her body.

"You failed me, Vivi. Your fault."

But lucky for him, he had a replacement in training. She was fresh and sparkling, and knew almost nothing about Gabriel's background. Yes, he would put Trini in the saddle for the next race. She would win it for him. She would be his new ward.

Chapter 5

Vor followed Armand and the mystery lady to the caves, her steps muffled by the crashing waves and hungry seabirds in the background. In truth, she could barely see ten feet in front of her if she squinted through the thick mist that had settled in. When they came to a huge boulder that served as a natural bridge to the path inside, Armand stopped and offered his hand to help the woman cross. A jolt of apprehension shot down Vor's spine when she saw the dark ebony hand the woman extended.

A slave? Was Armand bringing a slave to the property? Vor's mind flashed back to the women's faces she'd seen in sandstone the last time she'd been inside the largest cave. Was that woman and this woman the same? With the hood of her cloak hiding her face, she couldn't tell.

A sick feeling settled in Vor's stomach. She'd thought Armand seemed trustworthy—a good man. Was she a horrible judge of men's characters to get this so wrong? A shiver of apprehension snaked through her to see Armand's expression, which appeared rather furtive as he checked over his shoulder before he and the woman continued inside the cave itself.

Once she arrived at the boulder bridge, she hesitated, trying to decide what to do. Maybe this was close enough. Besides, as much as she dreaded the thought of telling Aila about the slave woman accompanying Armand, perhaps he had a perfectly good reason for being there and Vor was simply letting her imagination run away with her. Then again, she had absolutely zero experience with men.

Vor glanced toward the tunnel where the pair had entered. She knew the layout well. At the end would be a physical door on the right, and an open tunnel on the left. She remembered scary stories that Atli told her as a child, how he'd frightened her with elaborate stories of ghosts, hobgoblins, and devious mer-people. Her parents had also admonished her, warning that children who wandered into the tunnel that veered to the right were sometimes swept away by the tides, never to be seen again.

As she pondered further, she wondered who had put up the door and warning signs on birch bark, written in French and Norse, the Gaelic long ago crossed out since so few on the island could still speak it. The hair on the back of her neck rose at that thought. As far back as the first century, Romans used birch bark for their books. That detail told her the sign may have been posted before her father's ownership of the property. She stuck her hand in her pocket and fingered the green heart stone. This time it was silent, though warm, like a friend holding your hand in comfort.

"You volunteered. You finish the job," she muttered to herself, thinking of Aila back at the house.

Try the door and quit being such a ninny.

Despite her better judgment, she placed her hand on the doorknob and pushed. Nothing moved. Three times she tried. Three times she failed. She stared at the knob and caught the blue flash of energy that encircled it. Someone had placed a simple spell on it, but who? Again, she took a deep breath, shut her eyes for a brief moment to invoke the Goddess, but when she received no response, she decided to step into the left tunnel instead, to see if she could learn anything from what she found there.

The sounds in the cave were amplified, and she could swear she heard birds flapping and squabbling inside while she counted fifty steps as she descended into the huge cavern below. An earthy smell accompanied her descent. Bat guano.

She stopped, surrounded by complete darkness, and placed both hands on the wall for balance. It so unnerved her that the chill began to make her teeth chatter. She faced the darkness head on.

I am not going back without information.

As she took a moment to reassess her courage, she realized she didn't want to be brave simply so she could have something to tell Aila, or so her sister knew Vor could follow through with her promise. It was bigger than that. Her vision of a flood and the sight of Armand entering the cave at that exact moment ... There had to be a connection.

"Vor wants to please big sister, eh?"

Vor almost lost her balance at the unexpected voice. Moments later, she felt the weight of a huge bird on her shoulder.

"Raven? Is that you?"

"Who else, my dear? Why don't you remember to call on me in times like this?"

Vor swallowed. "I'm not typically stuck in dark caves by myself. Did I call you and not know it?"

"No time for jokes, young Vor. Are you here to do a job?"

"You wouldn't happen to have brought *Fitheach*, would you?"

It had been quite some time since she'd needed the sword she inherited from her great-grandmother Marsaili. Supposedly commissioned by the Goddess herself, it had gone straight to Aila as the first daughter in the MacAoidh bloodline, but she had quickly turned it over to Vor. It had been forged in Spanish steel, and the hilt was carved with a raven in flight, as seen from above.

The sight and touch of the sword always sent a thrill of excitement and a shot of courage to Vor when she needed it. She was just beginning to tap *Fitheach's* potential for magic, it appeared.

"Of course I haven't brought Fitheach with me, silly goose." Raven laughed, the sound echoing in the large cavern. Vor had never heard a raven spirit laugh before, and this was definitely loud. Too loud.

"Raven, please get off my shoulder, and be quiet. I don't want to scare off anyone, now do I?"

"Down, down, down. To the bottom we must go ... to raise you high," said Raven.

Vor shook her head, trying to make sense of Raven's words. "All the way to the bottom? Can't we just take a look at who's there and then go back the way we entered?"

"No. You must hit bottom."

"That sounds ominous, Raven."

"Which is why you should stay where you are." A man's rich, deep baritone voice filtered through the darkness. "My friend doesn't like visitors who make a lot of noise."

"Your friend?" Vor's hackles ran the length of her neck as she glanced around her, but she saw no one.

The man took a step forward and though she couldn't see his face, she saw that he was wearing a priest's robe. "Yes, I do see *you*. And I know why you're here, Vor. You think I find no value in this abomination created by women of your line." When he turned, she saw his face, his eyes growing huge as he showed her the *Book of Delsiran*. "Your mother, Eilidh, is an amazing woman when it comes to languages. Wouldn't you say?"

Vor's throat constricted at the mention of her mother. She wet her lips with the tip of her tongue, not sure what to say. "I suppose that's true." Her mother had told her men's eyes could not read that book, that it was forbidden. Had this man dressed as a priest read the painstaking cursive handwriting still legible from Saraid's time? She didn't know.

"Where did you find that book?" She tiptoed around the corner so he could see her in the dim light. "Why are you interested in that book ... if it's an abomination, as you say?"

The older man spoke Frankish, but with a peculiar accent. He shambled forward a few steps, dragging his priest's black cassock, the hood hiding his face.

"Oh, I believe someone would pay a great deal of money for this book."

"I think you're wrong ... sir. It's mainly a dictionary of everyday language." She was careful not to tell him any more than that.

"That may be so, dear child, but it reflects why women struggle in this world to this day."

The smell of sulfur suddenly filled the air, and she coughed several times. Her limbs felt weak and her senses dulled. She yelped when something warm and furry brushed her ankle and skittered away.

The man laughed, and a bony finger touched her shoulder. "You've met my friend, I see." He watched the creature scamper into the darkness. "What will you do with this *Book of Delsiran*, Miss Vor? What does it mean to *you*?"

His cassock was like none she'd ever seen, for it sported half a dozen pockets, and out of each pocket poked a sprig or root—herbs, most likely. Herbs that groaned and sighed. Herbs that smelled strongly and filled the air, their scent mixing with sulfur until she couldn't stop coughing.

"Are you a real priest?" she demanded in between catching her breath. "Or a ... a ... sorcerer?"

He laughed and closed the book. "Oh, I love your courage in asking, young Vor. Today, I am Father Alceste, exercising my bird watching hobby. However, you will meet me on the high seas as my ... *friend* ... Father Gabriel, soon." He stepped too close so that all she saw were his huge, black eyes.

Why do I feel so strange, like I'm floating?

"You will not remember the last part of this conversation, nor recognize me when you see me in my other guise. Do you understand?"

He placed a hand on her head. "By oak and ash and thorn, may the Goddess Book be gone ... until the rare primrose is born."

Had he said born or bloomed? Surely, it was the latter. *Until the rare primrose blooms?* What did that mean? But before she could dwell on it further, the overpowering yellow smoke completely enveloped Vor. She sighed and slid to the ground, unconscious.

When she awoke much later, Vor found the air inside the tunnel humid and sticky, and she smelled the crude aroma of bat guano on her clothes. She sat up and gazed around before rising on unsteady feet. As she stood in the left tunnel and wondered how long she'd slept, she realized none of this made sense. The scents of valerian and cowslip made her frown.

Footprints in the sandy soil bore signs of a large man. Who was he, and had he walked away and left her there when she fainted?

It didn't matter. She'd come to do something. Something for Aila. And it was important.

Very important. Now, if only she could remember what that was.

Chapter 6

When next Vor opened her eyes, she had the strange sensation of time being suspended. She heard a man murmuring as he read from a book in what she thought was Latin. He appeared to be a priest, dressed the way he was, but who was he and why was he there?

The priest knelt on the dirt floor of the cave, his deep voice barely a whisper. Every now and then, he pulled out an herb or root from a pocket and waved it around while closing his eyes. Vor recognized the familiar scent of valerian and closed her eyes to see what else her senses could identify. When she opened them a second time, only then did she realize her hands and feet were tied as she sat up against the wall of the tunnel. Her mind was still fuzzy as she recalled the smell of sulfur, and she wondered what the man was trying to do. He crouched near the ground and lit a lantern, using his hands to wave smoke into his mouth and nose.

Despite her hazy mind, Vor made a quick decision not to alert the priest that she was awake just yet. Based on what she was seeing, what she heard, what she smelled, her best guess was that Father Alceste, or whatever his real name was, was a sorcerer. And this must be a kind of dark magic he performed, though she'd never seen anyone actually delve into that kind of dangerous magic. She shook her head to clear her vision.

Her mother had warned her *never* to use dark magic, claiming it always came back to haunt you. *Don't even ask questions*, she'd advised. And yet, here Vor was, her heart beating like an ancient bass drum.

She listened as he continued his chants. Apparently, the birdman had strong mystical powers. She'd never seen her mother do anything questionable when she performed simple spells, and she felt certain her mother would never dabble in dark magic... for any reason.

Vor's family attended Church services due to her father's influence, but she'd never warmed up to any of the priests who came through periodically. Only her Uncle Padruig made her feel comfortable. For that reason, this priest's garb and its many pockets trailing herbs and roots sent a shudder of revulsion running down Vor's spine. As the man stepped back into the shadows, Vor wondered if he was real or an illusion. Either way, Raven had vanished, the coward. Once more, she was alone.

Barely moving her head, she glanced toward the main cave. From the corner of her eyes, she saw that there were other people shuffling about. Women, by the sound of it. She could call for help!

As if the priest had read her mind, he turned toward her and in his Flemish-accented French said, "I wouldn't do that if I were you. Those ladies are worse off than you. And if I just happened to get mixed up and send you off with them, you wouldn't like where you would end up or what you wind up doing."

Vor's face flushed with warmth. She was glad he couldn't see her.

She straightened her shoulders. "My father needs to be made aware of what's happening around here. I will see to it that he knows what you're up to."

Father Alceste leaned over her with a knife and Vor cringed, her heart racing. But instead of cutting her, as she feared, in two quick swipes with a sharp knife, he untied her hands and feet. A trickle of blood made its way down her wrist. "I've decided to let you go, but I want you to deliver a message to your father."

She stood and rubbed her wrists. "What is that?" she asked warily.

"Tell your father he has competition, eh?"

He had her full attention now. "Competition for what?"

"For breeding rights. With it, I can dismantle your father's business." He leaned over her with a sneer.

Vor's stomach churned. "Why would you want to do that? What has my father ever done to you?"

The priest lifted a hand and the yellow mist returned. "You will speak to him as soon as possible. Is that clear?"

Vor felt as if a piece of her had been plucked out, like weed in the grass. Who was he and what did he mean by all this?

"Do you understand?" he repeated.

"I hear you, and I understand."

He nodded in satisfaction and exited the main cavern to the footpath that led up to the cliffs. Vor followed. He stopped at the bottom of the path and gazed at Vor with those black eyes of his. "If your sister asks about Armand, you must tell her everything is alright. Can you do that?"

Vor nodded and turned to walk up the cliff path. She was glad to return to the light and escape the smell of bat dung and unwashed bodies, but she still needed answers.

As she reached the top of the cliffs, she was met by a smiling Armand. He paused and cocked his head. "I know Aila sent you to find out what I was up to with Izora. Tell her the business is about obtaining freedom. She has nothing to worry about."

Freedom? What did he mean? Vor stepped two paces away and frowned. She wanted to ask him, but she was still so dazed that she simply said, "I will." She glanced all about her feeling like she was finally snapping out of a trance. "Wait! Who is Izora?"

He paused and answered quietly. "Izora is an ex-slave, the head of the movement. She can be trusted completely."

"What movement?"

He took a step back and glanced along the empty cliffside to make sure they were alone. "That's enough for now."

She covered her ears with her hands. Her head spun like her great-grandmother's spinning wheel, making her dizzy. A movement? A strange priest doing incantations and warning her who to talk to and what to say? She shook her head, hoping to clear the cobwebs.

"Monsieur Armand, you must communicate with Aila, not me. And you need to speak with my father as well. Immediately."

Armand regarded her for a moment, then nodded. "I leave tonight for Frankia. There will be little time for talk before that, but I will try."

Vor had a hunch this wasn't something she wished to be a part of. Consequently, she held up her hands to stop him from speaking. "I'm staying out of this. This is your matter to clarify to the woman who will soon be your wife. If you have other women in your life, Armand, now is the time to tell them you're taken."

"I can't do that ... just yet."

"I won't be your go-between ..."

They both turned at the sound of falling rocks on the path behind them. A head bobbed into view, and Gemma appeared. She reached the top and paused to catch her breath.

"Pardon me." She started to hurry around them when Armand reached out and grabbed her arm.

"What were you doing down there? Did you go inside the caves?"

"Oh, I would never do that. We've been told many times how dangerous the caves are."

"Then why take this path down to the caves?"

Gemma looked at Vor and smiled. "Just getting a little exercise. I'm ready to return to work now." She freed her arm, then rushed back toward the house.

"What do you think?" Armand asked Vor, keeping Gemma in his sight until she disappeared inside the house.

"I'm not sure. But I do know Gemma can be a gossip."

Armand gazed off toward the house and nodded. "I have to find Aila before I leave tonight to take care of business back home."

Relieved to be out of the cave and breathing fresh sea air, Vor wandered back inside the great hall and went looking for her father to deliver Gabriel's message. The sooner her father learned about a new rival, the better he could prepare.

She found him near the training ring, where a two year old was being put through its paces. She put a foot up on the fence rail and watched for a few minutes. "Looks like you've got your work cut out for you with that one. She's a bit skittish."

He laughed. "Only a bit?" He turned and eyed the dirt on her skirt. "Don't tell me you've been climbing around those cliffs again? You know how that upsets your mother and me."

She didn't react to his words as the priest's message played through her brain over and over, like an obnoxious crow taunting her with its caw. "I met a priest while out. He said to tell you that you have a rival breeder and to beware."

Torleik stopped what he was doing, his face turning to stone. "What do you mean? Who is this priest and where did you meet him?"

Vor threw up her hands, feeling very tired all of a sudden. "I can't talk right now. I need to go inside and rest."

She turned away and headed for the longhouse.

"Vor? Are you well?" her father called after her.

She didn't turn around to answer him, too stunned by everything that had happened, but she did give a wave to indicate she was fine.

Vor passed through the great hall and climbed the stairs, intent on her next task—a nap. She went straight to her bedchamber. She removed her shoes and dove under the covers. She pondered Armand's cryptic message to give to Aila and wondered why he'd mentioned *freedom*, of all things. And why was Father Alceste in the caves with Armand and a woman who could be a runaway slave?

She'd heard all about what happened to people who were involved in slave trafficking. And what was this movement Armand spoke of? Whatever Armand's motives, she must tell Aila what he had said, but allow Armand time with her first.

A knock on her door revealed Gemma, a stack of clean laundry in her arms. Although miffed at the young servant, Vor painted on a smile.

"How was your day, Gemma?"

Gemma stuffed a pile of clean chemises in a drawer and grunted. "The same as every other day."

It didn't take a skilled seer to figure out that Gemma appeared especially sullen today.

Most of the children Vor's age were working in their parents' business, or else getting married and starting their own families. That didn't leave many young ladies with which to exchange news on the island. Vor hadn't even been born when Hallkel and Astrid had their one child together. Gemma was small and quiet. She reminded Vor of a mouse. However, she seldom showed off her best features, instead wearing washed-out colors that didn't help highlight her attributes. She'd begun working as a servant for Vor's family at a young age, as her older half-sisters Dagny and Ilse were now wives and mothers.

Puzzled by what she'd seen and heard on the cliff, Vor sat up, debating whether or not she should say anything.

Finally coming to a decision, she said, "Have you ever seen Monsieur Armand go through that large cave opening before?"

Gemma's smooth complexion turned rosy red and her eyes grew wide. She was clearly hiding something. "Mmm. I'm not sure about that, miss. Which one is he?"

"The handsome one with dark brown eyes, curly brown hair, and a dimple in his chin. The man I was talking to just a while ago."

She continued her task, shrugging indifferently. "They all look the same. I'm sorry, but I don't know, miss." Gemma arched a brow and paused for a moment, as if posing for a portrait. Then she shuffled over to the wardrobe.

How could she not know? He's all Aila had talked about since she'd made up her mind to marry him.

It was clear Vor wasn't going to discover anything useful this way. Gemma liked to play verbal games. Vor did not. It made her head ache. Vor sighed. "Never mind. Thank you, anyway, Gemma."

Vor wasn't typically the suspicious type, but there were times when she wondered if Gemma played dumb intentionally so she could stay with the family. Hallkel had been well loved. Sometimes that affection carried over into the next generation, regardless of personality or temperament. And sometimes, it didn't.

LAINE STAMBAUGH

All Vor knew was that if she was eighteen and pretty, like Gemma, she'd have left Orkney for something bigger a long time ago, which surprised Vor, now that she thought about it. Why hadn't Gemma left? Maybe there was something she wanted here, but what? Vor huffed in frustration. She had too many questions with too few answers. That had to change. Soon.

Chapter 7

Melun, Frankia

Vivienne gritted her teeth and eyed the imaginary finish line three laps ahead. The racecourse had been set up on the land owned by Xavier LaVelle, the well-known vintner and half-owner of Ivor, the horse she would ride in the King's Race coming up. It had served its purpose, but Vivi wished the weather would cooperate. She squinted as the exercise horse and rider flew past, spraying her face and arms with glops of mud stirred up by the horse's hooves.

I refuse to allow this stable boy to beat me, even if this is a practice run.

The sound of the horse's hooves vibrated up her spine. Too slow!

"Hah!" she shouted.

She reached around to her back pocket and found the whip. For some reason, Ivor was sluggish today and not responding to her commands. The track had been a bit wet early that morning, which Ivor detested. But that was no excuse. That left her with only one resource. She lifted her whip and, with a loud snap, cracked it on his haunches. As Gabriel had taught her, sometimes the great beasts needed a reminder about who was in control—just like humans.

As her hands worked the reins to encourage Ivor, she eyed the dirt track surrounded by a dense forest on all sides. She rounded yet another bend, Ivor's hooves pounding out a rhythm as he lunged forward. The smell of mud filled the air as Ivor's hooves churned the ground, shortening the distance between her horse and Thibault, the liver chestnut, ridden by the stable boy, and also the property of Xavier LaVelle. As she drew closer and saw the stable boy's shabby clothing, she couldn't help but smile. Though she hated to admit it, she lacked for nothing, including new clothes in bright exotic colors with shoes to match. She got whatever she wanted from Gabriel, her guardian, and although she was a small woman, she had a big temper, something she generally kept hidden until it suited her otherwise, like now.

"Hah!" she cried, striking the whip again.

Vivi dug her heels into the horse's side, the wind tearing at her dark locks as she pressed forward. Gabriel had announced they had an important race coming up against a hot young stallion bred and trained in the Orkney Isles. She would be ready if it killed her.

She pursed her lips and squinted into the wind. Vivi knew it was time to face the truth. She couldn't lose anymore races or it would be the end of her privileged lifestyle. She lifted off the saddle as she rounded yet another bend, the horse's withers now wet with sweat. Then she tugged at the inside rein as she plunged forward on the saddle, the rhythm of her shoulders matching that of the horse's strides.

She moved to the inside lane to try to get around the stable boy, her horse huffing from the effort, but she wouldn't be stopped. Gabriel had taught her that. Vivi needed to prove her worth or end up out on the street with no means of support.

Orphaned at the age of five, Gabriel had taken her in and raised her as his ward. It may not have been the most loving relationship, but she had everything she could ever want. As long as she pleased Gabriel, life was good.

Pulling her mind back to the work at hand, she watched as the dark chestnut colt, ridden by the stable boy, crossed over the inner line, crowding Ivor, who wasn't used to that.

"Get out of my way!" she shouted. What was the rider's name? Louis? Luther? "You cannot win!" She dug her heels into Ivor's sides. "Stupid boy," she yelled. "Who do you think you are?"

The "boy" turned to look over his shoulder. She scowled at the big grin he shot her. He was around Vivi's age, and about average size, as were most of the boys who worked in the stables. No girls competed with Vivi...ever. She knew nothing about Vor, the girl with the odd name who Gabriel hoped would be her opponent. But she knew she must win. That's all that mattered.

The stable boy's knees gripped the sides of the exercise horse as he leaned forward to shout in the colt's ear. Vivi frowned at the sudden burst of speed from the boy's horse. Gabriel would be watching her and he wouldn't be pleased if she lost, again, even if it *was* just a practice race.

She lifted the whip once more and saw the look of fear in Ivor's pink-rimmed eyes.

"I told you, Ivor," she growled. "We'll show those simple Orcadians what barbarians they are for trying to beat us. Now ... go!" She brought the whip down hard. At first, Ivor stumbled, then he quickly recovered. In no time, Vivi was riding even with the boy's horse. She lifted the whip to push them over the finish line.

The whip must have clipped the other horse, because it lifted its head and screamed in pain. Ivor reached out and nipped the other horse's ear, and before Vivi could regain control, both horses went down. She was thrown free, thank goodness, but her head hit the ground with a loud thud and her world spun.

Oh, Gabriel would have words for her. And they wouldn't be words of comfort.

Chapter 8

When Vor set out to do her chores in the stable the next morning, she was still pondering Armand's puzzling words and wondering whether to tell Aila all that he'd said. Aila had pestered her all evening about what she'd learned, but Vor had feigned fatigue and went to bed early. She needed time to make sense of what she'd heard. If she didn't know better, she'd think Armand was guilty of illegal activities, not to mention romantic liaisons he wasn't willing to give up. And if that was the case, wouldn't her father be aware? If Armand was smuggling slaves on her father's property, that could have dire consequences for her father and their family if the authorities found out. Now his livelihood had been threatened by a priest of all things. And yet she couldn't help but wonder if the priest had been talking about himself or someone else new to the island horse community?

When did things become so complicated?

Vor decided to wait to talk to Aila until she had more answers than questions. Otherwise, Aila might just balk for fear of a scandal, and that would be the end of any thoughts of marriage. But didn't she owe it to Aila to tell her right away?

She stepped inside Fillian's stall and gave his forehead a good rub as she greeted him. "Hey, handsome. You in the mood for some breakfast?"

"Oh, I don't know about him, but I could do with a nice, big bowl of porridge."

Vor turned at the sound of her cousin and best friend, Dalla. "Good morning to you. You're always hungry."

Dalla laughed and climbed over the gate. "I am, aren't I?"

"Did you ride here on this lovely day?"

"I walked. Cloud had her foal this morning. A colt. My father took one look and decided he had to have a Norse name worthy of a god. Ragnarok. Isn't that silly for a little pony?"

"Ragnarok." Vor let that mouthful of a name roll around for a moment. "What will you call him?"

Dalla gave her an impish look. "Rag or Raggie. Maybe Rocky." She laughed. "My father thinks that's sacrilegious."

They both laughed at the thought of Eilidh's youngest brother, Gregor, now a father of four. Dalla and her twin brother, Cameron, were Gregor's eldest at fifteen, twins running in their family. Dalla didn't come to Torleik's farm often, since it was about a mile walk, but when she did, she and Vor were inseparable. They shared a love of horses, and often exchanged tips and techniques they'd learned.

Fillian snorted and raised his head in greeting.

"Ah, Fillian says he's not sharing his breakfast this morning," Vor translated.

They both laughed, then set about feeding him oats and providing fresh water. When he splashed his drink on Vor's clean forest green apron-dress, she knew her day had officially begun.

But her mood changed as she got out Fillian's bridle and saddle. Her father stood to lose everything if Armand was found running a smuggling operation on Torleik's property. Her stomach plummeted at the thought. She desperately wished she had someone to talk to. She may not know everything about the big wide world, but she hated to think she was being naïve.

What is Armand up to?

"I thought I'd find you out here."

Both she and Dalla turned, startled to find Aila there. She looked as if she'd just rolled out of bed, her hair all scrunched up on top and her eyes puffy.

"You look terrible." Vor adjusted the saddle cinch.

"Well, thank you very much." Aila yawned. "I thought maybe a good ride on the shoreline might wake me up. Care to join me?"

Vor looked through the open doors of the barn and shaded her eyes with a hand as she confirmed a blue sky and soft clouds lingering on the edges. "Of course. It looks like it will be a sunny day."

Aila beamed a smile to both Vor and their cousin.

Dalla waved and climbed back over the stall gate. "I'll leave you two alone. I want to see your new filly so I can report back to my father. What's her name again?"

"Ninon. Look for Kolfinna's stall. She's showing off her little girl today."

"And I have no doubt she's justified." Aila was already headed for Kolfinna's stall where she spent several minutes examining the new filly. After she'd had her fill of looking at the little one with Dalla, Aila saddled her gentle mare, Primrose, and returned to the main area for their ride.

"You're right. Kolfinna is gloating and being stingy. She refuses to share her baby. I think I'd be the same way as a mother. But before we go riding, why have you been avoiding me and why won't you answer me about Armand and that ... girl we saw?"

As much as Vor disliked being evasive about Armand's activities, she didn't want to pass along incorrect information either, and as of now, she knew very little. But she could see by Aila's dour expression, she was distraught. Still, Vor was afraid that if she added any more worry to Aila's list, she'd bolt like a young filly.

Vor shrugged and kept her eyes down. "It's nothing, really. I think he was just showing the caves to a young relative of his that tagged along on the voyage from Frankia. She quickly turned her attention to her horse, hoping Aila wouldn't detect the little white lie by her body language. "Now, let's go for that ride!"

Atli hadn't come by to exercise Fillian that morning, so Vor had decided to take Fillian, a red chestnut bay, for a run to clear her head and come to some kind of decision before she spoke to Aila, but now her hand had been forced. Did she tell Aila what she suspected and risk ruining her chances at a wedding, or keep it to herself and hope to learn that all her worries were for nothing? Perhaps the ride would lend more clarity to her thoughts.

She guided Fillian to the middle of the stable and stood on a hay bale to help her up. But when she finally succeeded and glanced Aila's way, she saw that frustration clouded Aila's normally sunny demeanor as she stood there, gazing at nothing while Primrose nudged her pockets for a treat.

Vor could hold out no longer, so she decided on a half-truth. "I went to the caves yesterday afternoon to find out what Armand was doing down there."

"Yes? What did he say?" Aila paused with her hand on Primrose's mane.

"He asked me to tell you something. The only reason I waited was because I wasn't exactly sure what he meant."

To her credit, Aila's expression remained stoic. "And what was that?"

Vor thought about what her father would say. Stick with the facts. "I asked Armand what he was doing down there. He claimed he wasn't doing anything illegal, and that he was working on obtaining freedom, whatever that means.' He said not to worry." Vor shrugged. "Does that make any sense to you?"

Aila paled, then her face flushed bright red.

"What do you think he's referring to?" Vor asked, trying not to show her alarm at her sister's reaction.

"Well, considering he was hiding out in a former smuggling den, this made up bit about freedom doesn't bode well. Does father know?"

Vor shrugged and put a hand out to calm a restless Fillian who always seemed to sense her moods. "It sounds like Armand is trying to reassure you that he's doing nothing illegal or underhanded." *Or else he's covering his tracks.* "The next chance you get, be sure and ask him yourself."

"He could be dragging our father into something bad. Did you ever think of that?"

Vor made a sound between her teeth that caused Fillian's ears to perk up. Just then, she heard what sounded like footsteps near the barn door, but when she looked up, she saw nothing.

"Don't be so quick to blame Armand. We don't know the facts. Speak to him first." Then to Fillian, she said, "Come on. Let's go."

Aila appeared resigned, but she sighed and followed behind. Vor knew Aila would get to the bottom of things, one way or another. She wasn't the eldest child for nothing.

Gemma reached for another sheet and hung it on the line behind Vor's house.

"And then Miss Vor said maybe Mr. Torleik was being dragged into something bad by Monsieur Armand."

"Are you sure you heard correctly?" Gemma's mother, Astrid, picked up the laundry basket and walked around to the other side of the line. "Maybe that's not *exactly* what she said."

"I know what I heard, Mama. Something bad is happening down in the caves. And Miss Vor worries that her father is in the middle of it all." She hung the last clean sheet and turned to face her mother, hands on hips. "Shouldn't we tell the authorities? Don't we have that responsibility?"

Astrid pushed back a strand of blonde hair that had escaped her cap. "We owe Mr. Torleik. He helped our family get back on our feet when my first husband died in an accident. He was right there, taking care of everything, finding me a job and a place to live with two girls to raise. And you saw with your own eyes how close your father was to Mr. Torleik. He and Hallkel were like brothers. You can't just throw that away."

Gemma grabbed the empty basket. "You don't believe me."

"You shouldn't have been listening to their conversation in the first place. What were you doing in the stable, anyway?"

Gemma looked away. "That white horse had a new foal. I wanted to see it."

"Oh, that must be Kolfinna, Miss Vor's pony. What did she have?"

"A filly. Miss Vor wants to call her Ninon. It's French. Why would she give it a French name?"

"Maybe it's in honor of Miss Aila and Monsieur Armand's marriage." Astrid smiled and patted her daughter's shoulder. "You need to stay out of trouble now, Gemma. If your father was here, he'd be very upset by your gossip. Do you understand?"

Gemma eyed her mother for a moment, then shook her head as she headed for their cabin. "Those two will never get married now. Don't you know anything, Mama?"

Chapter 9

Vor scrubbed the dirt off her hands and turned to look at the chicken coop she'd just repaired. She could have left it for one of the male hired hands, but she always found a certain satisfaction in doing physical work herself. She had nothing to prove, other than being Torleik's daughter. Aila was the feminine sister. Vor was the one who liked to test her physical skills. After putting away her tools, she headed toward the house to clean up.

Her mother had invited a few neighbors and friends over that night to help celebrate the official engagement of their daughter, Aila, to Monsieur Armand LaVelle. As she cleaned off the mud and dirt, Vor had to smile. If one neighborly toast could guarantee a long and happy marriage, then she was all for it. Finally, they could all move on. She had no inclination to think about things like smugglers. No doubt they were all just stories, anyway.

Then why was the ebony-colored woman with Armand in the caves?

No, he'd said he had a good reason for being there, one that would secure his and Aila's future. Vor had to hope he was right. In fact, she noticed that Armand couldn't seem to take his eyes off of her sister at the party. Aila had donned a new gown in a light yellow-green, that set off her shining strawberry-blond locks beautifully. A ready smile was a good sign that all was as it should be.

With perhaps two dozen or so neighbors and friends circulating around the great hall, Vor's job was to keep an eye on the boys to make sure they didn't eat all the food set out banquet-style on the table. She eyed the scallops and crab cakes, cheeses and breads. Her father had saved three bottles of French wine for the occasion, and he poured generously until all three were gone. She'd expected him to quiz her about the message from the priest, but to her surprise, he kept his expression neutral, as though determined to make the day special for his eldest daughter.

"To Aila and Armand. May their married life be happy and fulfilled." He held up his wine goblet. "And to invite all of you to the King's Race, a horse race like no other, to be held in the afternoon on the twenty-third of June, ten days after the wedding." He glanced at Vor with a blank expression. "My daughter, Vor, has been honored by being asked to participate in that race, as one of two accomplished female riders, but has yet to respond *ja* or *nei*."

Vor felt all eyes on her, and heat flushed her face as the guests began to discuss the race. She hadn't expected her father to lay down the gauntlet just yet. Her neighbors clapped politely and she looked away until she felt a hand on her arm—her cousin, there to celebrate the happy occasion.

Dalla regarded her with an expert eye, as if aware that Vor was uncomfortable. "Is everything alright?" she whispered.

"I'm fine. I just have a lot to think about."

Vor picked up a crab cake and bit into it. She couldn't help closing her eyes and mumbling "delicious" at the exquisite taste. She couldn't remember them tasting so good before.

She glanced around the great hall until she spotted her father and Armand deep in conversation. Servants wove in and out of the crowd with trays loaded with drinks and food, and a spring breeze danced on the air through open windows.

Later in the evening, a loud knock sounded at the main door and drew her mother's attention. Vor didn't have a good view, but as the man stepped inside, she could see he was dressed in dark colors. Despite a warm summer day, he wore a black wool hood, so his face wasn't visible from the side. Her hand went to touch Graham's green heart stone in her left pocket, and she felt an uncomfortable jolt, like a strike of lightning. Something was about to happen. Vor's stomach suddenly turned sour.

"Who's that?" Dalla asked, indicating with her head the stranger at the door.

Vor shrugged, but she watched as her father immediately took over and her mother stepped away. They kept their voices low, so it was impossible to know what they were speaking about. Torleik's face typically wore a stoic Norse expression, but something the man said had clearly upset him, as his lips narrowed into thin lines. The whole conversation took no more than a few moments, but when it ended, her father nodded briefly, said something to Vor's mother, then left with the hooded man and his guards waiting outside.

"What's happening? Where did your father go?" Dalla placed a hand on Vor's arm.

Vor turned to her. "Could you please find Uncle Gregor and tell him to speak to my mother as quickly as possible? I'll round up Atli as well. Something's amiss, and it's got me worried."

"Of course. I saw my father speaking with Father Padruig just a moment ago."

Dalla quickly disappeared into the crowd as Vor made her way to her mother's side. Aila was there, but Armand had disappeared. Atli quickly joined them.

"Mother, what did that man want? And why did Father leave with him?" Vor inquired, clutching the skirt of her gown.

Eilidh didn't look her normally confident self, and that alone, made Vor stick hands in both pockets to test the stones. Still no activity, but the warmth they gave off reassured Vor.

"Come. Let's find some privacy in your father's office, and I'll tell you what I know. Aila, it's your party, so you stay here with your guests and try not to worry. Armand is with your father to offer support. This will amount to nothing, I'm sure."

Aila appeared about to protest, but nodded in reluctant agreement when her mother swept Vor and Atli away with her to the crowded room her father used as his office.

Once they were inside and the door was shut, Vor's mother turned to the pair. "Your father has been taken to the authorities for questioning regarding illegal activities in the area. Specifically, smuggling. Apparently, someone saw evidence of people coming and going from the caverns. There's been enough recent activity to suggest slave trading. Both your father and Armand have been seen near the caves, so it would seem likely your father would know if activity was taking place right under his nose." Eilidh clasped her hands, then squeezed her linen skirt. "I know this is baseless, but we have to allow the authorities to do their job."

"How did they find out about this recent activity?" Vor asked.

"Apparently, an anonymous tip was all it took. Probably from a neighbor."

Vor recalled her conversation yesterday with Aila, and how Fillian had been agitated toward the end. Had someone been there, listening? Gemma or Dalla? She supposed it was possible. Dalla would have questioned her. Gemma would have pretended she'd heard nothing, then slunk away. Either way, Vor had to know who had left the "anonymous tip" so she could rest at night.

If this was ultimately her fault, she'd never forgive herself.

Chapter 10

The next morning, Vor sat on the bench inside the *Kirkjuvagr* mayor's hall across the street from the local prison with her mother and Aila. She'd never been close to a prison before, and she wondered if Aila's legs shook the way hers did.

She'd tossed and turned the whole night, going over and over in her head what she could have done differently. How was she supposed to know someone was listening in on her private conversation? And how bad could it be if this misunderstanding was cleared up right away? She felt in her pocket for the green stone. It was cold. Cold as the sea.

"Father would never do what they're accusing him of. This is ridiculous. Everyone knows our father is an honest, law-abiding citizen." Vor hadn't realized she'd spoken out loud until the others nodded their agreement.

Her mother forced a smile and patted her daughter's hand. Then she turned to Aila. "Still no word from Armand?"

Aila's chin dipped, allowing her to avoid her mother's eyes. "No. Not yet. I don't know where he went or why he's not here."

"That's convenient," Vor mumbled.

"Not really," Aila responded, somewhat miffed.

"Now, girls, let's see what your father says. I'm sure there's a logical explanation for everything."

The office door opened, and a man dressed in black with a matching hood stepped into the hall. The hood reminded Vor of an executioner's hood, and it gave her goosebumps.

"Madam MacAoidh?"

Eilidh had retained her clan name upon marriage, and sometimes Vor thought that was a smart idea. In their province, the MacAoidhs had a much longer history than the Sorenssons.

Her mother rose quickly. "Yes?"

"I'm Sheriff Siggeir Ornolfsson. Please, come inside and you can join our discussion with your husband and the mayor."

Vor witnessed the anger her mother held in check, her hands clenched into fists at her side. Eilidh turned and addressed Vor and her sister in a calm voice. "You girls wait here. We should be bringing your father home soon."

"But we--"

Vor was cut off when the door closed in her face. She exchanged a look with Aila.

"Well, for pity's sake. This has gone far enough."

Aila paled and clasped her hands in her lap. "Maybe this is all my fault for considering Armand as a husband."

Vor shook her head. It was her own fault for speaking so openly about the smuggling operation and risking someone overhearing it. Why hadn't she been more circumspect and spoken to Aila in the privacy of her bedchamber? Well, it was too late now. "Let's see what happens today, and go from there."

Her mother must have been in fine form, because it didn't take long before the door opened and Torleik exited first, Eilidh trailing. Sheriff Ornolfsson wore a sheepish look, his eyes on the ground. Vor had never met Mayor Magnusson, but he had the appearance of a man who craved attention with a large grin and confident walk.

Vor rushed forward to hug her father, and Aila quickly did the same.

"Is this my fault? I didn't mean—"

Her father cut Vor off and smiled grimly. "No need for self-blame. It's one of life's misunderstandings."

Sheriff Ornulfsson stepped forward and freed Torleik's hands. "We apologize for bursting in on your engagement party yesterday, Miss Aila. Hopefully, your guests were understanding." He gave a polite nod to Torleik. "It's well-known you have been a model citizen and successful, generous businessman who has helped the people of our community since you first arrived, Mr. Sorensson. However, I hope you understand it is our duty to conduct a thorough investigation to find the smugglers. Until then, we must ask you not to leave your property, sell any of your land, horses, nor equipment—in other words, anything you may profit from at this time."

Torleik rubbed his wrists where the ropes had bruised his light skin and again gave a grim nod. "I understand."

Vor's stomach lurched. This would affect everything. The wedding. The horse race. Her father's business and reputation. Maybe even the house they lived in.

"And I will be waiting to speak with Monsieur LaVelle as soon as he is located," added the sheriff with a stern eye for Aila, who glanced away.

"As you indicated, I'm sure this is all a misunderstanding." The mayor shook Torleik's hand as if congratulating him for the economic assistance he'd gladly given back to his community on several occasions. If Torleik's assistance stopped, Eilidh's schools for girls and women would be in danger, and so might the future they'd worked so hard to achieve.

Vor's teeth began to chatter as she reached for her father's hand. As a family, they headed for their horses at the public stable.

All she could think about was her father having to start over, if any part of this was true. And all because she'd blabbed gossip in front of ... Gemma!

Vor had arisen early and gone to the special place her mother had named Saraid's Garden, as it was private and located around the corner of the manor where three large rowan berry shrubs formed a natural barrier. She seated herself at a table on the edge of the piece of property that faced the sea. The waves crashed against the shore and the gulls and kittiwakes were loud and raucous on that sunny day.

She opened up a journal where Aila had sketched a few possible wedding gowns, and began to study them. Not for herself, of course. But because it should prove an enticing lure for Gemma, who was obsessed with fashion. Vor was confident she'd show up in no time, once she told Dalla what she was up to.

When Dalla appeared with a pot of tea and two cups, Vor almost felt bad she couldn't spend time with her instead of Gemma. As Dalla poured Vor's cup of chamomile tea, Vor leaned forward. "Have you seen Gemma this morning?"

"Not yet. What's that you have there?"

"Oh, some wedding gown designs Aila came up with."

Dalla nodded. "So, the wedding is still on?"

Vor shrugged, adopting a casual attitude. "As far as I know. I suppose that could change at any moment."

"I saw Gemma picking vegetables earlier. Do you want me to get her? I'm guessing you'll want her opinion on the gowns?"

Vor smiled. "She does have a good eye for fashion. And with so many French guests in attendance, Aila is a bit nervous."

"Well, you can't blame Aila, especially after what happened with your father."

Vor flushed, but said nothing as Dalla turned away. "I'll go find Gemma and send her over."

Sure enough, Gemma came hurrying over in a few short moments. "Dalla says you're picking a wedding gown?"

"Aila wanted to be sure to ask your opinion. What do you think of these two drawings?" Vor knew to play to Gemma's ego and pretend the rest of them were country bumpkins. She would lap that up like a cat with a bowl full of cream.

"Oh, the blue one, definitely."

"But the blush color would look so nice with her strawberry blonde hair."

Gemma sat down across from Vor and took the journal in her hands.

"Perhaps. But I think a German princess wore something like that last year. Very similar description, as I recall." She pushed the journal back to Vor. "So, the wedding is still taking place even though the groom may be arrested at any moment?"

Vor tried not to frown. "Were you the one who told the sheriff, Gemma?"

Gemma took a moment to consider her response. Clearly, she didn't wish to admit she was the one to overhear Vor and Aila.

"Well, there have always been tales about things that happen in the caves. My father told me stories about selkies and faeries...and ghosts."

"Yes, but those are children's stories. You were at the caves. Did you report it and that's why my father was brought in for questioning?" She closed the journal and leaned forward. "Have you ever seen my father go into the caves?"

Gemma glanced toward the sea. "I don't have time for this."

"Gemma, you see everything. Everyone knows that."

She sat back and straightened her shoulders. "Are you suggesting I'm a busy-body?"

"It's alright. This might actually help if there's something you know that the rest of us don't. Something that might help my father or Armand."

Gemma rose from the chair and leaned her hands on the table, bringing her face closer to Vor's. "I know how you operate, Vor. I won't be manipulated. You're on your own."

With that, she smoothed the blue and yellow Norse gown she wore and walked toward the kitchen, chin held high.

Vor sat there by herself for quite some time, considering her next move. She was still sitting there, looking through Aila's journal filled with fashionable gowns of all kinds when Dalla returned, carrying a fresh pot of tea and a plate with cookies.

"You've been out here a long time. I figured you'd be hungry." She set the plate of cookies in front of Vor and poured her a warm cup of tea. "Your mother told me to tell you that from now until after the wedding, you all get only chamomile tea to drink."

"As if that will keep us calm!" Vor laughed. "She thinks she's so clever."

Dalla sat and nibbled on a cookie, staring out to sea. "Did you learn any useful information from Gemma?"

"Not really." Vor sipped her tea and followed her gaze. "I think she was holding back on something."

"What?"

Vor sat up. "When I suggested that she must have been the one to report suspicious activity at the caves, she clammed up and deflected my questions. But why point the finger at my father?"

"How odd. Do you think she knows something?"

Vor wrapped her hands around her mug. "That's just it. Gemma tends to know what's going on before anyone else. It's almost as if she has someone else on the inside, feeding her information."

"Why would she need that?"

Vor shook her head and stood. "I don't know. I think she feels less important than the rest of us. When her father, Hallkel, was alive, he was my father's best friend, and they did everything together. Now that Hallkel's gone, she's on the outside."

Dalla brushed back her white-blonde hair and tied it with a ribbon out of her face. "You know, now that you mention it, I saw Gemma talking to someone about using our property to access the cliff caves here. He was dressed as a priest and had an interest in birds. He called himself Father Alceste, a bird watcher. Don't know any more than that, but it was an intense exchange."

Vor thought of the priest she had seen inside the caves, the one with the odd herbs and incantations. She reached out and took Dalla's hands. "Can you remember what day it was? This could be important."

"It was Thursday. I remember because my parents took us on a picnic on Friday, the next day."

Less than a week ago.

Vor picked up the empty teapot while Dalla grabbed the empty mugs.

There must be something she could do.

Chapter 11

Vor growled, frustrated with how her talk went with Gemma. However, when her father called a family meeting as soon as they arrived back at the manor house from the prison, her shoulders sagged in relief to know her family wasn't going to wait to take action. Her father quickly assembled his three eldest children and Eilidh in his office, and then firmly closed the door. The servant, Mina, was put in charge of keeping the three younger boys occupied. Torleik gave specific instructions to them, no doubt knowing as Vor did, that he would need to make it clear to Graham why he must never speak of this event until it was resolved.

A small table sat in the middle of the cramped office where Torleik kept his horse breeding information. Vor loved going over the paperwork, as it brought her father's accomplishments to life. He'd shown her illustrations and letters exchanged among breeders all over Europe that explained the biological factors involved in producing a cream-colored horse such as Ivor. Or, how to combine the best qualities of a Highland Pony with an Arabian for added size to haul lumber from forested areas, as well as to create a handsome appearance and a pleasant temperament in the horses.

As a young lady, she wasn't supposed to be interested in breeding animals. However, she felt certain that once she was married and working on her Goddess projects, she would still continue working with horses. *If* her husband would allow it. She certainly hoped so.

Her father sat behind a huge oak desk imported from her Norse grandfather's study in *Nord Vegr*. Vor and Aila used to hide beneath it to escape the boys. Vor smiled at the memory.

Torleik reached for his mug. "Despite this setback, I think we should continue with the wedding plans as usual."

Vor sank onto a chair in the corner, determined to get to the bottom of this. "Is it true? Are you smuggling slaves? And either way, won't you need to publicly address that?"

"She's right," said Atli. "As soon as your creditors hear of this, all of your assets will be useless, if they're not already. And if you can't sell horses, you have no way to operate your business."

Torleik leaned his elbows on the desk, his brows furrowed. "Of course it's not true. But we can't do anything about that right now until we can find out what's known about the caves. Has anyone new come around asking questions?"

Vor looked down at her hands, wondering how much to tell her father. She was already in trouble for that careless conversation she'd had with Aila. After all these years of being warned not to enter the caves, should she admit that she had entered them despite her parents' admonitions? She glanced at her mother and shook her head, feeling sad all of a sudden. She decided to take another tactic.

"Looking back, I don't think I realized how much Gemma resented us for all you've given us through hard work and dedication." Vor studied a berry stain on her sleeve.

"You may be right." Torleik held up a hand and glanced at his wife. "You and Astrid are still good friends, aren't you?"

"Yes, of course. She's been like a sister to me."

He nodded, satisfied. "If you can find a way to have a casual conversation over tea or something, perhaps you can ask her how Gemma's been acting lately. If she's seen or heard anything about people using the caves."

"Tea with Astrid is always pleasant," said her mother. "Gemma is so sullen these days. I doubt she'd respond well to either Vor or myself."

For several moments, Torleik looked out the window that faced the sea, the sound of seagulls serenading them. When he turned back, his eyes were moist at the corners. "It makes me wonder how Hallkel and I shared everything, even a business. He never asked for more, nor was he greedy. I offered to give his share to Astrid after he died, but she turned it down. I wonder if Gemma knows that and thinks we somehow cheated her and her mother." Again, he turned his head toward the view of the shoreline below.

"I suppose that's possible," said Eilidh. "We as parents don't always tell our children what they need to hear at the right time. Knowing Astrid, as self-sufficient as she is, I doubt she told Gemma much of anything. She was in such shock when Hallkel passed on from that fever."

"Do we need to keep worrying about how Gemma feels?" Atli put a fist down on the desk, causing the papers to bounce and scatter. "If she's the one who spread this rumor that started all this, then–"

"We can't blame anyone without all the facts." Torleik rose, running a hand through his still-bountiful blond hair, now almost white. "Besides, Vor shouldn't have been speaking so openly about something she knows nothing about. We can't blame Gemma for that."

Vor wanted to melt through the floor. Her father had never addressed her in such a disparaging way. She vowed to make things right again as she turned, her cheeks burning.

"In the meantime, this is my property, and I'm responsible for what's been happening here. We will get to the bottom of this." For a moment, her father regarded each child, his pale blue eyes pausing on Vor. The accusation was there, as plain as day. She'd let him down in the most horrible and public way.

"None of this would have happened if it hadn't been for me," she whispered. She choked from the ache in the back of her throat.

Her father put a hand on her shoulder and forced a smile. "We'll figure this out, and we'll be fine."

Vor knew he was trying to absolve her of guilt, but it only served to reinforce her feelings of inadequacy. Then she recalled what Dalla had said about the priest at the end of their conversation, no doubt the same priest she had met in the cave. She knew it was time to tell him the whole story.

"I was in the caves."

"What?" her mother screeched.

"What were you doing in the caves? We've told you never to go there," her father scolded.

"I wanted to find out why Armand was headed that direction." She didn't add that Aila had asked her to go. Better that just one of them faced their father's wrath than both. "While there, I ran into someone in the caves who was dressed as a priest. He goes by the name of Father Alceste. He claims to have an interest in seabird nesting habits. I've asked around since, and both Dalla and Mina saw him skulking about this past week. The way they described him, I'm certain it's the same man. He may have found one of the cave entrances at the shoreline because Mina said he tracked sand into the front hall."

Just then, Mina knocked and entered the room to ask about a book one of the boys had left behind in the study. Vor's mother quickly procured it and then handed it to her.

"Mina, may we ask you a question?"

Surprised, Mina paused. "I suppose so, madame." She clasped the book in front of her as if to ward off any surprises.

"Vor says that you ran into a priest in the front hall last week?"

Mina nodded.

"What did the priest sound like?"

"He had a distinctive accent. Frankish, but slightly coarser."

"The priest I met had the same accent," Vor concurred.

Vor had no intention of mentioning she'd seen Armand down in the caves, nor that she'd stood so close to the priest that she could have reached out and touched him. Eilidh thanked Mina for her candor and watched her leave.

Aila sat silently, hands in lap. She was probably scared to death they would send Armand away and cancel the wedding. Vor could see her lips trembling. If their father didn't send Armand away, did that mean perhaps the pair were working together on whatever scheme they'd come up with? No, her father would never fall for something so underhanded. So evil.

Another family meeting took place that evening, and they reconvened yet again in the office. Vor had done some sleuthing since their earlier meeting and reported on everything she had gleaned about "Father Alceste's" visit in relation to his so-called interest in birds.

"We have the same birds as the other islands—kittiwakes, gannets, terns, oystercatchers, gulls, and puffins. Dalla didn't even say which one interested him. However, according to her, he and Armand seemed to know each other."

Her father nodded. "We'll talk later about your disobeying orders and going into the caves. But, meanwhile, good work, Vor. Anyone else have news?"

Those few words of praise relieved Vor considerably. She had a long way to go to be forgiven, but it was a start.

"I did some digging into horse breeding research and communication," said Atli, taking a seat near the window. "I found something interesting regarding our friend, Ivor, or *Ivoire*, as the Frankish call him."

"And what did you learn?" his mother asked.

"He was born and bred in Frankia on land owned by Xavier LaVelle—Armand's father. Ivor trains there, as well, with the rider, Vivienne Le Clerc."

Aila adjusted her embroidery project and kept her head down. "Armand told me he and his father aren't close, but surely he would have been aware that the upcoming King's Race was between his father's horse and ours."

"I have to agree. Why didn't Armand tell us that this was his father's horse?" Atli's blond brow arched upward. "Apparently, there's also another part-owner whose name I saw written on the registration form—Gabriel de Maci." Atli raked a hand through his abundant blond hair as he studied the registration.

"If Armand wasn't doing anything illegal in the caves, why does he keep disappearing?" Vor wondered out loud.

"Father, do you trust Armand?" Silence gripped the room as soon as Aila asked the question.

Vor watched her father's face for emotion, but once again, Torleik remained neutral as he checked a date on his calendar.

"I want to trust Armand. I like him. And I think he'll make a good partner for you." Aila's chin came up when she didn't hear the words she wanted to hear. "I see."

Much to everyone's surprise, she rose and gathered her materials. "I'm not feeling well. Excuse me." She walked across the room, opened the office door, then closed it firmly behind her.

Atli walked over to the window and looked out at the ocean.

"I'll go get her," Vor offered, and hurried after her sister. She checked all of the usual places—Saraid's Garden, Aila's bedchamber, the dining area, and the shoreline. No Aila. When she returned to her father's office, she felt like she'd failed once again. Standing just outside the door, she heard the conversation continue inside without her and paused to listen.

"What are we facing, dear?" her mother inquired of Torleik. "Tell us what we can expect so there are no unpleasant surprises."

She heard his chair creak as he shifted in his seat.

"I think we should put the wedding on hold until we speak to Armand. Perhaps that will flush him out, so we can have a serious conversation. As for the farm, if I can't sell anything to make a profit, we must get creative. We don't know how long this will last. We won't have access to our savings to fund your girls' school. At least, not for a while. You should plan to close it down for now."

Vor's hand went to her throat to keep from crying out. Close down the school?

Her mother was passionate about that school so girls and women could learn to read and write in a comfortable setting without the pressure of male interference or daily chores to vie for their attention. Vor could picture the range of emotions crossing her mother's face and nearly wept.

"What if Fillian wins the race? Can we keep the prize money then?" asked Atli.

"Not if we're the registered owners."

A long silence followed, and Vor debated going inside, so she couldn't be accused of listening in while standing in the hall.

"Just wait," said Raven.

Her head whipped around, but her spirit guide remained invisible on her shoulder.

"We could give Fillian to Vor as a gift," said her father. "They can't take the horse and money if it belongs to someone else, and Vor is of age to own property here in Meginland."

Vor chewed on the end of her braid.

"Fillian should go to me, if to anyone." Atli spoke up, anger crackling in his voice. "I'm the one who's put in the most time and effort with him."

"Atli may be right, dear. What if—"

"No, right now, we have to think about the prize money. We have no access to it if someone else in the family doesn't own Fillian. It's true that Atli is the more experienced rider and is of age. However, this race is intended for two *female* riders. The order stipulates that we must provide a female horsewoman or the race will be canceled. Vor has to ride Fillian, and she has to win. That's our only option."

Atli said nothing, but Vor couldn't blame him if he felt slighted. He'd invested hundreds of hours in training, exercising, feeding, grooming, and bathing the horse—everything one would do with a human child.

He'd be one more person she'd owe. But she could do this. Perhaps he'd take Kolfinna's new foal in exchange. Tears began to well up in Vor's eyes.

"*Now is the time,*" said Raven.

Vor pushed open the office door and stood up straight. "I couldn't find Aila."

"She's probably hiding somewhere. Perhaps reading under the apple trees?" Eilidh suggested.

"I didn't think to look that far. Do you want me to check on her?"

"Vor, we've been speaking in private," her father interrupted, indicating she should close the door. "What would really help me out is if you'll agree to ride Fillian in that race. I know you are reluctant, but we have no choice if we're to save the farm. We have three weeks to prepare. You can do this. What do you say?"

Vor had no other choice, if she was going to help her family survive. Besides, it would assuage the guilt she'd been feeling ever since she'd mentioned what she'd seen in the caves to Aila.

"If you want me to ride in the race, I'll do that. But I'll need Atli's help. He knows all of Fillian's quirks and strengths. I can't do this without you, Atli."

He glanced at her over his shoulder and shrugged. "Sure. Fine. I'll help."

Vor knew she had her work cut out for her. In the meantime, she would need to find a way to get back in Atli's good graces any way possible. She'd feel a lot more confident if she could find Armand LaVelle.

Chapter 12

Vor had a theory about bad things happening in groups of three. So, the next day, when another loud knock on the main door to the manor house disturbed their afternoon, Vor froze. She'd spent a good part of the day sitting in a comfortable window seat, making a list of ways to help her father's cause. In fact, she was so deep in concentration, she didn't even hear the knock until she saw Aila glide across the floor to lift the bar.

She couldn't hear what the person on the other side said, but it was definitely a man. Aila stepped back and invited him inside the manor house. She turned to Vor just as Fionne and Graham raced past, chasing after a runaway ball.

"Take the ball outside," Aila said, pointing.

The boys groaned, but gathered up the runaway ball and headed out into the rose garden.

"Vor, please fetch Mother. I believe she's upstairs in the sewing room."

Vor hopped up to obey, but her curiosity got the better of her as she passed by the man carrying a huge volume stuffed with loose pages. He had what some women would call a "sculpted" face, a long, straight nose, prominent cheekbones, and he wore a suit of fine gray wool, which helped indicate his status in society.

This gorgeous man did not muck out horse stalls for a living, that was for certain.

Vor hurried up the stairs and located her mother just where Aila said she would be, delivered her message, and remembered to slow down when the two descended the stairs.

As Vor's mother reached the landing, she paused to introduce herself. "I'm Eilidh MacAoidh, wife of Torleik Sorensson. How may I help you?"

The man gave a polite bow. "I'm Marcel Duran, and I represent the owners of the horse known as Ivor."

He spoke Frankish with a precise Parisian accent as he straightened the sleeve of what must be a very expensive black tunic with sleeve cuffs lined in black fur. To Vor, he had the look of an important man with little spare time on his well-manicured hands.

Aila stepped aside, a worried expression furrowing her brow. "Mother, this is the French king's debt collector. He wishes to speak with Father."

"Regarding what?"

"The registration papers for the horse, Fillian."

Vor placed a hand over her mouth to suppress a gasp. She recovered quickly, and remained silent. She was careful not to blurt out anything to make matters worse.

Her mother invited him in, then shut the door and sent a quick look to Vor and Aila, urging them to follow her to her father's office, the chancellery where Torleik's documents were kept. After they all found a seat in the cramped space, Eilidh glanced out the window. "My husband is harvesting the wheat crop right now. Is there a problem regarding ownership?"

"May I see the registration document, please? That may clear things up."

Vor's heart pounded in her chest. He must be there to determine whether the race should be canceled, if her father's credits were unavailable. Right now, the big red chestnut stallion was the only thing giving them hope for getting out of debt. Vor swallowed. Would he figure out they'd given the horse to Vor for just this reason the day before?

Eilidh paused briefly before approaching her husband's desk. "I can summon my husband from the fields, if you're willing to wait."

Marcel glanced at the stack of important-looking papers then shook his head. "Is the document close at hand?"

"Why do you want to see it?" Vor asked, unable to stay silent anymore. Did he doubt that she could ride Fillian in the upcoming race because their accounts had been temporarily halted?

While she was speaking, her mother poked her head out of the door and asked a servant to locate her husband. She returned and smiled, like everything was fine. "Our daughter here, Vor, is Fillian's owner. My husband reassured us the document was legal and at fifteen winters, Vor was of age to own property."

Vor caught on. Her mother didn't want to show Marcel the document because she'd only signed it the day before. Not that it was illegal. But it might appear suspicious. Like they'd planned for the transfer of extremely valuable horseflesh to another member of the family to work around the matter of administering fines for smuggling, if not prison time.

Marcel smiled, but it was with tight lips. "Again, may I please see the document? I assure you that is all I am here for ... at the moment."

Eilidh exchanged a look that Vor couldn't quite read. After a brief hesitation, her mother nodded, and Vor turned her back so Marcel couldn't see from which stack of paper she pulled the recently signed document. She took her time perusing the content, which coincided perfectly with Torleik's entrance. He appeared dusty and sweaty, but Vor thought him every bit like his wild Viking ancestors.

Her mother made quick introductions and stated Marcel's purpose, then Vor handed her father the document and stepped away. Torleik looked confident as he handed it to Marcel, and Vor tried to emulate that confidence by standing tall, shoulders back.

Marcel glanced at the paper, his brows dipping in frustration as he checked the backside.

"Is everything in order?" Torleik demanded. "If so, I need to return to the harvest. We must finish today if we want to process our winter grains early. Our people will be depending on that this winter."

Marcel handed the document back to Vor. Whether he was relieved by the turn of events or disappointed, he said nothing. "I heard from the sheriff that, except for livestock, any grain processed for consumption or sale will be held until this matter is cleared up." He set down his log book and made a notation. "The registration is in order. I see that a new date and owner were documented just yesterday."

Torleik smiled. "Is that not legal?"

Marcel's finger tapped the table. "The deed is ... fine. I must go now, but I will return if I have more questions. The sheriff asked me to tell you that he will bring you an updated list of all your assets so you can easily refer to those when needed." He gave Vor a pointed look as the new owner of a valuable race horse.

Eilidh opened the office door and escorted the handsome stranger to the main front door. When he left, Vor replaced the bar on the door and then leaned back against it. She couldn't help feeling that they weren't out of the woods yet.

Chapter 13

As Vivienne stood at the window of the common room at the village inn in Thjorsá, she gazed at the Atlantic Ocean in awe. At the sophisticated age of eighteen, Vivienne was typically a good traveler who didn't mind a lot of city walking on her own. However, she didn't care much for water crossings, and she was reaching her limit. By the time she arrived on the rock-strewn shores of northern Alba, all she wanted was an extra day of rest, and to return to her home in the Kingdom of Frankia. If the King's Race was taking place on Frankish soil, why did they need to make the short voyage to Alba? Gabriel had promised to explain, but so far, she was still waiting ... impatiently.

Gabriel had arranged for her to stay two nights in a relatively decent waterfront hotel he called a brief respite before the grind of preparing for a race. "You need a break," he'd said. "Perhaps, if you do well with a rest, you'll slide back into the winner's circle—where you belong."

She knew deep down that Gabriel wasn't simply being nice to her, even though she was his ward. If he was to give her beautiful things, he expected something in return from her. And she was running out of time. She must win this race and its generous prize money, or she just might end up on the street.

She winced at the painful lump on the side of her head. The dirt track had been hard on her, and she could still feel the goose egg-sized lump on the side of her forehead, while that stupid stable boy had managed to jump clear. Vivi didn't fall very often, and since then, she'd lain awake analyzing the incident from several different angles. The only reasonable explanation for the fall was that good-for-nothing boy. She'd scolded him for quite some time, throwing in a few curse words for emphasis. The stupid lad had stood there with a silly grin the whole time. At the end of that one-sided conversation, she decided he must be a simpleton. Maybe he'd been thrown one too many times. She'd shared that theory with Gabriel before they left Frankia, but he'd insisted she must put up with him a bit longer.

"For the good of the horse," he'd said.

As much as she wanted to argue with her guardian and tell him how contrary horses could be, Vivienne refrained from quarreling with him. There was something special about Ivor, or *Ivoire*, as they called him in Frankia. Not just the color of his rare ivory fur or pink-rimmed eyes. It was almost as if he were human and commanded those around him. Looked down on those he considered lesser beings.

Or, maybe she was the one looking down on others. She released a sigh, feeling confused as she gazed out over the ocean that seemed to go on forever. She loved the hustle and bustle of a big city like Paris, whereas *Kirkjuvagr* was a sleepy little port town. If she spent more than a day there, she got anxious. She still didn't understand the quick trip to Alba, but Gabriel had insisted, explaining it had to do with a new business project. And Vivi always obeyed Gabriel when he insisted she accompany him while traveling for his business.

Her head throbbed with all this thinking. Gingerly, she ran a hand over the lump on her head and wished she could be rid of it by race day. Race day was sacred to Vivi. Gabriel had taught her rituals used on occasions like this. She didn't know if they made a difference, but she liked how it made her feel close to her guardian to share what some may label as superstitious nonsense.

Through the inn window she caught a glimpse of the stable boy walking Ivor across the yard toward the stables. Ivor tossed his head and pawed the ground. Rain was misting heavily, adding to the gloom.

Vivi walked over to the door and opened it, but refused to step outside. "Hey, stupid boy! Ivor doesn't like the rain. He needs to be dry and warm—now!"

The boy, who was probably closer to her eighteen years, had interesting light blue eyes that turned up at the corners. When he heard Vivi's voice, he smiled.

"Hurry up! He's going to catch a cold!"

He must have thought her comment funny, because his expression changed to a grin as he waved her off and entered the stables. She slammed the door and muttered an expletive.

His insolence made her so angry that she'd almost forgotten to order dinner, which she did now. She made her way downstairs to the dining room where she ordered a bowl of nutmeg and squash soup delivered to her room. She'd have to speak to Gabriel about replacing that boy. She couldn't take much more.

When she slowly climbed the stairs to her room, she winced as her head began to pound even harder. The village was situated on the very tip of Alba, and Vivi suspected it was cold and windy most of the time. She closed the door to her bedchamber and waited for her bowl of soup and bread. After filling her belly, she didn't even bother to wash. She just burrowed under the warm blankets, grabbing two soft pillows for her aching head. She smiled to think Stupid Boy was likely staying in the stables with Ivor. She hoped he froze to death, and with that final thought, she drifted off to sleep.

She dreamed about Gabriel. They'd been arguing in the vestibule of an ancient church she didn't recognize, with priests and nuns everywhere, who raised their voices in harmonious song as they went about their daily tasks. A woman held up an old gown full of rips and tears, covered with dirt. She pointed to a spot behind her, and when Vivienne took a step closer in her dream, the woman gestured emphatically at something.

Curious to find out why the woman seemed so adamant, Vivi stepped closer still, then almost gagged at what she saw. A dead body covered with mold and maggots lay exposed, its head missing.

They stood outside now, in the dying light of day within a small cemetery.

Who has died?

Frantic to find out, Vivi grabbed Gabriel by the arm in the dream and asked where she should go. When Gabriel turned back to her, his face was different. She looked again. A small horse was visible in outline in place of where his head should be. She blinked three times rapidly.

What did all this mean?

Vivi opened her eyes and reached for a cool cloth to place on her forehead. She tried to remember the last time she'd felt this kind of terror. It made her heart pound and the sweat pour off her face and drip onto the bedcovers.

Something is coming after me . . . and I think it may be Gabriel.

Chapter 14

Gabriel awoke with a start, the nightmare subsiding. After a few moments, he grew accustomed to the darkness all around him and realized the thin walls of the inn did nothing to mask Vivi's sobbing in the room next door. It would seem they both suffered from horrific nightmares, something he wished never to re-visit. For a very brief moment, he considered knocking on Vivi's door and consoling her, but he knew it wouldn't help. She'd probably get angry. So instead, he sat at his window and looked out on the quiet harbor, pondering his next move.

He was so close to ruining Torleik, he could almost taste it. And right after he paid the sheriff to arrest him for smuggling people, he would go after that nosy chit, Vor. She didn't seem to know when to mind her own business. The slaves belonged to *him*, just like Vivi.

Vivi... He'd made sure she had no friends or allies to turn to, and that's the way he liked it. Fortunately, Vivi's abrasive personality chased off almost everyone who came in contact with her, making his job that much easier. But could he stand by and watch her lose the King's Race? He tried not to think about the prize money. That purse would put him in the position to buy Ivor outright from that fool, Xavier LaVelle, and charge a high stud service fee for the breeding program he hoped to implement by the end of the year. After Torleik lost all of his resources, including income, his livestock would be easy pickings for a cheap price.

"Don't overstep your bounds, son."

He swore and turned away from the window, his father's voice a nasty reminder of what a failure his old man had become before Gabriel's transition from priest to the King's Executioner. Surely, a triumphant rise. He couldn't wait to look him up and rub his prize winnings in his father's face.

With that thought, he lay back against the pillows, relaxed and calm as he slipped into deep sleep once more. The dream came quickly, but he couldn't do anything to stop it.

Gabriel watched his father make a fool of himself once again as he knelt on the tavern floor and wept, his hands covering his eyes. Would the man never learn from his mistakes? He was weak. And a fourteen year-old Gabriel wanted to be nothing like him. He leaned against a table in the corner of the tavern as Augustin Baptiste, his father's rival in the fabric and textile business, collected his winnings from several unsmiling men who'd placed bets on today's race and lost.

Gabriel knew this was the end of the line. He scowled at the man who'd given him life. His father had nothing left to cover his bet. Nothing that is, except their modest home.

His mother, Manon, stood at the entrance to the tavern, her body hunched over as she huddled against the cold evening. She'd forgotten her cloak, as usual, and hadn't remembered to brush her hair when she awoke. She hadn't been well. His mother came from a well-to-do family, the Verdiers of Champagne. Gabriel had seen a picture of her in her youth. Petite. Dark wavy hair. Big soulful eyes that pleaded with her husband to stop his reckless, impulsive behavior. Her blue wool work gown hung on her too-thin body, making her seem like a little girl, rather than a beautiful, grown woman.

Gabriel's stomach turned, and for a moment, he thought he might lose what little was there. He'd been working at the public stable mucking stalls and dreaming of riding a chestnut bay that belonged to a man passing through town. Calais was a Flemish port where people came to set sail for other much grander destinations. Like Paris, Germany, or Denmark. Some men went as far north and east as *Nord Vegr* or Russia.

Gabriel was dying to get away from all this chaos and see more of the world. He didn't need these people to keep him alive. And so he day-dreamed away the bad parts of his life, leaving not much that was good anymore.

When a man from the tavern came running to fetch Gabriel at the stable, he already knew his father was in trouble again. Antoine de Maci was predictable, and deserved what he got. But Gabriel had a soft spot for his mother. She'd never expected to end up out on the street, and here they were, a heartbeat away from the cold, damp night.

He loathed his father at that moment. Unable to withstand the taunts any longer, he took his mother's hand and pulled her outside. He didn't stop walking until they stood several blocks away. Hands on hips, he caught his breath.

"He's lost it all."

"*Oui*, I'm aware." His mother blew her nose into a kerchief.

He reached into his pocket. "I've saved a little money. Here. That should be two nights at a decent inn. Leave here and head for Reims. You have a sister there, *oui*?"

She nodded, her face miserable as big tears silently ran down her cheeks. "What about your father? Will you stay and help him find a way out of this situation?"

Gabriel felt the rage choking him, and it took a moment to tamp it down before he could speak. "I refuse to help him anymore."

"But he's your father."

"*Maman*, he has been given so many chances. So many opportunities. I'm not going to waste my time or money bailing him out. He must face the consequences." He patted her shoulder and pointed to the outskirts of town. "Go home and pack lightly. I will take you to Reims myself."

"You will leave him a note?"

He made a face. "He doesn't deserve even that, the bastard. I will come for you later."

"What if your *papa* comes home?"

"It's not his home anymore. That's why you should take only what you need. I will ask around and see if I can borrow a wagon and horse."

As he watched his mother shuffle down the road toward their home, he suddenly noticed how thin and shaky she appeared. He blamed his father for that, as well. Gabriel's life was about to change in a major way, and it was all because of a greedy, weak man. Gabriel gritted his teeth and fought off the rising rage.

Gabriel finished his work that evening at the stable and collected what pay he was owed. He hated using what little money he had to rent a horse and wagon. So he did the next best thing. He "borrowed" a small wagon that should hold his mother's belongings and could easily be pulled by one horse. Although he could get by with the old, sway-backed workhorse typically used with the wagon, when he stopped and peered into the stall of the chestnut bay he'd been day-dreaming about, he knew he'd never be able to give that horse back to its owner. Besides, he'd probably be arrested if he showed up here again.

That night, Gabriel cut all ties and left the only home he'd ever known. He told himself it was to protect his mother, but he refused to tell her he'd run into a curious stable hand who had to be eliminated in order to steal both the treasured horse and carriage wagon.

They arrived in Reims without trouble, and as Gabriel considered the fresh, sweet air scented by grapes that would one day become champagne, he knew this would be a welcoming place. His mother's older sister, Solange, was a taller, more cheerful version of her. His aunt invited his mother to stay as long as she liked, and she didn't ask questions about his father. As it is, she had her hands full helping to manage a vineyard that produced champagne, like so many others in the Reims vicinity. Between that and raising three boys and a baby girl, Solange seemed relieved when Manon appeared out of nowhere.

For those reasons and more, Gabriel felt reassured it was time for him to strike out on his own. He had no specific plan, but he knew he wanted to do something with horses. He named his new steed Roco, packed what few belongings he had in a saddlebag, and went to say goodbye to his mother.

"I know you and your father were troubled and didn't see eye to eye. But he loved you, Gabriel."

"If he really loved me, he wouldn't have gambled away all our worldly possessions."

His mother eyed his saddlebag, noting its sparse contents. "Where will you go?"

"I don't know. I might head south first."

His mother clasped her cloak together, a funny smile trembling at the corners of her mouth. "Have you ever considered the priesthood? You've always been a studious boy. You could put all that knowledge to good use."

Gabriel shrugged. "I'll give it some serious consideration. For you."

He thought about the stable hand he'd quietly dispatched with a dagger, then disposed of in a conveniently located bog. But he felt no remorse or guilt.

He smiled at his mother. She didn't need to know everything. "I'll talk to the priest in Reims before I go. How's that?"

"My good son," she murmured, then hugged him tightly.

Chapter 15

As *The Sea Raven* eased out of the harbor town of *Kirkjuvagr*, Vor watched her father laughing and playing with her brothers. It heartened her to see him back to his old self with the family. No doubt, he owed that to the authorities who had allowed him to attend Aila's wedding in Frankia while the investigation into possible smuggling activities continued. Thank goodness for the king's generosity in helping with expenses. She shifted her eyes to her mother, who was playing some kind of card game with Graham. While she knew they could have rescheduled the wedding to take place at their home, if necessary, her father had insisted Aila's wedding would be a splendid affair and the venue would be none other than a famous chateau called La Belle Rose.

Of course, adding Belle Rose to the mix was enough to increase interest and add a certain flair to the horse race, dubbed The King's Race, sponsored by King Louis. Now that she was bound for Frankia, Vor felt a constant nervous trepidation. She couldn't recall the last time she'd been so excited and anxious at the same time, so as the ship made its way down the coast of Alba and England, she took in everything with fresh eyes.

The ship stopped in *Thjorsá* first, to pick up Father Gabriel's ward, Vivienne Le Clerc, the other rider. With her horse, Ivor, at his home base outside Paris, she had no worries about caring for a horse. Which was to the horse's benefit. After less than a day, Vor had sussed out the fact that Vivi wasn't the nurturing type.

Since Vor had no sense of who her opponent as a rider would be, she had no expectations in that regard. Until Father Gabriel had boarded with great fanfare, leading a petite young woman with dark hair and a haughty air about her, she would never have anticipated such an obnoxious creature existed. Vivi was small in stature, but as tough as old shoe leather when it came to voicing her opinion. She appeared with two large trunks of clothes, and bragged about them constantly. Perhaps the worst thing was her mouth, which needed occasional censoring around the young boys. They, of course, thought Vivi was great fun when she deigned to play games on deck, which Captain Drogo forbade. But Vivi managed to wrap even the pirates around her little finger.

When she first met Father Gabriel, something nagged at her that Vor thought she should remember. His face was familiar, but she couldn't imagine how she could have met him before if he'd always lived in Frankia. Perhaps what bothered her most were his piercing, intense black eyes. He was one of those men who stood very close to her, which made her nervous. Furthermore, he smelled of burning wood, which she found odd. Not burning oak or ash or pine. Nothing specific. Just some kind of ash or dust. As she observed him throughout the day, Vor shuddered, sensing some kind of evil within him. She had no wish to discover what that might be, so she managed to stay on deck as much as possible with both parents or her brothers close by.

Unfortunately, the voyage wasn't all that smooth. Although they made good time with a satisfactory wind in their sails, Vor was still traveling with three mischievous boys and a horse prone to seasickness. As much as she loved her family, by the fourth day at sea, she was ready to strangle her brothers ... and Vivi with her big mouth. It didn't take long to figure out that her brother Atli spent the majority of his time in the cargo hold calming Fillian. But that wasn't the only reason he stayed out of sight. He would never come out and say it, but it became clear rather soon that he didn't like Vivi, which certainly was understandable as far as Vor was concerned.

Her first conversation with Vivi was an indication of things to come.

"So, why doesn't your brother look anything like you?" Vivi wanted to know. "You have that ridiculous red hair and freckles. And he's blond and handsome. An Adonis."

Vor had been enjoying a quiet, sunny afternoon until then. She shifted in an empty rower's seat since they didn't need all the rowers at the moment, thanks to a fine wind. She shaded her eyes and looked up at Vivi, who was dressed like one of the crew in brown leggings and boots, and a too-big white linen shirt with a belt cinched around her small waist. Vor considered a rude answer to the comment about her red hair, but couldn't bring herself to do that with her parents within hearing distance. Besides, she was used to it.

"Atli is my half-brother. He was born in *Nord Vegr*, and his mother died when he was two. His father, Torleik, married my mother when he was four. That 'outrageous red hair and freckles' comes from my mother's side—Clan MacAoidh." She sat back and studied her fingernails. "Any more questions?"

"Does he have a wife or lady friend?"

Vor wrinkled her nose. "Ask him yourself."

"He's staying down in the cargo hold with that puking horse. Do you have any idea what that smells like when you go down there?"

"Unpleasant?"

"He's avoiding me, isn't he?"

Vor scooted over to make room for Graham, who came to nap in her lap. "What do you think?"

"I think I'm going to beat you in that race without any trouble."

"You brag a lot, Vivi. But where are your recent wins? That makes you and Ivor fair game."

Vivi grimaced and turned away, muttering something unrepeatable under her breath.

"I don't like her," Graham whispered, laying his head on a blanket draped over her lap.

"Good for you. Always trust your instincts about people," she whispered back.

He nodded his agreement and yawned.

"I'm hungry" he said.

She glanced up at the sunset on the horizon in the west. "I'd guess we'll have dinner soon. Maybe in an hour. Can you wait that long?"

"Uh huh."

"Sleep now. You never know when the sea will get rough again."

Graham nodded off almost immediately. Vor watched Vivi laughing and joking with other crew members who didn't bother keeping their voices down. Pirates were like that. Loud. Boastful. Liars. Vivi fit right in.

After supper, Aila and Vor lounged in the small cabin where they shared a bed, while their parents occupied the captain's cabin. Graham slept inside with them. Fionne and Erik were excited about bunking under the stars with the pirates. Vor had no idea where Gabriel and Vivi slept, and she really didn't care.

"I can't get over how much she brags about herself," Aila said as she brushed her hair before retiring. "I wonder where that comes from. The need to make yourself look better than others."

Vor set aside her shawl and crawled under the surprisingly warm bed covers. "Father once told me it comes from being insecure inside. People act the opposite to make up for their shortcomings." She put her arms on top of the covers. "Atli said she was orphaned when she was really young, then raised by Gabriel." She punched her pillow. "If I were her, I would never trust Father Gabriel."

"Why is that?"

"He's a priest, for starters. So, why doesn't he act like one? And why is he into horse racing?"

"It does seem a bit dubious, doesn't it?"

Aila put away her brush and climbed under the covers. Vor leaned over and blew out the candle, and they settled back on the pillows.

"You and Armand seem much ... closer. At least, he seemed reluctant to say goodbye when he boarded the ship to return home."

"We do seem a bit closer, don't we?"

"Just think, in less than a fortnight, you'll be sleeping with him."

Aila made a little noise and covered her mouth.

"Was that a yay or nay sound?"

"I think it was more of an eek. Don't remind me of things like that."

Vor chuckled. "I can't wait to see your new home. Armand says he has lots and lots of servants to wait on you."

"Hmph. I don't really need dozens of servants. Though one would be nice. I asked Mother if I could bring Mina, but she said no. I think she's getting used to having the help."

For a while, Vor enjoyed the smooth rocking motion of the ship, glad the waves had settled into a motion more conducive to sleep. It was also a time for her to delve deeper into the secrets and mysteries of the past few months. One mystery had her particularly vexed. Each day at their main meal, Vor would gaze at her mother, trying to remember something. By the third day, she felt she was going crazy trying to recall something to do with her mother. Something important. She voiced this concern one night with Aila.

"I feel like I'm losing my mind. How could I forget something if it's supposed to be so important?" Vor punched her pillow.

"Don't kill the pillow, Vor. We don't want to anger the pirates."

"Pirates. Right. By the way, why are we sailing with pirates?"

"You know what Father said. It has to do with the ship's large cargo hold for animals, and a design that makes the ship travel faster in the water."

"Still. I don't know anyone who sails with pirates."

"Father has become friends with Captain Drogo. That's my theory, anyway." Aila settled the blanket over her. "You know, it may be that you're more nervous than usual about the race, because it's turned into a big event. Perhaps that's what's got you frustrated."

Vor sighed. "I suppose that's possible. It just feels like time is running out. What if what I'm trying to recall doesn't come to me in time?"

Aila patted her arm. "It will. You're good with obligations and dates. It will come. Meanwhile, relax and stop obsessing about it.

Vivi is having fun. So should you. You may never experience an important event like this again. Focus on that."

"But Father's horses ..."

"You can't control that."

Vor knew her sister was right, but her conscience wouldn't let go. "If I win the prize, everything can go back to the way it was."

"Then focus on winning."

Vor remained silent for several moments. "That's so simple."

"Yes, it is."

After a brief pause, Vor turned to Aila. "Has Mother asked you again about the Goddess Charge?

Aila sighed deeply. "I confess, I didn't really listen. The idea of using that book upset me so badly. Mother said we would discuss it before the wedding." Vor jumped to her feet and peered out the porthole.

"It's a full moon," Vor said, then turned to Aila. "A good time for a confession. But you can't tell Mother."

"Oh, Vor, what have you done now?"

"I went back into the caves before we sailed ... "

"After all of mother and father's warnings?" Aila tsked.

"I found the book, old and falling apart, on a high shelf. I couldn't pick it up because someone had put a spell on it. It almost burned my fingers."

"Who would put a spell on a dictionary?"

Vor frowned, her mind whirring. Something about Father Gabriel had seemed familiar. Those eyes. Suddenly, she bolted upright, excitement making her heart beat faster. "Of course! Father Alceste and Father Gabriel are the same person, but he goes by Alceste when he's out bird watching or snooping around. He was the one reading from the book. It sounded a bit like Latin. I wonder if I might ask Gabriel to undo the spell so I can get the book back."

Aila sat up, pulling the blanket with her. "Oh, Vor. You should know better not to trust Gabriel or to believe in things like conjuring. It's superstitious nonsense. You know that."

Cold now, Vor climbed back in bed and hugged the bedcovers to her chest. "You don't believe me."

Aila lay back down and stared at the ceiling. "It doesn't matter what I think. In the morning, when you're fresh, tell Mother everything you think is relevant. Let her decide what to act on. You need to get some sleep. And so do I. Goodnight, little sister." She turned on her side, her back to Vor.

Vor hadn't expected this. She shivered and turned to face the other wall of the cabin. Aila was probably right. But she had to make someone understand that what happened to her was real.

She sat up again and peered over at Aila. "Are you still awake?"

"What now?"

"I think, under the right circumstances, it's a book for making magic. When I followed Armand into the caves like you asked, I couldn't open the door to the tunnel on the right. So I went down the tunnel on the left to search for the book. I found it. But when I went back, Gabriel put a spell on me, and I couldn't see the book anymore. Maybe he rendered it invisible?"

Aila groaned. "You can't tell mother I was involved in any of this."

"I would never tell Mother you asked me to follow Armand into the caves. It's just that I need you to believe me about what happened. Father Gabriel spoke some words and then created some sort of awful yellow smoke. Sulfur, I believe. I've heard it said that witches or sorcerers are able to produce sulfur."

"So, you're saying Father Gabriel, an ordained priest, is a witch?"

"Or sorcerer," Vor added in a small voice.

"We'll continue this conversation tomorrow, Vor. Just don't say those words aloud while aboard ship. You hear me?"

Vor curled onto her side, hugging a pillow. "I understand. Pirates can be very superstitious, can't they?"

"You say the wrong words around them, and they'll make you walk the plank. I'm not joking."

Vor let those words sink in as she clutched her pillow against her stomach.

"I know you're going to obsess over this," Aila continued. "My advice is to wait until you get back home and look for the book again. Once you've done a thorough search, and it's still missing, *then* tell Mother. She'll know what to do." Aila paused to yawn. "I assumed she would bring the book with her and give it to me in Frankia, the same way her grandmother Marsaili sent it in a trunk with her belongings when Mother moved to Meginland to marry Father."

"Which means ...

"Either she has the book—"

"Or she knows where it is."

An icy tingling made its way down Vor's spine.

Chapter 16

Aila was right. Vor couldn't stop thinking about the book. In the full light of day, a tendril of fear crept up Vor's neck as she stared out over the ocean and once again wondered what to do about the missing book. Did her mother have it...or Gabriel? If her mother had it, she would have said something to Aila by now, surely. And hadn't she seemed distracted lately? Worried? But that could be due to the hustle and bustle of the wedding. She'd no doubt been concerned about how they would afford this trip with their hard-earned money unavailable. Fortunately for them, the king had heard of their plight and had offered to pay their expenses to and from Frankia so that the King's Race could go on as planned. He'd even provided for incidentals along the way, so that she could experience Paris for the first time, saying it had to be a young woman's dream come true. Still, whatever the reason for her mother's anxiety, Vor must find out without causing a major stir right before the wedding and the race.

Cool water sprayed her from the bowsprit of the ship. She turned her attention to the bright red flag with the beady-eyed Raven. *The Sea Raven.* It was true none of the pirates had bothered the girls, other than the occasional whistle of appreciation. Fortunately, they kept their hands to themselves, and called Aila and Vor "mademoiselle." Vor had no complaints, and Vivi seemed to have discovered several besotted men who regarded her as something exotic, so she wore a smile for the majority of the voyage.

Vor had read about pirates, or corsairs as they were known in Frankia, privateers who worked directly for the King of Frankia, known for attacking the ships of Frankia's enemies. From what she'd learned, most ships piloted by corsairs carried official *lettres de marque* that made their actions legitimate in the eyes of the Frankish justice system. Should they be captured, that letter gave them the status of a war prisoner rather than a pirate, the latter carrying the punishment of hanging. They were typically ordered by the King to attack only enemy ships. This provided revenue for the King, as they were required to hand over a portion of their booty.

Vor shivered at a sudden breeze. She'd forgotten her cloak, so hugged herself to stay warm. As she watched the ever-present gulls entertain with their antics of diving for fish and squabbling over what the pirates tossed them, it occurred to her that she was at an age where she needed to trust her father to take care of her, but at the same time, she needed to take some responsibility for her own well-being. Since she'd fallen out of favor with her father, she felt like a little girl once more. One who had misbehaved. She sighed into the wind, surprised how much it hurt. This fall from grace.

As they sailed past the eastern boundary of Alba's coastline, not even stopping for food and water, Vor felt a crushing loneliness take hold as they moved further and further away from her homeland. Even though her family was aboard ship, it finally sank in that her life would be forever changed once Aila's marriage took place. She may never see her sister again, for all she knew.

The ship's speed held steady for the majority of the trip, which helped her stay calm inside her small self-imposed cocoon.

As the pirates settled into their routine, she grew used to their voices barking out orders, almost as if it were a typical British naval ship. The steady rush of waves against the hull was a powerful reminder of Nature's whims, and she had to force herself to stay awake several times during the afternoon after little sleep the night before.

Armand wasn't joking when he'd said the ship was fast. It was almost as if the gods had gathered together to blow the perfect amount of wind into the sails, because they completed the trip in five days.

In the Flemish port town of Calais, Vor watched the pirates disembark and head for their favorite bars and saloons to celebrate the end of the voyage with familiar comrades.

She had to smile when she saw Atli unload an anxious Fillian, who picked his way carefully down the gangplank.

Please allow me to hold onto Fillian and keep him healthy.

Captain Drogo and a few of his men carried their trunks and travel belongings to an inn for the night. They would leave for Paris the next day.

"I am so glad to be off that horrible pirate ship," said Aila as she and Vor freshened up for supper. "I can't imagine what Father was thinking, making arrangements with a pirate captain."

"Well, as Armand said, it was a fast ship. They may have dressed more colorfully, but at least they left us alone. Did you know pirates have a code of honor not to harm women on their ships?"

Aila tilted her head. "I guess that explains their good manners, for the most part. We should consider ourselves lucky."

"Still, I'm glad to have solid ground beneath my feet. So is Fillian, by the way." Vor described Fillian on the gangplank and Aila laughed at the image.

Vor reached in her sack and found her hairbrush, gave her hair a good brushing, then put the last of her belongings back in her sack. "If it's still light out after we eat, maybe we can walk around town and get our bearings."

"That would be nice. We may never see Calais again."

Once they felt somewhat revived, they joined the other family members in the dining room, easily taking up one long table. Shortly afterward, Drogo, Gabriel and Vivi entered with a young man Vor didn't recognize. He was quite good-looking, with light brown hair that brushed the collar of his work tunic, and his light blue eyes turned up at the corners, lending an exotic air to his features. He smiled and nodded as Gabriel introduced him.

"This is Ivor's trainer and exerciser, Luc Frontier. He'll help you take care of your red stallion until the race is over," he said to Vor.

Vor blinked, guessing him to be closer to Aila's age, seventeen. To Gabriel, she said, "Thanks, but we don't need help with Fillian." She turned to Atli. "Do we?"

Atli wore that combative expression she'd learned to avoid. "We can take care of Fillian just fine." He indicated where his three brothers sat in a row, impatiently waiting for their food. "Vor and I can handle most of it. And my brothers will fill in when necessary."

Erik and Fionne sat up straight and tried to look intelligent. Graham ignored everyone to play with a toy horse on the table.

"I'm so hungry, I could eat that horse," groused Vivi, rubbing her stomach.

"That seems kind of crude, considering the subject of the race," said Atli, gazing at her over his ale. "I thought riders had more empathy for their steeds."

Vivi had changed her clothing, and wore a pale strawberry tunic belted over a dark blue skirt. For once, she appeared feminine with her dark hair pulled back, and Vor couldn't help but wonder if she did it to attract Vor's brother, Atli.

Vivi ignored Atli's comment. "So, Gabriel, what should we tell them about the team Ivor and I make?"

"Nothing unkind, my dear. Now, you should order a meal to keep you fortified for tomorrow's sojourn."

In other words, shut up and eat.

Vivi stared at Vor, as though noting Vor's frizzy red hair, which needed a good wash. "I see you didn't take my advice and avoid the cargo hold. You stink like vomit."

Vor had no intention of allowing the other woman to intimidate her. She pasted a smile on her face. "I'm aware I'm not my usual neat and tidy self. It's hard to maintain good hygiene on a pirate ship." She turned away, her cheeks flaming.

"Oh, ain't that the truth now, princess?" Drogo looked from Vor's frizzy mess of red hair to Vivi's delicately curled locks, which hung loose on her shoulders.

Vor shrunk inside, having never felt so unsure of herself before.

Anxious to see Fillian for herself before she retired for the night, Vor followed the irascible Vivienne le Clerc from the Bones & Barnacles Inn to the public stables, four blocks away. Aila was ready to get some sleep, so declined to join them.

Vivi had a habit of turning her head with one ear toward a speaker, reminding Vor of a horse. Her ears didn't actually move, of course, but it was an interesting observation. That, and how she liked to walk, scuffing one shoe on the right. Had she injured her leg at some point?

They entered the stable, and Vivi turned to pin Vor with dark brown eyes. "Where is the handsome Adonis? I was hoping to spend some time alone with him."

Vor frowned as Vivi glanced around at the other horses.

"Adonis? Oh, you mean Atli. I don't know. Probably hiding from you. Leave him alone and focus on the race."

Vivi pointed a finger. "As for tonight, I expect you and your sister to be quiet. No laughing, giggling, or anything that keeps me awake. You understand, Stinky?"

"Fine by me." Vor ignored Vivi's jab. Instead, she looked up in time to see they'd stopped in front of Fillian's stall, where Atli fed Fillian fresh hay.

"Sounds like you have a wild night planned." Atli set out a new bale of hay for Fillian to work on, then glanced up.

Vor hoped she didn't have to play mediator for Vivi and whomever she spoke to or insulted over the next few days. Vor really must tell her half-brother not to engage in conversation with the woman. Vivi would argue with the King of Frankia, if she thought she could get away with it.

The two continued to banter back and forth. Vor sincerely hoped that didn't suggest an attraction of any kind between her brother and Vivienne. Fortunately, Atli appeared to ignore Vivi's haughty remarks and as they prepared to leave said to Vor, "Bring me back something with meat. Beef, preferably. I'm wasting away here."

"You're in fine form today. See you later, brother."

Vor whispered a farewell to Fillian and petted him between his ears, then followed Vivi out to see what delicious dessert creations they could find at the Bones & Barnacle. Or not.

Chapter 17

Vivienne's nightmares were beginning to invade her daydreams, and she was having a hard time keeping everything straight. As she sat back against the inn's unmade double bed, she wished Gabriel was there so she could get to the bottom of whatever was ailing her.

She had worked so hard these past weeks to keep her temper in check, and figured she needed good public support if she was to keep riding. However, being around Vor and Atli was like sleeping with a dog with fleas. They naturally rubbed her the wrong way. She'd pleaded with Gabriel to have her own room at the inn in Calais, instead of sharing her private time with strangers. Vor and Aila were used to it, so Gabriel finally let her have her way. And yet, late at night, all alone, Vivi was loath to admit she could use some company.

Vivienne clutched at the bedcovers when she heard men's voices outside her door. Afraid they were drunk and might try to enter her room, she shoved a table in front of the door. Gabriel had warned her to beware of such men, especially with the crew from the pirate ship lurking nearby. She wished she had that big, strapping Atli as a bodyguard right about now. Then she might get proper sleep. She would never confess this to Vor or Atli, but she enjoyed making him uncomfortable with her undivided attention.

Vivi's thoughts turned to Marcel. She often dreamt of the debt collector. Those dreams soothed her, made her feel safe. Of course, she barely knew him, yet he was fine to look at, if she were honest with herself, and she thought he had shown polite interest in her, as well. And although not as fit as Atli, he had appreciation for money that she thought translated into caring for her in the way she deserved. With the prize money from the race as her dowry, and her looks as leverage, she felt confident she could talk Marcel into marrying her so she could get out from under Gabriel's thumb.

But then she frowned and pressed on her forehead. Since her spill on the racetrack, her headaches had increased. She knew something was very wrong with her, but did she dare say anything to Gabriel? He was counting on her to ride Ivor to the finish line and win that prize. He might not trust her if she told him she wasn't feeling well. Besides, the race would be behind her in just over a week. She could seek help then.

Gabriel kept telling her to get more sleep. But sleep had become the enemy. When she closed her eyes, strange dreams came to life. Dreams of her childhood. Sometimes just images. Weapons with blood. People with no heads. Had she witnessed something awful when she was small? What had really happened to her parents? Gabriel had told her since she was a child that they both died from a fever within a week of each other. But these disturbing memories were now her constant companions, and each dream took her further and further back in time. She didn't want to go there. She didn't really want to know, did she?

She inhaled and shuddered.

"Your father did a bad thing," Gabriel had told the five-year-old Vivienne all those years ago. "And the king was very angry. So your father had to pay ... with his life."

Vivienne sat very still until the shaking stopped and the memory faded, then reached for a glass of water. Before she could take a sip, it spilled all over her skirt, and she cried out as she attempted to dry her skirt with her hands. But try as she might, the memory of that night kept returning.

Gabriel held onto the little girl with the lisp.

"My father?" she'd asked.

"He was executed, my dear."

"Exe...scuted?"

"Yes, my dear. He was killed by the King's very own Executioner."

Beads of sweat gathered on her upper lip now as she recalled her words. "What did he do?"

Gabriel circled her in the dream, his dark eyes mesmerizing. "Your father was an apothecary. He made a potion requested by the king. Unfortunately for your father, that potion killed the wrong man, which made the king very, very angry. So I took out my sword and I swung it ..."

"No!"

Vivienne remembered hearing someone scream.

Supper at the Bones & Barnacles Inn wasn't exactly gourmet eating. The public room was almost full the next morning, so Vor reluctantly agreed to share a table with Vivi, then tried her best to remain optimistic about the food. She ordered what she hoped would be simple fare for their first and last night in Calais. Surely the cooks couldn't ruin something as basic as lamb stew with fresh baked bread on the side.

Vor took her time chewing her stew. It wasn't half bad, but not the freshest mutton. Vivi didn't seem to care, and ate quickly, then jumped into a long discussion with someone at the table next to her about the superiority of European-bred horses. Vor felt perfectly comfortable not contributing. Instead, she closed her eyes and let her thoughts drift. When she opened them again, she spotted Luc, Ivor's exerciser and trainer, standing near the door to the Inn. Vivi waved him down into a vacant chair and kept up her conversation with the person at the other table. With Luc's arrival, the other customer finished off his mug of ale and left the tavern, having lost his knowledgeable female audience.

Vor was about to mention the race, then thought better of it. She had no interest in a knock-down drag-out fight.

Luc ordered the stew and a mug of ale then rested his hands on the table. When Vor's gaze shifted from him to Vivi, Vor immediately noticed her red-rimmed eyes and pale face.

"Vivi, are you alright?" Vor asked. "You look ill. Maybe Gabriel can give you something to make you feel better?"

"No! I'm fine. It's probably just a headache from the noise people are making." She finished her meal and rose. "I'm going to rest now. The walls are thin, so you and your sister better not make any noise in your room tonight. I'm a light sleeper."

Vivi turned and left the dining room, as Vor and Luc stared, speechless.

"How odd." Vor wiped her mouth with a napkin. "That's the lightest insult I've received tonight. I wonder why she's off her game."

"She's been yelling at me and the horses in the cargo hold pretty much nonstop," Luc offered. "She may have strained her voice."

"She went down in the cargo hold? I don't want her anywhere near Fillian."

Luc's eyes slid to two burly men who were arm wrestling at the bar. "I didn't see her go near your horse. Instead, I think she went down there to flirt with your brother."

"She must have really wanted to see Atli if she'd go below deck. She gave me a bad time about the smell earlier."

Luc laughed. "The longer I know Vivi, the more complicated she gets."

To help her sleep, Vor accepted a cup of chamomile tea from the serving woman, then sat in quiet contemplation for a while. Luc continued eating and kept his silence, for which she was grateful.

Several moments slipped by before she finally shared her thoughts. "How hard did Vivi fall from Ivor last week? Did she hit her head, perhaps?"

His hand went up to his own forehead, and she noticed a cut, likely from the gravel. "I think she landed on her backside, so if she hit her head, it would have been on the side or back."

"Was Gabriel there? Did he rush to treat her wound?"

Luc pushed aside his empty bowl. "Now that you mention it, he's been making her take a tonic of some sort every evening, a sleep potion, I think."

Vor sipped her tea, thinking about Vivi. Then she saw Luc rub at his forehead again. "Are you alright?"

He shrugged. "I have some bruises, but nothing's broken. One of the hired men at the house cleaned up my forehead and put something on it. It's just a scratch, almost healed."

"I'm glad to hear that." She glanced around, then leaned in closer. "Do you know what made the horses stumble and fall?"

He finished off his ale. "Probably the whip Vivi likes to use. Ivor felt that, and stumbled. Then he ran into Thibault, the exercise horse I was riding during a practice race. Thank God the horses didn't break anything."

A horse whip. Not good.

"I agree." Vor leaned her arms on the table and rested her head in her hands, her heart aching for the horses. "Did the back of Vivi's head bleed?"

"I don't recall. But I've seen her touching a spot on the side. She must have a lump there."

"That would seem likely."

He leaned forward. "You're not going to use this information against Vivi, are you?"

He'd lowered his voice to a whisper, causing Vor to lean even closer. "Not at all. It's just that my mother's a healer, so I'm trying to think if there's anything that could help her."

Luc was silent for a moment, his light blue eyes searching her face.

She broke into a smile. "I know I'm considered the enemy in this race, but what I really want is a good, well-matched competition. It's to all our benefits."

Slowly, his shoulders relaxed as he sat back. "I believe you."

"Thank you. Now, I'm off to get a good night's sleep. I look forward to seeing Ivor in the flesh. So far, he's like a ghost horse in my mind."

Luc rose and smiled. "You won't be disappointed."

She was surprised when he stuck out his hand. Despite being a competitor, she reached out and shook it. "I'll see you in the morning, Luc Frontier."

He nodded politely, and while she didn't know if he could be considered a new "friend" because of his affiliation with Vivi and Gabriel, at least he seemed like a fair and even-tempered young man. Besides, she liked the way he leaned in when he spoke and the slight rasp in his voice. He smelled like salt from the sea, and peat from the fire.

She climbed the stairs and felt her hand tingle where he'd touched her. Though she couldn't say why, that made her smile.

Chapter 18

A shrill woman's scream woke Vor in the early morning hours, bringing her fully awake within seconds.

"That's Vivi!"

Vor shook Aila and jumped out of bed, grabbing her shawl.

"Wha—what's wrong?" Aila gurgled, not quite awake.

"I just heard a scream. Vivi may be in trouble."

Vor stepped into the corridor and knocked on Vivi's door. It took a few moments before she heard something being scraped across the floor and pulled away from the door. When Vivi opened the door, she looked feverish and disoriented.

"Why did you wake me up?" she demanded, her lips forming a pout.

"You woke us up with your scream. Don't you remember?"

"That's ridiculous." Vivi put her hand on the door and started to close it. "Leave me alone so I can get my sleep." Then she stopped and looked around her room, as though noting the furniture arrangement. "Who's been in my room?" She turned in a tight circle, eyeing everything, then stilled. "I was dreaming of Marcel. He asked me to marry him."

Vor exchanged a puzzled look with Aila just as her mother and father appeared from down the hall, wearing their nightclothes.

"Well, congratulations, then." Vor made a quick decision to just go along with Vivi's delusions, not wanting to stand in the hallway any longer. "I wish you and Marcel all the happiness in the world."

Vivi squinted. "Who's Marcel?" She leaned in closer. "I know you. You're out to grab any man who's not attached."

"Vivi, you're causing a commotion," said Gabriel, suddenly there among them. "Let's go inside, and we can talk about this privately, so the others can get their sleep."

Sleep was in short supply as Vor made her way to her room. As she began to wake up and face the day, she made a last-minute decision that today was the day she'd ask Gabriel what he was giving Vivi that could affect her in such a strange way. No more sitting on the fence and hoping for the best. Therefore, they all enjoyed a hearty breakfast upon waking, and then gathered outside the inn where Gabriel was double-checking the bridles and horses that would pull the heavily loaded wagon. Vor chose that time to approach him.

"Excuse me. Father Gabriel, as you know, Vivi woke us up screaming last night. I think something is giving her bad dreams and making her seem confused. I'm really worried she won't be able to ride in the race. My mother is a healer. Would you mind if she takes a look at Vivi when we stop for the night?"

Gabriel finished fiddling with the bridle and stared at her. "If you insist, mademoiselle. Let her sleep during the day. She'll be better tonight."

Vor considered it a truce of sorts, and nodded. She quickly filled her mother in so she could observe Vivi during the day, which made Vor feel somewhat better. She had to admit, she hadn't known Vivi long, but she might just be starting to like her, warts and all.

The group started out for Paris while fishermen were just beginning their day in Calais. A mist-like rain fell for quite some time. Torleik and Atli had constructed a temporary cover over the wagon to help keep the sun and rain out, which Sister Marie Claudette, the nun who had asked to accompany them part of the way, greatly appreciated.

Armand had returned to the chateau before they arrived by ship and retrieved his personal mount, Roman, a pale gray stallion with dark gray mane, tail and socks. Sitting comfortably in the saddle, he led the group south toward his family home. Atli rode beside him, trying to control an excitable Fillian, clearly happy to be back on solid ground once again.

Vor had no choice but to ride in the wagon with Aila and Vivi, while her mother rode with the driver. The younger boys alternated between walking and riding with Torleik or Atli. As Vor eyed Vivi's massive travel trunk, she realized she had nothing special to wear for the race. In fact, she had only a clean work tunic and leggings, and a fresh gown in her travel sack. That bothered her considerably, not because she wanted to look especially fancy, but because she wanted her parents to be proud of her, and more than anything, she wanted to feel confident. As though she belonged. She may never have this opportunity again to show them what she was made of. She *must* win.

And then, when she returned home, she would find the *Book of Delsiran*. She didn't like facing the extra challenge of being so far away at this time. But if she was very organized and wasn't in Frankia for too long, she just might be able to find it before her mother noticed it had gone missing.

Vor's thoughts turned to Gabriel, who spoke quietly with Sister Marie Claudette as he walked next to the wagon. He wore an old, frayed black cassock and carried himself a bit stooped, like an old man. At first, Vor thought it was a disguise, but later decided he really had aged since she'd met him. The price of performing dark magic perhaps? Once again her thoughts scrolled back to the missing book. If he had taken it, what could he possibly want with it? She felt the hair at the back of her neck rise.

To rid herself of the feeling, she turned to Luc, who was chatty that morning. He and Atli were discussing the attributes of the Frankish draft horses that Gabriel had purchased to pull the wagons. Luc seemed very proud of how much weight they could pull, and every so often he offered to drive the wagon to give the driver a break.

For the first time in a long while, Vor thought about finding a husband, especially after Aila's long and difficult search for one. Vor was determined not to agree to an arranged marriage. If only she could find someone confident enough in himself to accept her as she was and who valued education. She eyed Luc again, but immediately shook her head. Her parents would never accept him. He was too "common" in their eyes. Unless she'd misjudged her mother and father somehow.

At last, Vor turned her attention to Vivi who appeared even more tired and grumpy after the other night's nightmare.

Enough is enough.

Vor jumped down from the wagon and sidled up to Gabriel. "Mmm, Father ..." Alceste? Pardon me for interrupting," she said, nodding at Sister Marie Claudette. "May I speak to you in private?"

"Of course, mademoiselle." Gabriel guided his horse away from the wagon. "What do you wish to ask?"

Vor swallowed, hoping he didn't think she was butting in where she wasn't wanted. "As we discussed earlier, I'm concerned that Vivi may have had something to eat or drink that is making her ill, and she's only getting worse as the day progresses."

Gabriel chuckled, as if he thought that funny. She was glad she'd remembered not to use his name in front of Sister Marie

Claudette as it seemed clear that he didn't wish to be recognized by her. But why? That was the question she'd asked herself since the start of this journey.

He sobered and his dark eyes narrowed to slits. "Well, as you saw last night, my Vivi is high-strung, which makes it hard for her to sleep through the night. I gave her a sleeping draft in her wine before bedtime."

Vor processed that information, wondering if it could account for Vivi's other symptoms. "That doesn't explain the scream. I think she was having a nightmare." She glanced briefly over her shoulder. "Are you a healer, Father Gabriel, that you should be treating her? Is it possible that something in the sleeping potion makes her ... not herself? I'm more than worried about her, to be honest."

Luc and Atli stopped talking, clearly interested in Gabriel's response. As if an omen, Vor saw a brilliant monarch butterfly land on Gabriel's shoulder, the yellow a stark contrast against the black fabric. She wished she could ask her mother what it meant, but Eilidh was conversing with the nun.

"The sleeping potion I gave her is indeed strong, so I suppose it's possible it could have caused the nightmares, perhaps making her forgetful or clumsy at times."

"When I knocked on her door and awakened her, she mumbled something about Marcel, a debt collector. For some reason she thought she was to be married to him. Is that true? But when I asked, she said she didn't know anything about him. That seems odd."

"Odd, indeed. Thank you for telling me. I'll take care of that. My daughter is *not* marrying a bill collector, if I can help it."

His daughter? But Vivi claimed she was adopted. Vor said nothing. Maybe he loved her *like* a daughter. It was all very confusing.

After the midday meal, Vivi appeared to feel better, and had opted to walk for a while. Erik and Fionne were fascinated with the feisty lady with the "bad mouth." To Vor's surprise, she did seem to clean up her language with both Eilidh and Sister Marie Claudette nearby. Vor had a momentary image of Vivi taking communion with Gabriel, and it left her with a big grin. At some point in the late afternoon, however, Vivi stumbled and fell to the side of the road, losing both her breakfast and midday meals.

Atli and Luc stopped the horses and wagon and leaned down to tend to Vivi.

It was several moments before she stopped vomiting and wiped her mouth. Atli handed her a clean cloth and she smiled wanly before taking it. Once that was done, Atli picked her up and gently placed her in the wagon next to Sister Marie Claudette.

"You must have eaten something last night that didn't agree with you. Why don't you ride the rest of the way with us and try to get some sleep?" the nun suggested.

"I agree. Rest is what's needed. And drink from this," said Gabriel, handing her a water flask.

Vivi's hands trembled as she gripped the flask and took a drink. She ignored Gabriel, and instead nodded toward Atli. "Thank you for your help, Monsieur Atli. You are very kind."

Vor was shocked when her tall, handsome brother, who normally was so stoic, blushed a deep pink to the roots of his blond hair then turned to Gabriel. "I would go easy on putting things in her food or drink for the next few days, sir. She obviously had a bad reaction."

Gabriel frowned at Atli, then scowled at Vor. "It's none of your business—either of you. I know what Vivi needs, so stay away from her. Vivi works her best when she's isolated."

Standing as tall as she could manage, Vor defied Gabriel. "What you're giving her is making her weak and sick. Do you want her to lose the race because she doesn't have the strength?"

She didn't see the slap coming, but she felt the sting across her cheek.

Gabriel gritted his teeth. "You will stay away from my Vivi until after the race. Am I clear?"

Atli took a step closer to Gabriel. "Don't ever lay a hand on my sister again, or you will know the pleasure of a Norse blade in your gut."

"Atli!" Torleik barked. Atli immediately relaxed and put away his knife. But the hate in his blue eyes remained.

For a moment, Vor feared Gabriel would pull out that lethal-looking hunting knife he carried. She scuttled away from him and climbed back in the wagon.

"Gabriel ..." Vivi started to say something, but suddenly vomited again over the side of the wagon. This time, her stomach was empty. Sister Marie Claudette patted her back and murmured soothing words.

Grateful for his intervention, Vor's eyes trailed her brother as she silently offered her thanks.

Atli brought Fillian closer to the wagon. "Are you alright?"

Vor touched her still warm cheek from Gabriel's hand and glared at his back. "I'm fine. But that man had better watch out before someone here turns him into a toad."

"Can you really do that?" Luc jumped into the conversation.

Vor grinned. "Wouldn't you like to find out?"

The walls of The Spotted Dog Inn were thin, but if Vor thought someone would hear her call for help, should the need arise, she was sadly mistaken. This was the kind of place where no one asked questions. Sister Marie Claudette had indicated she was fine sleeping in a dry, comfortable empty stable stall, while Atli, Armand, and Luc slept with Fillian. That left Vor's parents, Vor, Aila and Vivi to fend for themselves in the small guest rooms. The last single room was claimed by Vivi, who made a show of traipsing up to the attic. Once again, where Gabriel slept was a mystery.

Later that evening, Vor had a relaxing dinner, knowing they were more than halfway to Paris. She and Aila returned to their room to retire, where Vor rubbed a damp towel on the window so she could see out.

"Have you seen Luc? Before we parted, I slipped a note into his coat pocket regarding what to do if he sees Gabriel make Vivi eat or drink anything today. He should be returning to check on her soon. Did he read it? Did he forget?"

Aila shrugged and pulled the bedcover up to her chin. "Maybe he was distracted with everything that's going on." She threw back the bedcovers and moved to the chair near the night table. "I wonder if we could get some tea."

Vor began to pace the small bedchamber. "I'm really worried, Aila. This is all so strange." She stopped abruptly and folded her arms over her chest. She was about to say something when a knock came from the other side of the locked door.

"I wonder what our dear Vivi wants now."

Vor opened the door expecting to see Vivi asking to borrow something from Aila as she had done twice already. Instead, Luc stood there, glancing over his shoulder.

"It's about time," she said, fuming.

He turned back to face her. "What?"

"Didn't you get my note? I put it in your coat pocket. How is Vivi?"

He heaved a sigh. "I didn't see your note. However, I think she's getting worse. And she still insists she's engaged to Marcel, the debt collector. I take it Gabriel hasn't had that talk with her yet."

Vor ushered him in. "If she's physically and mentally unable to ride, what will happen with the race?"

Luc shrugged, his blue eyes wandering around the room. "I don't know Gabriel well enough to predict that. I suppose he could find someone else—another female—to ride Ivor."

"But why would he poison his star rider? He stands to earn a large purse if she wins."

Before Luc could answer, a shadow appeared in the doorway, and a moment later, Gabriel stood before them, casting a pall on the previously cheerful room.

"I heard that last part, Monsieur Frontier. If Vivi can't ride by tomorrow morning, I've decided we'll either have to find someone else to ride or forfeit the race. Normally, there's no one else Ivor tolerates, and some days, he doesn't even put up with her. If Vivi, or someone of her caliber, doesn't ride, we all lose."

Luc stared at Gabriel, and Vor wondered what was going through his head, because he didn't look happy. Surely, Gabriel didn't mean to replace Vivienne at this late date. Who would he find who could step in with such a challenging horse?

Gabriel smiled at her and placed a hand on her arm, which sent chills barreling downward to the fine tips of her fingers. After a moment, he let go. "Not to worry, she has ridden through worse."

"Worse?" Vor rubbed her arms to rid herself of the chill. "But surely you will want her healthy."

"Oh, but aren't you the smart one, Mademoiselle." He shrugged. "She'll be too distracted when the king attends to worry about her health."

"The k-king will be attending?" asked Luc as he raked a hand through his hair.

Gabriel smiled wide. "Ah, did I forget to mention that? After the race was postponed, then moved to Frankia, King Louis was suddenly available to attend. Is that not wonderful?"

If Vor didn't know any better, she'd say Luc looked terrified at the thought of being presented to the king as the groomsman. She couldn't blame him. She just hoped he wasn't hiding something from his past that could come back to haunt both him and Vivi.

"We'll discuss that in more detail later," said Gabriel. "In the meantime, we're going to have our mid-day meal together tomorrow in the tavern, and then we'll start our final journey to Belle Rose. Ladies, I am told your father has rented a nearby cottage for your family that's within easy walking distance to the racetrack. Tomorrow night, you will stay with them."

At long last. Some semblance of normalcy with her family.

Vor watched Gabriel shuffle away, stooped and old. It was all an act. She knew that now.

Chapter 19

Vor had no choice where she and Aila slept the next night. The Spotted Dog Tavern and Inn was a popular inn on the road to Paris, so Vivi, who'd been assigned the largest vacant room available, had to share with the sisters, much to her dismay. When Vor finally sank into an uneasy sleep, she dreamed of her home completely flooded, all the tapestries and furniture ruined. Her mother raced around, trying to save items, but there wasn't much to salvage. She saw her father's horses drowning, their screams too much like those of humans to ignore. In the dream, her father was trying to save each and every last horse, before humans and horses alike submerged beneath the water. Then, the horizon washed away into nothingness.

She awoke abruptly, and sat up in bed on the mattress edge, hoping she hadn't disturbed Aila. Or Vivi, who slept on her side, facing the wall, her breathing even. Vor had worried all day they might have to call off the race altogether. If that happened, she would have no way of repaying her father for everything he'd lost. She wrapped the blankets around her to stave off the chill.

She still couldn't understand why Gabriel would poison his own rider. There must be something in it for him. Then it came to her as though a chill air had breezed in through the partially opened window despite the mugginess of the evening.

Perhaps Vivi was no longer winning. Hadn't Gabriel mentioned the possibility of replacing her with another rider?

Vor lay there for what felt like hours, but couldn't get back to sleep. The air felt warm and stuffy. She peeked out the window curtain and saw how black the sky appeared away from the city lights, and how bright the stars seemed. In an effort to be alone with her thoughts, she very carefully reached for her night robe, then at the last minute grabbed her warm shawl. Stepping into her shoes, she quietly made her way downstairs. The only person in the common room was the inn owner, who sat next to the dying fire dozing. Vor tiptoed across the room and very quietly opened and closed the main door of the inn, so he wouldn't stir.

The first thing she noticed when she stepped foot outside was how cold the night air seemed. She was glad she'd thought to bring her shawl. All she wanted was a bit of fresh, cool air, and then she'd head back and likely be able to sleep. She sat down on the porch step and pulled the shawl close, looking up at the stars and breathing deeply.

Only a few moments had passed when she heard a rustling sound. Afraid it was an unwanted guest who'd become drunk or lost, she started to rise.

"Don't get up. It's me. Luc."

She was glad it was dark, so he couldn't see her hot, red cheeks. "Oh, I'm sorry. I didn't see you."

"Can't sleep?"

"No. You?"

He hesitated, then sank down on the step next to her. "No. How is Vivi tonight?"

"She's sleeping and breathing normally."

"Do you think she'll be alright?"

Vor thought about that for a few moments. "I wish I knew what Gabriel was feeding her, and why. Something is affecting her mentally, that's for sure."

"Your whole family is here, *oui*?"

"Yes, I'm so grateful."

"Did I hear right, that your mother is a healer? Perhaps she can shed some light on this."

"Maybe."

Luc allowed the silence to settle like the warm shawl around her shoulders. "Do you mind my asking what has you so troubled this evening? It can't be just Vivi."

Normally, Vor wouldn't confide in someone she'd just met, but Luc's gentle ways were calming. She gulped down her trepidation and then told her story about her father and the caves. She hated how her voice shook at the end. "I love my father. But he didn't deserve to be held in prison. There was no evidence of his involvement."

"So, do you think your new brother-in-law is the one involved with smugglers?"

She pulled her shawl tighter. "He says he's not involved and that Aila should trust him. But he gives no explanation. I hate it when a man says 'trust me.'"

Luc chuckled. "That has to be frustrating. Hopefully, your father is gathering facts and clues, and doesn't want to say anything about Armand and the smuggling until he knows for sure what's going on."

Vor rose and tipped her chin up to the sky. "You're probably right. My father is like that. Facts first. Accuse later."

When Luc stood beside her, she noticed he was just a few inches taller than her—not that it mattered. He had a closer sense of personal space than any man she knew, and she wasn't sure how she felt about that. She could feel his body heat, and his hair smelled like woodsmoke.

"So, if your father hadn't been taken in for questioning, you might not have agreed to ride in this race?"

Vor turned and really looked at him for the first time. His clear blue eyes drew her in, working their magic on her.

She nodded, then chose her words carefully. "What's worse, earlier tonight, I had a dream ... that scared me."

"A dream about what?"

"A flood. It ruined our house and drowned the horses. I believe it's somehow connected to the race and my father's horses. I confess, I'm a little superstitious."

He smiled and took her hand. The sudden feel of warm skin on skin sent shivers of excitement ... and fear shooting through her.

"I think most of us are. You're not alone. Speaking of superstition, it's been said you can see the future. Is that true?"

Vor stared at his hand holding hers. "Sometimes, seers, or those who possess the gift of second sight, are accused of witchcraft because others don't understand where their gift comes from. They think it's evil, from the Devil, so it's not something I like to talk about."

Luc let go of her hand and took a step closer. "You're the last person I would describe as evil."

Vor sighed in relief. "*Merci.*"

She looked up at the window where Aila and Vivi slept. "I should go back inside and try to get some sleep. You, too."

"*Oui.*"

She was just about to turn away when she felt his hand on her arm. He pulled her toward him in what felt like slow motion, and kissed her lips until she felt them tingle. She backed away, both shocked and giddy, all at the same time. For one brief moment, she stood still, gazing at him in the torchlight, noting his wide-set-eyes, his full lips. What was she doing cavorting with the opposition?

Embarrassed and uncertain about her mix of emotions, she turned her attention to what she knew best. Horses. "Not to change the subject, but we need to get up early and run the horses tomorrow."

He laughed at the abrupt change of subject. "Ivor is staying at the manor house that belongs to Armand's father and his wife. The home and extensive property is called La Rivière, and includes its own race course. I hope you meet them. They're good people. Armand has three half-sisters. I think you'll enjoy them." He stepped away and waved a hand. "Good night, Mademoiselle Vor. I look forward to working with you tomorrow."

Luc turned and disappeared into the darkness, whistling a lively tune.

Vor felt her heartbeat begin to slow again, and held her hand over her chest until it returned to normal. In the future, she must be more careful. After all, she had just kissed a man who stood to gain a lot if she lost this race.

As Vor greeted the new day, and the caravan made its way to Paris, she wasn't quite sure why she felt embarrassed to be around Luc. It had all happened so quickly. Their surprise meeting. The kiss. She ran a finger across her lips, recalling the brush of his mouth against hers.

Aila had slept late and Vivi remained in the room until the last moment, so Vor had little time for privacy or to discuss what the kiss meant with Aila. In the meantime, she wanted nothing more than to arrive at her final destination so she could focus on the race.

Vor chose to walk the last portion of the journey alone. It felt good to stretch her legs, but she kept her eyes on Gabriel, noting that his stoop was less noticeable today. She realized she was becoming suspicious of everything and everyone, and she didn't like the feeling, especially when it came to Luc. And yet she couldn't help feeling at a slight disadvantage when it came to him. After all, he had been hired by Gabriel to take care of Ivor so he had a vested interest in seeing Vor lose. Did that mean the kiss last night and pleasant conversation was meant as a distraction, and nothing more?

My first kiss. Why did she have to question its intention?

Instead, she turned her attention to Vivi, who rode in the wagon with Sister Marie Claudette, her movements lethargic and tentative. Something was definitely wrong with her. Worried, Vor chewed her bottom lip until it bled. Yet, as closely as she watched Gabriel and Vivi's interactions, she failed to see him give her anything that appeared to be medicine or a potion. She was hesitant to get her mother involved, wishing to spare her the priest's awful temper. On the other hand, without her mother's expertise identifying poisons or other treatments, Vor felt adrift, but then she heard Gabriel and the nun talking and her ears perked up.

This would be Sister Marie Claudette's last day with them, since Gabriel had promised to drop her off at her new assignment, the abbey at the Basilica of Saint-Denis. Gabriel took great pleasure in telling the story of the first bishop of Paris, Saint Denis, who was martyred for his faith by decapitation around 250 AD.

"That didn't stop Denis, *non*. He picked up his severed head and he walked ten miles while preaching up a storm on the theme of repentance!" Gabriel laughed and slapped his knee. "An abbey appeared on site for those who wished to worship him. Then came the building and restoration of the magnificent basilica." Gabriel turned to Sister Marie Claudette. "Have I left out anything important, Sister?"

Sister Marie Claudette shifted in the wagon bed and glanced at Vivi. "No, I believe you've been very thorough, Father Gabriel."

Vor's little brother, Graham, who had caught up with Vor, stood rooted to the ground, his mouth open. Vor swooped in and turned a disapproving eye on Gabriel. "You have to be careful what you say in front of little ears. You've frightened Graham." She patted the boy on his shoulders and hugged him to her. "It's only a story. Don't worry. Father Gabriel's headless saint will not be greeting you at the basilica."

"Oh, don't ruin the fun, mademoiselle." Gabriel glared, then quickly turned that into a grin as he pointed down the road. "There's the basilica, Sister Marie Claudette. Your new home."

Luc stopped the wagon so she could get a good look from the hill where they had a spectacular view of Paris in the distance to the south, and the village of St. Denis immediately below them.

"Oh, my," the nun breathed, crossing herself.

Atli dismounted and shaded his eyes. "The Lord works in mysterious ways. I've been told the people here are somewhat contentious and need the fear of God drilled into them."

"Maybe we should drop off Vivi with the nuns, then," teased Luc. "She would be an excellent teacher-nun."

Vivi's cheeks puffed out. "I would *not* be a good nun! So, forget about it and get us to our inn, Stupid Boy."

The nun frowned at the name Vivi called Luc, but that didn't stop Vivi. She turned to Sister Marie Claudette. "I don't mean to rush you, Sister, but I need to find a new silk tunic to wear in a few days when I beat Vor on that old horse of hers."

"Old horse!" Vor put her hands on her hips. "Fillian isn't even three years old. How dare you!"

"Well, I guess this is a good time to say goodbye," said the nun, giving a brief wave. "I'll walk the rest of the way. I can't have the good sisters thinking I rode all the way and suffered no hardships." Sister Marie Claudette gave them an impish wink. "I thank you for the good company and for watching out for bandits. God be with you." She waved at everyone, then turned and walked down the hill with surprising speed.

Vivi stood outside the wagon, a determined look on her face. "Old hag walks better than I do."

"Too bad she had to endure hardship every time you opened your mouth," said Luc. Vor wondered if he was baiting Vivi or standing up for himself, finally.

"We don't have time for this. Let's keep going until we find our inn for the night."

Atli had taken a break from scouting ahead, and made a point to pass by Vor and state loudly, "Sounds like Captain Vor is in charge for the time being."

Vivi didn't bother disguising her feelings. "I'm going to rub your face in the dirt at the end of that race. So, you better stay out of my way, little girl."

Vor frowned, stunned that Vivi would threaten her so publicly. Even worse, no one jumped to defend her.

Chapter 20

Vor was impressed with the size and luxury of Armand's home, if one could call La Belle Rose a home. The chateau had housed or entertained numerous princes and princesses throughout the generations, according to Armand. Vor glanced around at the gold gilt frames that enhanced portraits of the many male and female ancestors. It was almost overwhelming, when paired with the furniture.

As they explored the guest room assigned to them, Vor was pleasantly surprised to find a huge bed with curtains and a canopy covering. Pink and green stripes with gold accents adorned matching bedcovers and curtains.

Vor tested the mattress filled with brambles and aromatic heather, the scent of summer in Scotland, then hopped up to peek out the window. "So many bright flowers—even at this time of year." She pointed. "And look, over there. A fountain where the driveway ends. It's so sparkly in the sun." She clasped her hands to her chest. "You're so lucky that this will be your permanent home."

"I'd be a silly girl, indeed, not to love this," Aila said quietly.

Vor thought her sister's voice sounded subdued for the occasion. "Where are your trunks?"

"In the master bedchamber ... with Armand's things. The wedding is tomorrow, so I'll sleep with you tonight, and then I'll be Armand's wife tomorrow night." Aila followed it up with a sob, then looked away.

Vor was so exhausted from trying to fix everyone's problems, she felt almost guilty that she had no more will left to help. But she gave Aila a hug and said, "I know you're anxious. You really should talk to Mother tonight, while you can. I'm still learning how to handle these sentimental emotions."

Aila nodded and swiped at the tears. "I will. Don't worry about it."

Vor reminded herself their stay was for one night only. Tomorrow, she would pack up her belongings and have them ready for Atli or her father when they arrived late in the afternoon to take her to the cottage her father had rented. When she was told the name of the cottage, it made her smile. *Le Jardin de Citron*. The Lemon Garden. She couldn't wait to find out if the lemons were a grove, a few trees, or a whimsical name with no real meaning.

Vor had met Armand's mother, Genevieve, earlier in the day, and had decided that she was a rather nervous woman, who relied considerably upon either Armand, when he was there, or his sister, Clotilde. Armand's sister remained unmarried and devoted to her mother, Genevieve, even though she must be close to thirty. Vor had expected the sister to be haughty and reserved, but she'd begun to think she was shy more than anything else, particularly when she volunteered to show some of her artwork to Vor.

"Whatever you do, do not bring up the subject of my father's second family to my mother," Clotilde instructed her. "The scandal is still somewhat new, and my mother isn't handling it well."

And it was true, Genevieve had immediately started sobbing loudly, and rushed from the room to climb the stairs in order to spend the remainder of the day lying in bed. The scandal would be borne by the children their whole lives, Vor knew, while Xavier would still be rich, therefore, imprudent on occasion, but able to do as he pleased, for the most part. Vor hadn't had time to discuss Aila's thoughts and feelings about any of this, but she had no doubt her sister would stand beside her husband, because Armand believed in taking care of both families, as the only son and heir.

Vivi, Gabriel and Luc were now officially guests of Xavier, Armand's father and Jacqueline, his second wife, at La Rivière, and it was decided that the riders would use their home and race track as a base, to simulate race conditions as much as possible. The third day would be The King's Race, and Vor knew that to win, she needed to know that race course with her eyes closed. It was almost impossible not to feel butterflies, so, on the following day, while Aila was getting situated in her new place of residence and dealing with last-minute wedding details, Vor decided to practice on the new track. Therefore, she headed for the barn where she mucked out the stalls, fed, watered, and brushed the horses, then spent the next two hours riding around the track. Afterwards, when she returned to the barn, she decided to keep it low-key for the horses, who were extremely sensitive to nervous anxiety.

Vivi had found an empty stall to place her trunk with her race clothes, and an old full-length mirror to prop up in one corner. Given permission by the acquisitive Vivi, Vor couldn't stop herself from looking at the pretty silk tunics in a variety of bright colors Vivi had to choose from.

"Red is *my* color. Like this one, called 'scarlet'." Vivi carefully folded the red shirt and put it back in the trunk. "You know, Vor, if I were you, I'd ask my father to buy me a new silk tunic for this race. A nice, rich, bright color, so people can see you coming and going. That may be all you get out of this event." Vivi giggled, then glanced over her shoulder with a sly look. She turned back to face the full-length mirror and held up an emerald green tunic.

Vor frowned and looked back toward the stable entrance. "You don't pay much attention, do you, Vivi? I don't have money for a new tunic. Neither does my father until this smuggler mess is over."

"Luc mentioned your father's trouble with the authorities."

"Did he?" Vor would have to be more careful who she told in the future. "As for my tunic, I will find something to wear."

"Well, you better hurry. It's less than two weeks 'til race time." Vivi rummaged through her trunk, and eventually pulled out a teal blue tunic. "I could loan you one of mine. But I'll have to look for something that might fit you, as you're taller."

"Don't bother." Vor turned away and swiped at a lone tear.

"Who just said 'don't bother'? That better not have been you, Vor. You don't give up on anything."

Her heart swelled when she heard her father's voice and turned to see him and their family coming through the stable doorway. Before she could burst into tears of happiness, she rushed to hug her parents and brothers.

"Where is Aila ... and Armand?" She almost forgot to ask about him.

Her father hugged her, then held her away from him, his brows forming a deep "V" in his forehead. "They'll be here shortly. Armand is still getting her settled at the moment." Vivi paused while carrying a saddle to another location, and let it drop to the ground, just missing Vor's toes. "Ah, we haven't met formally. I saw you on the ship. You must be Vor's parents. I'm Vivienne le Clerc." She looked directly at Torleik and batted her eyelashes.

Vor tried to suppress a groan of embarrassment at Vivi's falsely cheerful voice and flirtatious manner.

Torleik turned and glanced around the stable. "Is Gabriel around? I had some things I wanted to discuss with him."

"I'll see him later for supper and tell him you were looking for him. I'm sure he'll make time for you as soon as possible."

Torleik nodded and made way for Aila, who finally appeared, no doubt having finished moving into her new home. She stepped aside for her little brothers, who were already checking out the horses that came and went.

"Is this Ivor, the horse that's running against Fillian? Why are his eyes pink?" Fionne demanded in his straightforward manner.

"Where is Fillian?" Erik wanted to know, his eyes scanning the nearby empty stalls.

"Is Atli here? Where's Atli?" Graham asked, sticking close to Vor. She saw his hand caressing the green stone in his pocket, as if the stone were a pet mouse. He'd been doing that ever since she returned it to him on their arrival at the chateau.

Aila appeared pale and quiet, but she smiled as she made a point of giving her little sister a hug. "I spoke to Mother last night," she whispered into Vor's ear. "I'm less anxious now."

"I'm so glad. In a month, you'll be an old married lady."

Aila gently nudged her shoulder. "Don't say that. I'm not old!"

"Is your wedding gown ready to go? Do you need any adjustments? Genevieve says one of her servants is an excellent seamstress."

"Good to know. But unless it shrunk or I expanded during the voyage, it should fit just fine."

She was smiling again, and Vor congratulated herself on helping do her part to talk Aila through whatever troubles she faced.

Vor glanced at Vivi, who was conversing with Eilidh near Fillian's stall gate. Good. Her mother could make her own assessment of Vivi without Vor's influence.

"You have to come see where I'll be staying. It's amazing." Aila gently tugged on Vor's arm, pulling her toward their mother and Vivi. "Mother, sorry to interrupt, but before we discuss more wedding details, I want to show you and Vor around Belle Rose. Ms. Vivienne, you're welcome to see it as well."

Vor smiled at the way Aila said Belle Rose. She made it sound like a living, breathing person.

"I have too much work to do," said Vivi, without looking up from where she polished Ivor's saddle until it gleamed in the light.

Thank goodness.

With the wedding only two days away, and the race 10 days after that due to the timely arrival of good weather, Vor needed some quiet time without Vivi's inane chatter.

Her thoughts turned to the couple's special day. Armand had seemed calmer and more attentive of late. That's what Vor hoped to find in a mate someday. Someone who listened to her thoughts and dreams, who laughed at her silly attempts at jokes and thought her the most beautiful woman in the world, red hair and freckles included.

She brushed off the hay that clung to her gown and waved at her father. "I'm off to wander the chateau with Mother and Aila."

Torleik smiled and waved goodbye, but there was a hint of sadness in his eyes. Vor couldn't help but wonder if perhaps he was feeling insecure about their homelife in Orkney. As if his business was pulled out from under them—everything he had worked so hard to gain for his family—gone.

Vor felt a little odd not having dinner with her family at the Lemon Garden Cottage. On the other hand, she felt like a true adult dining at the chateau as a guest of Armand and Aila on their first night as a couple. Gabriel, Vivi and Luc rounded out the guest list, as she experienced her first taste of sophisticated Frankish cuisine and customs presented by Genevieve and her daughter. The matriarch clearly enjoyed entertaining as she sat at the head of the table that night, smiling at Gabriel, who wasn't wearing his usual cassock, but rather a black silk tunic over braies. Vivi dressed in an emerald green tunic over a black skirt, with a gold chain necklace, whereas Luc donned a simple clean white work shirt. Vor noticed that he fidgeted as he glanced around the huge dining room with its ornate chandeliers and wall sconces. She had to admit the massive woven rugs dyed in pastel blues, pinks and golds were meant to impress royalty and commoners alike.

The slightly plump Genevieve employed excellent cooks and greatly enjoyed her food, Vor deduced as she devoured her meal of grilled asparagus, freshly-caught trout in a thick white sauce, and fresh bread and butter. For dessert, they were given a small tray of cheeses to choose from. The excellent red wine was not from LaVelle Vineyards, but more than adequate as it slid down Vor's throat with ease. By the time Gabriel poured her a fourth glass, Luc moved it out of her reach, earning a definite frown.

"I'm not drunk," she whispered.

"Good. You have a lot of work to do tomorrow. And I promised your father to bring you over to their cottage tonight ... sober."

She glared, then softened her expression as she realized she did feel a bit giddy. "That reminds me." She leaned closer to Luc's ear. "I'll have some questions for you later, when we're on our way to the Lemon Garden Cottage. Don't let me forget."

For a moment, Luc gazed at her, a smile materializing. He quickly regained control and gave her a stern look. "Of course, mademoiselle."

She may have gazed at him a beat too long, because her cheeks flushed and she had to look away, embarrassed that she'd shown her hand in front of all these people she didn't really know, except for her sister. She reached for her water glass.

Fortunately, Aila was paying attention to Armand. Whereas Gabriel seemed to be enjoying the sound of his own voice, so he dominated the conversation, with occasional comments from Vivi.

For the next half hour, Vor created a mind game where she observed and took in Frankish ways of expressing themselves she hadn't learned in text books. Hand gestures and emotional outbursts appeared to be the norm, making her wonder if that came with living in a chateau. But in the end, she missed her younger brothers and was relieved to be heading back to the humble cottage where her family was staying.

At long last, the evening meal came to a conclusion, and Vor and Luc said good night to their hosts. Now that dinner was over, Luc would escort her to the Lemon Garden Cottage stable.

As Vor waited for Luc to saddle Fillian, she glanced back over her shoulder at the chateau, all its windows lit by chandelier candles. Her father would say that was a waste of a good candle. She smiled into the oncoming darkness, counting her blessings that she was no relation to the mysterious Gabriel.

Unfortunately, she wasn't paying attention when Luc lifted her into the saddle, as she suddenly seemed to fly through the air. She let out a squeak of alarm.

Luc laughed. "Caught you by surprise, didn't I?"

Vor turned her nose up. "No, you did not."

He hopped aboard a borrowed dun-colored horse named Gideon while she settled into Fillian's saddle.

"*Oui*, I did surprise you. Now, so you don't forget and complain I stole your things, your belongings have been delivered to the Jardin cottage. You'll remain there with your family until after the race."

"So, you'll be staying here, at the chateau?"

"*Oui.* Armand invited Gabriel, Vivi and I to stay here. Armand will travel back and forth between the chateau and the Jardin cottage, as needed." He straightened in the saddle. "Now, over dinner, you said you had questions for me. What is it you wish to ask me?"

Vor looked at the road ahead, then up at the night sky, so many stars visible. "The other night... why did you... kiss me?" She put a hand on the MacAoidh broach holding her cloak closed. "Was it to distract me from the race? Or...?"

Luc's mouth formed a wide "O," but he recovered quickly. "Honestly, I just couldn't ignore those beautiful lips. I wanted to know how they would feel beneath mine."

"And how did they feel?"

Moonlight shone down, enough to allow him to focus on those lips once again. He smiled. "I may need to refresh my memory."

Vor felt heat wash over her cheeks and was glad he couldn't see that he had caused it.

Luc suddenly appeared contrite and straightened in the saddle. "That was presumptuous of me. That kiss. I apologize. I never meant to distract you from the race, before or now."

She would have said "No, you didn't distract me—not at all," but Luc had spurred his horse ahead of her and she raced to catch up.

Chapter 21

Vor might have noticed more details during her sister's wedding if she hadn't been so preoccupied. It didn't take long to determine that peach was Aila's favorite color, as peach-colored ribbons adorned bouquets and wreaths alike. In fact, Aila must have secured every peach or pinkish flower in bloom in Paris.

Genevieve coordinated the decorations, and like the guests who kept arriving, the décor was lavish. Aila was assigned her own personal servant, an ex-slave woman from Africa, named Izora, who crafted a wedding bouquet of peach and pink-colored peonies and roses that gave off the most heavenly scent.

Upon waking that morning, Vor made arrangements for Aila's bath to be filled while others raced around to finish tasks before the wedding breakfast. Just as Aila was about to dip her toes into the steaming, fragrant bath water, a knock at the door caught their attention. Vor walked to the adjoining room and opened the door to find Armand, his expression sheepish. He held an ornate box out to Vor.

"I wanted to give this to Aila as a wedding gift—to wear today," he said in a low voice, so as not to be overheard.

Vor stared at the box, thinking Armand was naïve if he thought her sister could be bought with jewels. But when she opened the box, she gasped.

"Tell her it belonged to my paternal grandmother. I wanted Aila to know how special she is. Despite what you think, I only want the very best for her. I know I'm not supposed to see the bride until later, so could you please be sure she puts this on?"

Vor took the box and touched the sapphire pendant set in gold.

"I'll tell her what you said." She looked up, wanting to believe in this young man, but finding it hard to do so until he provided a good alibi for his recent comings and goings. She shut the door and returned to the other room, setting the box on the table beside the bed.

"Who was that?"

"It's a surprise. I'll tell you later," said Vor, with a mischievous wink.

She and her mother helped Aila bathe and wash her long silky hair in rosewater. When the bride-to-be rose from the bath and was wrapped in a thick warm towel, her skin and hair gave off the lovely scent of roses. Vor and her mother ushered Aila into the adjoining room.

Eilidh had made a new chemise for Aila to wear beneath her gown, and the ivory linen felt as smooth as silk as Vor helped Aila pull it over her head. With reverence, Vor lifted Aila's wedding gown off the bed and approached her, surprised at how sentimental it made her feel.

Aila lifted her arms and let the gown slide down over her hips. "You've been mentioning my wedding a lot lately, Vor. Are you thinking about your own wedding someday? Or is it the race that has your attention?" She raised her arms so her mother could fasten the ties on each side. Once secured, she leaned closer. "I've seen you with Luc. He's quite handsome."

Vor took a step back and turned her face so Aila wouldn't see her hot, red cheeks. "I don't know what you're talking about. I've got plenty of time 'til I wed, right, Mother?"

Eilidh smiled gently, most likely remembering herself at the same age. She reached out and patted Vor's arm. "You take your time, sweetheart. We're in no hurry."

Vor's mouth dropped open as she hadn't expected that answer. To distract herself, she set Aila's shoes where she could easily step into them and then stood back.

"All we need now is to do your hair ... and maybe add a little blush to make your cheeks not so pale." Eilidh made room at the vanity table, then turned to Izora, who had given a quick rap at the door, then entered to help with the remaining wedding preparations. Eilidh handed her the hairbrush.

Izora moved gracefully across the room with Aila in tow, and seated her in front of a tall mirror, then stood behind her. Neither Vor nor Aila had ever seen a person from Africa, and Vor was intensely curious. Izora worked quickly and with skill, as Vor watched. She couldn't help but wonder if this was the same hand she'd seen Armand take when he helped the mystery woman cross the ledge near the cave openings.

"Izora, have you ever been to the Orkney Isles?" Vor asked, then waited with baited breath for the reply.

Izora's dark eyes met Vor's greenish-blue eyes in the mirror. The young woman hesitated, considering her answer. "I... am not sure, mademoiselle. My travels have taken me to many places. I do not recall all of them."

Good, non-committal response.

Aila's eyes fell to the fancy box on the bed. "What's that? Did I hear Armand's voice earlier?"

"I'll show it to you when Izora finishes your hair."

Aila's wedding gown fit her tall, slender figure like a glove, molding to her curves, the soft blush color a beautiful backdrop to her strawberry blond hair piled atop her head. She wore a short veil, which would be raised only at the end of the ceremony. Her gown was in the French style, a satin ivory and peach fabric with long sleeves and a modest square neckline.

When Eilidh opened the antique box Armand had dropped off and lifted out a gold chain with a sparkling sapphire pendant, all four of the women let out a collective sigh. A bright blue oval sapphire sat in a gold crown setting, a gem fit for a queen. Aila inhaled deeply, as if she couldn't believe it was hers. Or that Armand could afford something so precious. She walked over to the window and allowed the sunlight to caress the gem, causing prisms of light on the ceiling and walls.

"That is truly stunning," said her mother.

"And probably worth a fortune..." Vor caught herself from mentioning money, as that just reminded her of her father's debt.

"It suits you, mademoiselle," said Izora.

"I don't know if I can wear this. It's too valuable." Aila turned it over and inspected the workmanship.

"But Aila, Armand wanted you to wear it today," Vor said.

Aila reached into the box and opened the note. She read it, then heaved a huge sigh. "Sapphire is known as the stone of wisdom and royalty," she read. "Its color symbolizes loyalty, faith and devotion. This belonged to my grandmother on my father's side."

"Maybe that's his way of saying good things will come, and you should remain loyal to him." Her mother gazed at the sun outside. "We must hurry now. The breakfast is prepared, and we don't want it getting cold, or we'll never hear the end of it. Come here and hold still, Aila."

Aila appeared reluctant as she lifted her veil and allowed her mother to attach the chain around her neck. The pendant rested perfectly in the square neckline of her gown, and Aila touched it again, as if she couldn't believe it was real.

The door opened a crack, and Genevieve poked her head in. "We're ready for the bride." Her sharp eyes didn't miss the sapphire pendant, but she said nothing as she escorted Aila to the top of the staircase where Aila would descend on Torleik's arm.

Genevieve had hired a French troubadour to provide music, and he played a light march-like entry on his lute. Two other musicians joined the lute player when Aila reached the bottom of the stairs. How lucky her sister was to be a part of this new world. As much as the sisters squabbled, Vor was going to miss her terribly. She looked away, and brushed at a tear.

Fortunately, the ceremony was short, and when it was over, Armand kissed Aila with Frankish gusto, then invited the guests to the late wedding breakfast. Vor felt like she was wandering around in a dense fog. This place didn't feel like home, and she couldn't let go of a niggling suspicion that Armand was guilty of something.

Izora made herself scarce during the meal, but Vor did spot her whispering to Armand near the end. What was going on with those two? When Vor's eyes cut to Aila, her sister was fingering the sapphire around her neck and gazing at Armand with tight lips. Was she wondering if she'd just married a smuggler ... or someone who womanized his servants? And would a sapphire like that keep her quiet if he was?

Luc had never given marriage much thought. But when he saw that sapphire necklace around Aila's throat, he wondered just how profitable Armand's business dealings really were, anyway? The second thing that occurred to him was how lovely Vor looked in her Norse gown with the carved brooches securing the shoulders of a moss green outer gown much like an apron, with an undergown of pale red. Gold embroidered sleeves and hem tied the look together, and the beads and necklace added to the unusual attire that evoked whispers among the guests.

Luc was seated across from Vor at the wedding breakfast, with Vivi next to him. Vivi had remained quiet all morning, and he could see Vor was concerned. Gabriel made a brief appearance to congratulate his business colleague, Xavier LaVelle, Armand's father and co-owner of Ivor. As soon as this day was over, Luc knew he'd be required to give all his attention to race preparation. He could already feel the intensity building for the race.

And, of course, after Vor had told him about the smugglers, he'd promised to help her find the true culprits using the caves back on the island. Furthermore, he was surprised to see that Izora worked for Genevieve, which made him wonder how much she knew about her son's business dealings outside of France.

He looked up at the head of the table, where Aila and Armand had eyes only for each other. He wished them well.

After the breakfast, guests were encouraged to take it easy and wander around the chateau grounds. When Luc wandered outside to visit Armand's kennel of mastiff hunting pups, he was surprised that Izora followed. No one else was at the kennel, so she put fresh water down for the pups.

"Monsieur Luc, all is well?" she inquired.

"*Oui.* I believe so. How are things on this side of the world?"

He squatted down to play with two older pups, each already close to eighty pounds. At times like this, he wished he had a home to go to, a place where he could relax and not worry about details like who was conducting illicit business and where. And how to deflect accusations that were baseless. He picked up a stick and gave it a good toss. Both pups chased after it.

"The pups that were ordered will be ready soon. Do you have a preferred date of receipt?"

Luc scratched his head, certain that she was hinting at something that could cause trouble for him. Even prior to Vor's revelation, he had heard rumors of smuggling, women no less. "What does Armand say?"

"The sooner, the better. Only, your help is needed to procure them."

The dogs returned with the stick Luc had thrown, and he wiped it clean. He'd been hoping for a bit more of a respite here in Frankia. He couldn't recall the last time he'd taken a day off. Besides, he would like the opportunity to get to know Vor better. He liked talking to her. She listened, and she was smart. For that reason, he hadn't made arrangements for his next job, but he felt safe in telling the truth.

"I must remain through the race. Any time after that should be fine. Check with Armand if that is acceptable."

"*Oui*, monsieur."

Izora pulled apples from her pockets and handed one to each dog. Luc had heard from a fellow groomsman that, in moderation, apples were beneficial for the dogs. She then moved over to the youngest litter and gave them fresh food and water, stopping to play with each pup.

"Just out of curiosity, were you assigned to work the kennels?"

Izora grinned, her teeth straight and white against her dark skin. "Oh, I love animals. I volunteered. I could work here forever, as long as pups keep appearing."

Luc laughed. "Be careful what you wish for."

He waved and headed back to the chateau, hoping to see Vor before the race.

Chapter 22

Vor supposed it was normal to feel exhausted after a wedding of that nature. As a result, she slept in a bit longer the next morning, a rare luxury. She also tried to get used to the fact that Aila would no longer be at her beck and call, and vice versa. Prior to this, she'd always had her big sister around.

Vor hadn't realized how conservative Aila was when it came to drawing attention to herself. She clearly had no intention of wearing the sapphire in front of so many strangers any longer than necessary. After the wedding breakfast, Aila retired to her bedchamber to change, and with Vor accompanying her, Aila removed the necklace and handed it to Izora to put back in its ornate box. "Please ask Armand to return this to a safe place."

"*Oui*, madame."

Izora left them alone and closed the door. Aila's delicate brows came together as she watched the woman leave. "I know what you're thinking, Vor, so you might as well just say it while I'm here."

To distract herself, Vor picked up a hand mirror. "Alright, what am I thinking?"

"I saw the look on your face when you first viewed the pendant. You thought it was stolen or smuggled goods. In other words, you still don't trust that Armand is telling you the truth." Aila sat on the bed she now shared with Armand. "That's only natural, considering what we've all been through lately. I must admit, I feel the same way."

"Then don't you think you should ask him if he stole the pendant? He knows you doubt his trustworthiness. Just put the question out there and see what he says."

"Perhaps..."

An insistent knock at the door drew their attention. Vor frowned, preferring her remaining time with her sister not be interrupted.

"Vor! Are you in there? Open up!"

"Vivi," said Vor, as if that said it all.

She opened the door and found Vivi standing there, holding a package, and wearing a lovely pale blue gown with delicate ivory lace trim. Her hair was combed to the side, and she had the appearance of a young schoolgirl.

"Oh, I'm glad I found you. Luc has offered to take us on a brief tour of the *cité* to see some of the important construction. He says we'll start at the Seine."

Vor ran a hand through her hair. "What about getting ready for the race? It's only ten days away."

Vivi giggled. "Actually, Gabriel said we've been working hard these past couple of days, so it's alright to take off an afternoon. It'll probably only be for a couple of hours anyway. Do you want to go?"

Vor hesitated. "I promised Father I would train for the next ten days until the race."

"You should go," Aila encouraged. "I heard him say just yesterday you and Fillian were in good shape."

"Well, then... maybe two hours won't hurt. I did put in extra time yesterday and the day before." Vor tried not to feel guilty, but she didn't want to disappoint her father, of all people.

"*Oui*! Besides, I brought you something else to wear, mademoiselle." Vivi opened the package and held out a rich indigo blue tunic and matching skirt. "This color should look wonderful with your hair and complexion, *n'est-ce-pas?*" She caressed the fine wool and smiled. "I think the handsome Monsieur Luc is sure to notice you in such a fine outfit."

Vor narrowed her eyes. "What are you up to, Vivi? Last time I saw you, you called me 'Stinky'."

Vor clenched her back teeth at Vivi's high-pitched laugh.

"Stinky?" inquired Aila.

"Don't ask." Vor reached out and took the outfit. "Thank you. Just this once, I'll go with you, but we need to be back early."

Vivi clapped her hands. "I will wait with Monsieur Luc downstairs." She rushed out, leaving Vor surprised.

"I'm suspicious. She has *never* been that nice to me."

"Let's see what you look like in that blue. It's exquisite material. I may have a belt you can borrow that would cinch in your waist nicely."

"Vivi must want something. That's probably why she's being nice."

"Don't be so cynical. We're in Paris. You can take a few hours to sightsee."

"I don't trust her."

"Nobody said you had to. You'll be with Luc. Just enjoy yourself."

When she slid the tunic and skirt on and attached the silver chain belt Aila brought her, Vor had to admit she felt good. She twirled in front of the mirror, then waited as Aila attempted to tame Vor's hair with a comb before braiding it.

"You know what? Let's leave it down for a change." Vor turned to regard her image in the mirror.

"Good idea. You'll look soft and feminine for... two hours."

"Hmph."

When she'd finished brushing out the thick, reddish-chestnut hair, Aila sat back and inspected Vor's appearance from head to toe. "You look beautiful. Now, go have fun."

Vor gave her sister a hug and hurried down the long staircase, feeling fifteen for the first time in a long time.

Luc was pleased to have a lovely lady on each arm as they started out on their walking tour of his favorite city. Whenever he was in Paris, he liked to stroll along the Seine River to see what progress had been made on the latest architectural projects. But having companions to discuss what they saw made it all that much better.

Vor seemed curious about her surroundings, and asked dozens of questions. And he couldn't help but admire her in a feminine tunic and matching blue skirt, with her hair flying in the breeze. Normally, he wasn't one to notice things like that, but lately, he found himself noting everything about Vor. He decided he liked her hair down.

They stopped and he pointed out the impressive spires of a new cathedral going up. "That's *Notre Dame de Paris*, or *Notre Dame* for short."

"What was here before?" Vivi straightened her collar.

"Two earlier churches. And before that, a Gallo-Roman temple dedicated to the Roman god, Jupiter."

Vor's eyes grew huge. "So, it predates Christianity by quite a bit?"

"It would seem so. About ten or twelve years ago, a bishop here in Paris had the idea of converting the two old buildings into a single building on a much larger scale. As you can see, construction continues."

"What are those strange arches sticking out?"

Luc nodded, appreciating Vivi's plain way of speaking. "Those are called flying buttresses. They're designed to hold up thousands of pounds of stone, but are visually striking, as you can see."

"And what is that building across the river?" Vivi pointed.

Vor's eyes darted over the beginnings of even more grand architecture in progress.

"That's the first university to be built in Paris. People typically call it The Sorbonne, after its founder, Robert de Sorbon. It's part of the University of Paris, and offers a curriculum on law, medicine, theology, and the arts—with an emphasis on training the poorest students in the city."

"Do they accept female students?"

Luc regarded Vor for a moment, assuming this question must be very important to her. "I wish I could say yes, but to my knowledge, not yet."

"Why would you want to sit in a classroom day in and day out only to have all those boys ogling you?" Vivi asked. "I would be a nervous wreck."

Vor chuckled. "I would think you'd love being ogled."

Vivi stuck out her tongue.

Vor put her hands in the pockets of her cloak and shrugged. "I don't know. I guess academia runs in my mother's family. My mother was the same way. Always had her head in a book."

"Can we stop for some tea and scones now? I'm starving." Vivi put her hands together like an angel praying.

The sun had disappeared, and a cool breeze caused Vor to shiver. She pulled her cloak tighter. "Brrr. I didn't expect it to be this cool." She held out a hand and frowned. "And it's starting to rain."

"Okay, ladies. That's the end of my tour. We're only a few blocks from the chateau."

Vivi suddenly appeared pale and feverish. "I... I'm not sure I can run that far. I seem to be short of breath."

"We'll prop you up between us," said Vor, looking at Luc.

"I'm not so sure we can..."

"Let's give it a try."

Vor's eyes were soft and pleading. It made Luc wonder if she and Vivi were better friends than they let on. Or, was she acting friendly and helpful to make an impression? He'd been around manipulative women and girls for far too long. It was hard to think of them as being genuinely interested in someone else's welfare.

But he had to admit, there was something unique about Vor's greenish-blue eyes that spoke volumes about her character. He gave a quick nod. "You take hold of her on that side, and I'll support her on her left side. With the two of us, we'll have her back in no time."

They rushed through the narrow Paris streets, no longer interested in sightseeing. For that reason, they beat a downpour by mere moments, and shook off the first drops as they entered the chateau and called for hot tea.

Aila came gliding out of the salon as if she'd been doing that her whole life. "Oh, I'm glad you made it before the deluge. Luc, you must stay for supper, *oui?*" She smoothed her light green gown and accepted Armand's kiss on the cheek as he entered through the front door behind them. "Mother and Father will be here. The boys will eat at Armand's father's home with Sister

Marie Claudette. I would like for them to get to know their three step-cousins."

Vor reached into her pocket, and a buzzing vibration from the two remaining stones surprised her. They were waking now. But for what purpose?

Gabriel's right eye twitched—not a good sign. He was glad no one else was around the stable area at the Lemon Garden Cottage that late in the afternoon as he paced back and forth near Fillian's stall. Time was running out. In ten day's time the race would take place, and Vivi hadn't bowed out gracefully due to "health" problems as he'd hoped she would.

He'd planned and prepared Trini so carefully. It never occurred to him that Vivi would take a stand and insist on riding. In the past, she'd gone along with whatever he told her to do. Now, she appeared to be under the influence of Vor and her mother, the healer.

Damn those meddling women!

Shadows were beginning to appear in corners of the stable, and the few other horses there settled in for the night with their oats. While Gabriel pondered how to get Vivi out of Ivor's saddle and Trini in, he heard voices coming closer. One was clearly Vor, but he couldn't place the other until they stopped in front of Fillian's stall.

"You've been so busy riding, I couldn't find you," said Graham, a bit of a pout in his voice. He sniffled for good measure.

"Well, I'm here with you now, my little man. What's on your mind?"

He dug a hand into a pocket and set something on his palm.

Curious as to what the boy showed her, Gabriel spotted the green rock crystal Graham held out to Vor. She inspected it and turned it over a few times to look at both sides.

"This is beautiful, isn't it?" she said.

"Does the stone have a name?"

"It sure does. It's called aventurine."

He tried to repeat the sounds. "Uh... ven... cha... rin."

"You've got it. There's a legend that says if you put aventurine close to two other stones containing certain properties, it creates a little pocket of magic that lets you see into the future."

"Ohhh. Can you show me the magic?"

"Not right now. I'll show you later, though."

He nodded that he was alright with that. "You can put this in your pocket for good luck during the race."

"Are you sure you want to do that?"

He hesitated. "You'll give it back after the race, won't you?"

Vor cupped his dirty little face in her hands and kissed his forehead. "You bet I will. I promise." She hugged Graham to her and he giggled.

All Gabriel could think about is whether or not she noticed the dirt and grime clinging to the front of the boy's shirt. One of the reasons he hated kids. Grubby little hands.

"We should go into the house now. Say goodnight to Fillian."

Graham peered over the stall door. "You got to run your fastest on race day, Fillian. Don't forget."

Vor took him by the hand and led him out into the garden.

When Gabriel left the shadows, he wondered why Atli wasn't there. If Gabriel had known the horse would be left alone before the race, he would have fed something to Fillian. But no. He'd check in on Vivi and see how she was tonight. If she seemed a bit too perky and awake, he could always slip something more potent into her nightly glass of wine. Maybe, if her health continued to deteriorate, he still had time to convince her to bow out, but the clock was ticking. If only the woman wasn't so stubborn.

Gabriel strode to the end of the stable where a woodland extended well beyond the Lemon Garden Cottage. He felt the anger building at the ingratitude he must suffer.

Vor's family was slowly luring Vivi into their lair and away from him, her guardian. *How dare they!*

But then, if Vivi pulled herself together and won the race in just over a week's time, he'd let her back into his good graces. No, it would be better to hedge his bets with Trini. She was a winner in the making. First, he must see Trini win the race, then he would destroy that book written by women to fool their men into complacency. He would use that Delsiran book against them and take everything he desired. His plans all started the day after tomorrow.

He set off at a brisk pace toward La Rivière, Armand's family's home. And while he walked, an idea took root. A wonderfully wicked idea. He could almost taste the triumph, long awaited, but worth every moment. He closed his eyes and sniffed the air, expecting to smell the win as he inhaled.

By the time Gabriel reached La Rivière, huffing and out of breath, Trinette was just finishing her practice with Ivor. The sun had disappeared and darkness encroached, but the determination was clear on her young face as she put Ivor through his final paces. She had a light touch, as opposed to Vivi, and Gabriel was pleased. She listened to instructions well and didn't talk back. She made no demands and didn't seem to mind the extra workouts Gabriel assigned in the ten days leading up to the King's Race.

The only fly in the ointment was her guardian, Izora, who knew nothing about his arrangement with the girl. Gabriel had no doubt she would launch a major protest when she learned Trini had been working for him. The girl confessed she preferred not to sneak around, but her love of horses was a powerful incentive. The stables at La Rivière and La Belle Rose made her dark eyes grow large every time she stepped inside the stalls. She'd been told by Izora to steer clear of Vivi, and so far, so good. He wanted no more drama from Vivi at this point. What he wanted was to quietly dispose of his fractious ward.

Consequently, it had been an easy matter to increase the potion he'd been feeding Vivi in food or drink this past month, but he was at the max without killing her. At this point, she was having trouble even getting in the saddle without help.

Eight days passed quickly before the dreaded morning of the race was close at hand. Gabriel must time it as near to the last minute as he could before letting Vivi know she wouldn't be riding Ivor. He needed to be ready. However, right then and there, he made a magnanimous decision: if she was looking strong and showed proper gratitude for all he'd done, then *maybe* he'd give her one last shot. He would love to see Vivi and Ivor beat the heck out of Vor Torleiksdottir. But he'd have his backup ready to go in case.

He looked around the stable, and not seeing Vivi, he walked up to Trini on Ivor. "Trinette, your riding skills have improved to an astonishing level. I think we made a good choice on your riding instructor. How do you feel in the saddle?"

Though willowy, Trini grinned and raised her chin. She may be taller than most successful riders, but she reminded him of a little brown sparrow that came to his window almost every day, waiting for its mother to feed her. A tenacious young lady, she rarely gave up or complained.

"Oh, I love riding, Father Gabriel. I could ride all day. Especially Ivor."

"Good. Good." He crossed his arms and gazed off in the distance. "How would you feel riding Ivor in the King's Race the day after tomorrow? I'm not sure Vivi is up to it, and I think you'd make a fine replacement. I'll even split the prize money with you, let's say 60% for me, 40% for you. That's a lot of money for a young girl to have in her possession. You don't have to respond now. Think about it, and we'll confirm right before the race starts."

After a brief hesitation, she asked, "How come you get more money if I'm doing all the work?"

Gabriel coughed in surprise. *She's a shrewd little negotiator.* "I had to hire and pay a trainer for you. I also paid for some of your equipment, such as your saddle, and the racing tunic you will wear is pure silk."

Trini appeared to give that some thought, then smiled. However, her grin slowly faded. "I would love to be in a race like that, but Izora won't like it. She told me I shouldn't mingle with Mademoiselle Vivienne or ..." Her light brown skin paled considerably as she looked away. "Or you, Father Gabriel." She patted Ivor. "I'm sorry, but I must decline."

For a moment, Gabriel considered her honest response, and couldn't help comparing her to Vivi and her whining. He grew weary of their constant battles and Vivi's increasing demands. He was well aware that she knew too much about his various business endeavors. In the end, he wouldn't be able to let her walk away. But now that Vor and her family had butted in, he'd have to be extra careful. Darn those women. Why couldn't they mind their own business? If he could dispose of both of them, life would be easier.

"Why don't I have a talk with Izora? Would that be okay?" he suggested.

Gabriel had no intention of bringing Izora into the mix. He didn't care if she was Trini's legal guardian or not. She'd been acting all high and mighty ever since Genevieve had given her emancipation papers. What a mistake. Genevieve was a fool who would get what she deserved. Izora... he had something special in mind for the proud young woman from the Fatimids in North Africa.

But first, he had to get Trini in Ivor's saddle without too much fanfare.

"I'll see if I can arrange bonus money for your trouble. That shouldn't be so hard to do. We'll talk again tomorrow. Meanwhile, get some rest tonight."

"*Oui*, monsieur."

"Where are you staying? Does it include a good meal?"

"Oh, *oui*, monsieur. Madame Genevieve's cook is the best. He saves dessert for me each night."

"You have him save your desserts from now until after the race. We don't want you gaining too much weight, do we?"

Trini cocked her head, then glanced down at her flat stomach. "But Izora says..."

Gabriel felt stymied at every corner. He growled in frustration and felt huge, angry veins popping out on his forehead. "I don't care what Izora says. Or any other woman's opinion, for that matter." He forced himself to calm down. He'd have time enough later to deal with the *Book of Delsiran*, and the women who used it as a sword to conquer men who stood in their way. "You and I will be partners for the King's Race. After we win, I'll take you anywhere you want to go. How about that?"

For someone of such a tender age, Trini regarded Gabriel with knowing eyes. "I would like to go home."

Gabriel combed his greasy hair with his fingers. "Then, that's where we'll go. *If* you win." He stuck out his hand, and she shook it with a sparkle in her eyes.

This will be like taking bonbons from une bébé. Now, for Vivienne le Cler.

Chapter 23

When Vor awoke early on the day of the race, a new blue silk tunic lay across the bottom of her bed. She jumped up and gave a whoop of pleasure, knowing her brothers were already awake and making noise in the main room. As she washed and dressed, she thought of Vivi's offer to lend her a tunic. Or lend her money to buy a new tunic, but then she would owe Gabriel. Thank goodness her mother had taken care of this final detail and a sticky situation had been avoided. Vivi may have appeared quiet and cooperative lately, but Vor knew better.

She paired the royal blue tunic with black leggings and boots. When she saw no sign of Atli, she went ahead and borrowed a black leather belt from him and cinched it comfortably around her waist. Next, she brushed and braided her hair, and was about to leave her bedchamber when her mother knocked and entered, carrying a tray of tea and food to break her fast.

"Oh, Mother! Thank you for the shirt! It's perfect."

Eilidh deposited the tray on a table and turned to embrace her second daughter.

"You should eat something. I have a feeling it will be a very long day. Atli told me the winners will meet the king and queen later, and have a light supper with them. Afterward, there will be a formal presentation of the prize money."

"You're assuming I will win. What happens to the loser?"

Eilidh shrugged. "I haven't a clue."

Vor sipped her mug of tea and mumbled, "Probably get thrown to the lions."

Eilidh moved around the room, picking up and folding clothes, and appearing preoccupied. Vor didn't know if the timing was right, but to have her mother's attention all to herself was such a rarity.

Vor took a deep breath, wondering how to word her question without offending.

"Have you ever used dark magic to produce a certain outcome ... for the good of others?"

Eilidh dropped a shoe she'd retrieved from under the bed. "Why do you ask me that? You know we don't use dark magic in our family."

Her mother's voice had increased in volume, and Vor knew she'd upset her. She quickly put down her mug. "I apologize. I was just curious."

"It's best to keep your focus on that horse. Slip into the shirt so I can see if it needs hemming, then you can take apples to him."

Once again, her mother had neatly averted the conversation. Vor did as asked, and yet she still needed to find the *Book of Delsiran* and defeat Gabriel's dark magic. She would need to address that soon ... if she was to redeem herself in both her father's eyes, and to appease the Goddess.

"I'll get some apples from the cook on my way out."

"Her mother stepped back and plucked at one of the sleeves of Vor's new tunic. She considered the way it draped. "It needs just the right feminine touch." She reached into the leather pouch she normally kept around her waist for herbs and pulled out a matching blue ribbon. "Hold still." She moved around to Vor's back and lifted her heavy braid. She made deft work of attaching the ribbon so it could be seen from afar, then marched Vor over to the long mirror leaning against the wall so she could see herself. "What do you think?" Eilidh raised a hand to cover her lips. "Oh, my. I can't believe we're encouraging you to do such a dangerous thing."

Vor tried to make her mother smile. "We're just riding horses and going around a track. It's only a mile-and-a-half. Nothing dangerous about that."

"I don't trust that woman not to try something."

"Vivi? Well, I don't trust her either, but I'll be watching." She hugged her mother one last time. "Thank you so much for the tunic. It makes me feel like a winner already."

"It's time to go!" Torleik's voice boomed from the other room.

Vor hustled to the kitchen and grabbed two apples, as she doubted Vivi would remember one for Ivor. She stuck them in her travel sack and followed her father and the three boys outside.

Atli had Fillian saddled and ready to go by the time they reached the stables. Vor gave the stallion a pat on the neck, then accepted Atli's leg up into the saddle.

"Is that my leather belt?" Atli narrowed his ice-blue eyes and took the reins.

Vor merely smiled and shrugged, to which Atli shook his head, but let it go.

The others rode their own mounts or traveled by wagon to cover the relatively short distance to the racetrack as Atli guided the family toward the racetrack. Vor felt proud in her brightly colored tunic, as she headed her entourage atop such a magnificent animal.

The scene was chaotic as they arrived. Vor had never seen so many people in one place in her life. And to think, one of the reasons they were there was because of her. She reached down to caress Fillian's muscular neck. Atli was forced to walk close to Fillian, and as they approached the stable, he glanced up to see how she was doing. They couldn't hear each other over the roar of the crowd, so all she could manage was a grin.

Vor enjoyed the festive atmosphere and the aroma of fresh baked goods that filled the air around them. Vendors sold everything from buttery, flaky rolls and bread, to small carved toy horses that resembled Fillian and Ivor.

Since the racetrack was configured in an oval, everyone in the first ten rows would be able to see the entire race. Temporary seating had been added, and Vor was surprised to see the spot where the King and Queen of France would sit.

"Alright, boys. Stay close. I don't want anyone getting lost in this crowd. Erik, Fionne, keep an eye on Graham."

Although her mother's voice was full of authority, the boys ignored her, then jumped down from the wagon and took off in a hurry. Atli guided Vor and Fillian into the stable, where Fillian would wait until they were called to the starting line. Vor hopped down and offered fresh water to Fillian and her father's dappled gray horse, Justice, while he unbridled the draft horses. She was surprised she didn't see Vivi or Ivor, but they'd be there soon enough.

She checked her pocket for Graham's stone, and smiled in satisfaction at the warm touch. She was busy sorting her thoughts when a familiar male voice interrupted. "Are you nervous?"

Vor smiled as she spotted Luc outside the stall. He was regarding her new outfit as he stepped inside the gate.

"I'm not usually so anxious, but this crowd is like none I've ever seen before." She pushed her braid back.

Luc grinned and stepped behind her. "Parisians love horse races and getting dressed up. You look nice in that color." He held her shoulder still, then reached to retie the blue ribbon at the end of her braid.

He always smelled so good... like a home fire. Today, he smelled of citrus and pine. For a moment, Vor felt flustered. "Why... why aren't you with Vivi and Gabriel?"

He shrugged. "I'd rather be here."

"You're in the way here," said Atli, approaching with a stern expression, then stopping to brush Fillian's gleaming flanks. "Now is not the time to distract Vor's focus."

"He's right. We can talk... later." Vor started to squeeze his arm, then pulled her hand back like it was on fire. "Let's wish each party the best, and go our separate ways for now."

Luc nodded and glanced momentarily at Atli. "I can't guarantee Vivi won't try something. I think she's getting desperate to win again."

"I understand. We both have our reasons for needing to win." Vor pulled out an apple for Fillian, who was eager for the treat. She handed the other apple to Luc. "This is for Ivor. I imagine Vivi will forget to give him a reward."

"And if she remembers?"

"Then, *you* can have it." She reached out and playfully pinched his cheek.

"Thanks. Be careful, Vor."

Luc wore a reluctant expression on his face when he exited the stable and faded into the outside crowd. Vor didn't have the time to analyze what it all meant, but she appreciated the warning about Vivi, which came as no surprise.

When the racers were finally called, Vor once again mounted Fillian. One thing she always did before a race was to whisper into the animal's ear for a few moments. She was doing just that when she spotted Vivi dressed in red and standing next to Gabriel, who scanned the crowd, as if searching for someone.

Vivi's scarlet tunic, draped over scarlet leggings and black boots, was startling to behold, a man's black leather belt cinched around her tiny waist. She spotted Luc and waved him over.

"She looks like the Pope in all that red," Atli groused under his breath.

"Now that you mention it..." Vor chuckled, but secretly, she wondered how Vivi found the confidence to draw attention to herself that way.

"Where have you been, Stupid Boy?" Vivi demanded of Luc.

"I'm here now."

"You are such a brat. And a traitor. I saw you flirting with Vor."

"What is it you wanted?"

"I... can't remember."

"Vivi," said Gabriel, lowering his voice. "May I have a word with you in private? It can't wait."

She handed the reins to Luc. "I'll be right back," she said, giving him a big wink.

Vor thought Gabriel seemed subdued, under the circumstances. She would love to hear the conversation they were about to have, but as Gabriel led Vivi away, she knew there was no chance of that. She turned her head to admire Ivor, who stood about ten feet away, shaking his tail at flies and chomping on clover.

To Vor's surprise, a tall young girl dressed in yellow and black appeared from somewhere in the crowd, and exchanged a few words with Luc. He didn't seem surprised, helped her mount, then led the horse to the starting line.

"What in the world is happening?" Vor jumped down, took the reins from Atli and then walked the short distance to where Luc and Ivor were gearing up. "Is there a problem?" she asked

Luc as she shivered in her silk tunic when she recognized the new rider. "Trinette? What are you doing here... on Ivor?"

The girl smiled wide. "Father Gabriel asked if I could help out by riding for Mademoiselle Vivienne, who hasn't been feeling well."

Vor swallowed. "I hadn't heard that. It does appear that Ivor tolerates you better than most."

Ivor took that moment to turn his head and shake it in the affirmative.

"Oh, Ivor's been an angel since I first arrived." She reached down to pat his long neck. "Father Gabriel gave me plenty of time to get used to Ivor, and for Ivor not to be afraid of me."

Vor caught herself openly staring. How could she have missed that? She closed her mouth. She wanted to ask Luc if he'd known this was coming, but he was watching people in the crowd in the direction Gabriel and Vivi had gone.

"Father Gabriel must have great faith in your skills and abilities. Have you ridden in a race like this before?"

Trini's light brown cheeks blushed as she smiled. "I've won a few races. But they weren't this big."

"Is Father Gabriel paying you a portion of the prize winnings?"

Trini sat up tall in the saddle, and her face took on an impenetrable look. "I'm not supposed to talk about that."

No doubt because he's cheating you.

Vor's instincts nagged her to withdraw from the race or protest. But the look on Trini's face made her hesitate. And the prize money called. "Did Father Gabriel promise to take you home if you won?"

Again, Trini refused to look Vor in the eye. She was clearly struggling with something internally and Ivor shuddered, his legs twitching as he waited for a command.

Not knowing what else to do, Vor tried locating Izora.

"Are the racers ready?" a race official shouted.

Vor bit her lower lip, the pressure building. What to do? What to do?

She turned quickly to find her father standing by her side. While she was explaining what was going on, a flash of red silk hurtled right at them. Vivi stopped just in time, causing Ivor to rear up on his two hind legs. But Trini had him under control in no time, and everyone turned to Vivi.

"Get off my horse! I'm riding Ivor, or *nobody* rides him. Is that clear, little girl?"

Practically spitting her words, Vivi's flushed face almost matched her red silk outfit as she tried to pull Trini off the horse.

Suddenly, Gabriel appeared, and Vor was never so glad to see him. "Vivi, stop that deplorable behavior at once! You're going to hurt someone."

"Why is *she* here? *I'm* scheduled to ride."

"She's here because you haven't been winning races. And changing a name on the schedule is not a complex endeavor."

Vivi looked like she was about to explode.

Clearly worried by her response, he reached into his robe and carefully produced a ceramic jar of water. "Calm down, my love. Here, drink this. It will help you relax."

She knocked the jar out of his hand. "I don't need to relax, you imbecile! How can I win that prize money if I don't ride?"

Vor felt bad for Vivi, even though she wasn't the most polite person in the world. And yet, she was appalled at how Vivi addressed her guardian. Lucky for them both, Torleik suddenly appeared.

"That's enough," Torleik said in a low voice, as if not wishing to draw attention. "If you wish to discuss whatever needs discussing, I'll let the king know of the delay."

"No delay." Gabriel took Vivi roughly by the arm and started to force her to go with him.

At the same time, Torleik and Atli helped Vor back in the saddle and escorted her quickly to the starting line. Luc followed their lead, and guided Trini aboard Ivor.

Gabriel whirled around and pointed directly at Luc. "Do not let her go until I give the word."

"*Oui*, monsieur."

Vor wasn't surprised when Izora made her way through the crowd, and arrived with Clotilde, Armand's sister.

"Trinette, what are you doing here? Are you alright?" Izora aimed her question at the girl, but her eyes returned to Gabriel, flashing daggers. "Why is Trinette here? And on that horse? What are you planning, Father Gabriel?"

Gabriel paused for a moment to regain his composure. He then explained the mix-up with the riders. At least, that's how he termed it.

"Mix-up, my ass," hissed Vivi, her eyes narrowing. "It's all Gabriel's doing." She then turned her focus to Trini.

One of the race authorities timidly approached, and Vor wondered what would happen now. "The King is asking why the race hasn't begun. Is there a problem?"

Vor regarded Gabriel, who went into his cooperative mode—in case the King was watching, no doubt.

"Mademoiselle Vivienne is not feeling well today. Rather than reschedule the race, would King Louis approve a qualified substitute rider?" He held up his hand and indicated Trini, her eyes huge at all the fuss.

"And how is she qualified?"

Gabriel gestured to Trini. "You may speak. Tell the man about the races and prize money you have won to date."

For a moment, Trini hesitated.

Vor wondered if she would tell the truth, or make up stories that no one could dispute?

"You don't have to answer, Trini. Get down off that horse and come with me."

Izora held out her hand, and Trini obeyed. They then disappeared quietly into the crowd, Izora's head held high, Trini's dark eyes staring at the ground.

Vor frowned, as confused as everyone else. To her surprise, Vivi accepted Luc's help mounting.

Gabriel looked at the place where Trini and Izora disappeared in the crowd, a slightly wistful look in his eye. But then, moments later, his brows dropped into a deep furrow, and he was all business as he turned to Vivi.

"Have you got each of my instructions in that crazy head of yours?"

"Of course I do. Now, hand me the reins."

"My new business success is riding on you, love."

"No pressure, I see."

"You must focus, Vivi. I mean it. Either that or I will have to turn to Plan B," Gabriel muttered, then handed her the reins and stepped back.

What had he meant by that? But Vor had no time to ponder his cryptic words because Fillian kept snorting and pawing the ground, eager to get going. Vor's heart began to pound and things in the background grew fuzzy. She had to work hard to hold Fillian steady.

The Mayor of Paris held the red flag in one hand and after a long hesitation for dramatic effect, he let it drop. The crowd roared and rushed to their feet as Vor's stomach suddenly lurched. They were off.

Ivor surged ahead and took the lead. Although Vor could feel the wind against her cheeks and her leg muscles pressing against Fillian's sides, he was slow from the start, but at least he was responding to Vor's commands. She was used to a smaller arena with a much larger field of competitors, and she hoped Fillian would know how to deal with the situation. There wouldn't be time to make corrections for any mistakes.

"No mistakes allowed," she whispered into his ear as she leaned forward, her face almost touching his neck.

The track was damp from an early rain. She could feel his legs pumping out a steady rhythm, the sound of pounding hooves echoing inside her head as the shouts from the crowd grew in volume.

The Frankish were calling out their countrywoman's name. "Vee-vee. Vee-vee."

"We're going to make a move, Fillian," whispered Vor.

Fillian's eyes were on the road ahead, but she thought she saw him nod. Vor edged him closer to the railing, knowing she would most likely have only one shot at this.

"Ha!" she yelled. "This one is for my father. For everything he's worked so hard for. "That *we've* worked so hard for."

Vor's heart raced as she felt the jarring of sinew and muscle beneath her, heard the roar of the crowd and the sound of hoofbeats pummeling the earth. The lead could change at any moment, and Vor needed a plan. Out of the corner of her eye, she saw Vivi lying almost flat against Ivor's back, his legs pumping out a steady rhythm as the noise from the crowd grew in volume.

That girl can ride. I may have underestimated you, Vivi.

She must have recovered from whatever Gabriel had been putting in her food and drink.

Vor used her knees to guide Fillian toward the inner railing.

Vivi didn't like that and began cursing. "Get your damn horse out of my way! Who do you think you are? The Queen of England?"

Vor gave in to a small smile. Steady as he goes, Atli had advised. Little by little, Fillian inched closer to the railing.

Vivi went into the first turn, lifting her bottom above the saddle. When she came out of the turn and realized Vor and Fillian were right there, Vivi reached for her whip.

"This is what we've waited for, Fillian," Vor crooned. "This is *your* race."

It started with an opening about half an inch, which quickly became an inch. Vivi's whip came down and Ivor lunged away from the railing and drifted left. An opening the size of a horse appeared, and into that void slid the big red chestnut, all the while never missing a beat, his muscles gathering beneath Vor and then lengthening 'til his limbs stretched out as far as they could. He reached and reached, his heart pumping. By the time Fillian demanded his rein, Vor was happy to give it.

Into the second and final loop around the track, Vor held tight to the reins, her legs controlling Fillian's speed. When they emerged from the last curve into the critical straightaway, she had to squint to see the finish line with the wind causing her eyes to water. All this time, she felt confident she was far enough ahead of Vivi and Ivor not to worry, so she never looked back until it was almost too late.

From the side, she spotted Ivor's pale legs almost even with Fillian once again. The crowd was on its feet, shouting, "Vee-vee! Vee-vee! Vee-vee!"

Vor had never been in a race where she wasn't the favorite, and she didn't like it. She talked to Fillian again, and he listened, ears pricked back.

They were about ten feet from the finish line when an object appeared on the road. A box. With something shiny on top. As she drew closer, Vor could tell what it was right away because she'd been dreaming about it for months now. A large, shiny hunk of aventurine glistened with green sparkles. It was sitting right there, waiting for her. But Vivi saw it too and started to slow down.

Vor heard someone call her name. Her father? Atli? Luc?

She rubbed Fillian's forelock and whispered, "Not for us ... not this time."

They never slowed down, and while Vor knew this could be a test by the Goddess, it could also be a trick by Gabriel or Vivi.

She and Fillian crossed the finish line and never looked back.

Chapter 24

Vor crossed the finish line in a blur, her heart pounding. It began to subside as she remembered to pull back on the reins and slow Fillian to a walk, through the haze of the roaring crowd.

For their part, the people in the crowd didn't seem to know what to do when she crossed first. Their Frankish countrywoman, Vivi, had stopped to admire the green crystal placed in the road, but when she jumped down and attempted to lift it, it disappeared, box and all.

It took Vor only a few moments to realize the crowd couldn't see the stone, so had no idea why Vivi searched the stands, as if looking for someone to blame. When she finally crossed the line, Vor jumped down and reached out her hand in a sign of good sportsmanship. Vivi dismounted and looked at Vor's hand for a moment, then reluctantly reached out and shook it. Yet, her eyes flitted over the crowd.

"Gabriel made that stone appear. He meant it for you, didn't he?" she growled. "Once again, he ruins my life. I counted on that prize money to move away and start over."

Vor handed Fillian's reins over to Atli and accepted his hug. Before she was engulfed by her family, Vor leaned in close to Vivi. "I suspect Gabriel used dark magic to conjure the stone he knows

I've been seeking. He put it there because he thought I would choose magic over my family."

Appearing stunned by Vor's revelation, Vivi handed Ivor's reins to Luc, who handed them to someone else as Vivi tried to recover.

"There you are, Luc. Cool Ivor down, water and feed him. I'll be at the stalls later to check on him." She grimaced.

"Are you hurt?" Vor asked.

For a moment, Vivi regarded Vor with a frown, then watched as Luc hopped up into the saddle and took Ivor for a walk. "You won the race. You can quit being nice to me."

Vor watched Luc and Ivor ease through the crowd. "Why are you so rude to Luc, calling him names all the time?"

Vivi smirked. "I call him what he deserves. He doesn't complain. As a matter of fact, I think he likes it. It's just a game." They walked to a well between the track and the stable, and both took a long drink from a pail of water. "Are you worried he's not tough enough to take it?"

Vor looked around for something to wipe her mouth on, other than her silk sleeve. "Not at all. I just think it's unnecessary."

A female servant standing nearby grinned and congratulated Vor on the race, then held out a fresh towel, which Vor used to dry her face and mouth. "Thank you. Look, I know we're not exactly best friends, but if you need help, just say the word and I'll be there. I'm guessing here, but I don't think you have a particularly healthy relationship with Gabriel. If I were you, I'd start with that." She reached for another towel and handed it to Vivi, who hesitated. At last, she took it and wiped her face.

Vivi loosened her shoulder-length chestnut hair from the leather strap that had held it out of the way. Using her fingers, she massaged her scalp and moved away from the well.

"You need to understand. Gabriel pays for everything. I have no money of my own. Every time I win a race, the prize money goes to Gabriel. He gives me a small allowance and pays for my clothes. I can't just walk away." A tear slid down her cheek. "I don't know what I'll do now. I th–think he's replacing me with that girl we saw earlier."

Vor cocked her head. Was Vivi playing the "poor me" role to fool her out of her prize money? She regarded Vivi's fresh tears and the way she held her sore shoulder. She quickly came to a decision she hoped she wouldn't regret.

"Why don't you come to dinner tonight? I'm sure my mother won't mind one more guest. She can tend to your shoulder. Maybe we can come up with a solution together to get Gabriel out of your life. The whole family will be at the Lemon Garden."

"Oh, I don't know. People make me anxious. That's why I prefer horses." She hesitated. "Mmm, will Atli be there?"

"As far as I know. I'm sure the boys would love to see you."

Vivi gave a crooked smile, a sign of hope. "Well, alright. But if Gabriel sees me try to leave Xavier and Jacqueline's home..."

"You mustn't let him see you."

Vivi hesitated for a moment, then glanced at the crowd dispersing all about.

"Well, alright. I'll be there."

"Just don't call me names in front of my brothers, or I'll never live it down."

Vor felt relieved to finally hear Vivi laugh.

Vor had never invited anyone over to eat, so she hoped her mother and brothers wouldn't make a huge fuss. After all, it was just Vivienne le Clerc, an average girl like her. Well, maybe not.

She sent Vivi on her way just as her family appeared, the boys their normal rambunctious selves and thrilled with Vor's win, therefore generating a lot of noise. Torleik took a moment to give her a big hug, then smiled down at her, giving a nod.

"I knew I could count on you."

Aila and Armand appeared, and after eyeing a subdued, yet happy crowd for the event, they walked with Vor and Atli to the stable, Aila's arm entwined with Vor's. "You inspire me to try harder. Did you know that? When you race like that, it gives me courage to not be so scared."

Vor didn't want to admit it, but she was feeling shaky. Had she done the right thing in offering to help Vivi escape Gabriel's influence? And yet something didn't feel right about the way he'd been acting lately. But what?

You're worried Gabriel will take revenge on you.

Aila halted mid-stride. "By the way, you and Vivi are invited to dine with the King and Queen of France for the midday meal tomorrow, where the queen will present you with your reward money for the race."

"I wondered when that would happen, since I didn't see anyone rushing to bring me heavy bags of coins," Vor teased as she looked around for her mother. "I just wish I could forgo the meal with the king and queen. My table manners could use some work."

Aila smiled and gently brushed back some stray hairs that had escaped Vor's braid. "It's a good thing, really. I've already heard people in the stands saying they want a re-match next year between the two horses."

Vor disengaged her arm and smiled weakly. "A year is a long way away."

She looked around for Luc, but didn't see him anywhere. Vivi had disappeared, and there was no sign of Gabriel, which Vor thought odd as Ivor's co-owner. Armand's father, the other co-owner, was present. He had a huge grin on his face and shook his son's hand, clearly as proud of Ivor as he could be, even though he came in second. Already, people were lining up for stud service.

Next, Eilidh and Torleik took Fionne and Graham back to the Lemon Garden, after also having received an invitation to dine with the king and queen. Finally, Aila and Armand left to prepare for their meal at court the next day. Not ready to leave just yet, Vor watched while Atli and Erik bathed Fillian, then groomed him until his coat shone brilliantly, and his black mane and tail were combed with equal results. Standing back, Vor realized she felt differently since her name had gone on Fillian's registration form. He was the first thing of real value she'd ever owned, and she took great pride in giving him the best environment possible. Before she left, she even checked his hooves for stones and the soundness of his legs.

"Anything else, my prince?" she teased the bay. Fillian gave an emphatic nod of his head and nudged her pockets for a treat. "How did you know that's all I had room for in this tiny pocket?" She pulled out a carrot and he gently took it from her hand.

At last, she was ready to call The King's Race done and over. "When can we leave for home?" she asked Atli.

"I'll talk to Father and have a better answer tomorrow. Don't you want to spend extra time in Paris—shopping, perhaps?"

Vor made a face and followed him to the main door of the public stable. "I have everything I need." She stopped to gaze across the stable and watched as Fillian reached for his oat bag. "We're not going to leave Fillian all alone here tonight, are we? We should take him with us. Lemon Garden has a small stable. You and the boys can take turns checking on him, and he'll be a lot closer."

Atli considered her words and gave a slow nod. "That's a good plan. You run ahead with Erik, and alert the stable hands. I'll get Fillian's equipment and bring it to the cottage stable."

Pleased she'd thought of it, Vor went to give Erik the news.

The cottage at Lemon Garden was older than Vor's home on Meginland. Much older. But that just meant that the plants, trees and shrubs were older, too, and bigger than what Vor was used to.

"It's like this," she explained to Vivi when they sat in the pleasant air that evening after supper. "Norsemen settled in the north of Alba and its isles over three hundred years ago. The first thing they did in the Orkneys was to cut down all the trees to build houses. That's why there are so few large trees there. Some landowners have imported and replaced trees, but not many grow as fast or as big as trees like these here. That oak tree over there is over two hundred years old!"

Vivi nodded, as if trying to appear impressed. "Didn't religious groups like the Druids use those old trees for sacrifices?"

Vor looked away, feeling her face grow hot. "None of us was alive back then. Who's to say what really happened? But I suppose it's possible."

Eilidh appeared with a tray of chamomile tea, which Vor knew she'd need to sleep well that night. Though things had been fine at dinner, rather than measure every word that came out of her mouth, Vivi tended to blurt out whatever she was thinking. The only time she was short on words was when Graham asked her why she'd slowed down at the end of the race.

Vor gave her a warning look not to tackle that, so Vivi answered the second part of the question with a white lie.

"Ivor put so much into the race that he needed a rest near the end."

"But you lost the race because of it," said Fionne, the competitive son.

"Fionne, it's complicated. Let's not bother Vivi with something out of her control."

Fionne shrugged, then went to the rear of the garden to play with Erik and Graham.

"I'm sorry about that. Boys aren't very subtle, are they?"

Vivi leaned back in her chair, appearing relaxed and content in her black gown. As for not liking children, she had been surprisingly entertaining with the boys. When she bent forward, Vor noticed the gold cross she wore around her neck.

Is she a Christian? Now, that would surprise me.

"I guess it's time we talk about Gabriel, anyway," Vivi sighed.

Vor poured more tea. "How long have you known Gabriel?"

"He took me in when I was five—right after both my parents died."

Vor fingered a biscuit on her plate. "The dreams you've been having. Nightmares that wake you up? What are they about?"

Vivi twirled a lock of hair near her cheek. "They always have Gabriel in them. And they don't feel like dreams anymore. They're more like ... memories."

Vor realized the facts of the matter were quickly becoming more complex, and she suspected Vivi needed an expert of some sort. Could her mother help?

"Has Gabriel ever... harmed you or anyone you know? He was so angry when I asked if he'd put anything in your food or drink." Vor left it at that and waited to see what Vivi would say.

Her eyes followed the graceful stems of a birch tree near a pond as stars began to appear in the night sky. "What he gives me at night helps me sleep. For a little while. Until the nightmares come. We've tried several herbs and spells. Nothing helps. A physician would only bleed me. Which makes me even weaker."

"When did Marcel Duran propose to you?"

Vivi sat up. "What? Are you crazy? Why would such a handsome man want to marry me?"

"You've told us more than once that Marcel is your fiancé. Is that not true?"

"Are you saying that to be cruel?" Vivi shot up out of her seat.

Vor thought about how calm Aila could be. "Not at all. I'm just trying to understand. In fact, I doubt Gabriel would want you to marry a debt collector, anyway. At least, that's what he said. He wants someone better for you. He told me so himself."

She didn't bother to add that it probably had more to do with how much money her prospective husband might make, or his occupation. She had a feeling Gabriel was simply looking for someone to help him with his various business schemes. But Vor would never say that out loud.

"I told you I was engaged?" Vivi looked very young at the moment. And vulnerable. "Why would I do that?"

Vor rose from her chair and looked up at the stars. "I don't know, but if you want to start a new life where you have control of some of these things, you'll need money. And a regular occupation where people respect you. Like a teacher. You could be an equestrian teacher for young girls."

"A what? E-ques..."

"Equestrian. It's from Latin and means someone who rides horses. You could teach young ladies how to ride. Ladies from good families."

"Do those families have money?"

"Indeed, they do. Once they learn how skilled you are, you may be able to charge as much as you want for your services."

Once she'd said the words out loud, Vor knew she was on to something. "You could travel from family to family, staying in each of the homes as long as they need you." She picked up an empty mug. "In fact, you could start with Xavier and Jacqueline's three daughters. Once you finished with them and word got out about how capable you are, you could make a lot of money pretty quickly. You could start by using Paris as your base, since you're already here. Later, when you have more money, you can try someplace else." She set down the mug. "What do you think?"

Vivi sat down again and gazed at the garden at night. "It sounds too good to be true."

"We'll find a financial consultant to help." Vor waved her hand in excitement. "We'll ask Marcel Duran to make suggestions. How about that?"

Vivi wrapped her hands around her empty mug. "How soon can we make this happen? The longer I'm with Gabriel, the more I... I fear him. I know so many bad things he's done."

Vor tried to push down the feeling of dread that settled in her middle. "Out of curiosity, what would Gabriel do with all that prize money?"

Vivi shrugged. "He's been working on a new business venture. I wasn't supposed to hear him, but I think it's in Alba and Orkney. I don't know what it involves." She placed a hand on the birch tree trunk. "And as I said before, I think he planned to replace me if I didn't win this race."

"That's awful!" Vor said.

"I've noticed a girl hanging around a lot. She's about thirteen, fourteen. Very quiet. But she watches me all the time. And I've seen her talk to Izora, so they may be related. I think her name is Trinette."

Vor shook her head. "Well, it's clear you need a new beginning with a career you can be proud of. If you worked as a ladies' equestrian trainer for five years and saved all your money, you would have enough for a sufficient dowry to marry a decent man. Maybe even Marcel."

"Do you really think so?" Vivi's expression was wistful. "Five years is a long time."

"That's just a number. It all depends on you. In any case, let's start with you not swallowing anything Gabriel gives you to eat or drink for the time being. Don't let him see you refusing, but find a way to never ingest anything. I'll speak to my mother who's a healer. She might have some ideas. And you must not stay with Gabriel anymore. It's time you were on your own. I'll speak to Jacqueline tomorrow and see what she thinks of our plan. I'll also make an appointment with Marcel Duran, as well. If nothing else, you'll meet someone who knows numbers."

Vivi jumped up and hugged Vor tightly. "I want to put Gabriel behind bars for what he's done. That man is a monster, and I refuse to let him turn me into one, as well."

Nausea rose in Vor's throat at the sound of Gabriel's name. She tightened her shawl. "I don't know if we're strong enough to defeat Gabriel on our own, but we can certainly give it our best try."

Vor saw a spark that hadn't been there before, but now shone brightly in Vivi's eyes.

Chapter 25

The day after the race, every muscle in Vor's body felt sore and over-used. Consequently, it wasn't the best day to meet the King and Queen of France, but Vor managed to pull herself together. Today she'd finally receive the silver coins that would help her family survive until they could prove that the smugglers were working of their own accord.

Shortly after noon, an envoy from the king came to escort her and her family to the royal court of King Louis and Queen Adela. Her mother had unpacked another new surprise gown for Vor that she'd purchased from the stipend the king had given them to make the trip. It was designed in the Norse style in summery shades of blue and yellow. Vor felt proud to wear it as they walked through the stone courtyard of the palace. When they arrived at the door that led into the great hall, Vor spied Luc off to one side holding Ivor's reins while Atli held Fillian's. Everyone gravitated toward the two horses, who appeared jumpy, despite the apples each received.

"Magnificent animals," said King Louis, running his hand down Ivor's neck. "I enjoyed that race, especially with two females in the saddle. Very exciting, indeed."

He glanced at Vivi first. "Mademoiselle Vivienne, whatever made you stop your horse to dismount? A very unfortunate decision on your part, wouldn't you say?" His beady blue eyes narrowed.

"Ivor stumbled, and I thought it was better to check his leg than to risk he'd go lame, your highness." Vivi gave a perfunctory smile then performed an awkward curtsy. She had clearly prepared a response to everyone's burning question. She looked away, as if satisfied with her words. Did the king believe her?

He shrugged, as if she, and what came out of her mouth, was of no consequence. Vor debated coming to her aid, but quickly dropped that idea. No point in making a grumpy, judgmental person angrier. Especially if that person happened to be a king.

Vor felt bad that the king hadn't been kinder to Vivi, as she was a wonderfully skilled rider... most days. The king placed his feet wide apart and clasped his hands in front of him. "You, on the other hand, Mademoiselle Vor, were spectacular. How did you overcome that slow start—and, unlike your predecessor" — he shot a glance at Vivi — "without a whip?"

"I would never use a whip on an animal, your highness. After all, patience is an important attribute when working with animals." She then remembered to curtsy as she had seen Vivi do, and saw the queen hide a smile behind her hand.

The king turned to Torleik. "Very commendable. You must be a proud father. I can tell your daughter has both compassion and determination."

"She is brimming with determination, your highness," said Torleik with a grin. "She's working on the compassion part."

The two men chuckled, and with that out of the way, they entered the great hall and turned to admire the tables loaded down with all kinds of food.

"You must be hungry after a run like that," said Queen Adela. "We have a banquet set up in your honor. Please, join us." She swept an arm back, indicating the whole family, and the boys' eyes grew huge as two servants walked by carrying a whole roasted pig between them. "Mademoiselle Vivienne, you and Monsieur de Maci must join us, as well."

The banquet was set up in such a way that all the guests dined together at the same table. Vivi sat across from Vor and ate quietly from a plate that contained little. She didn't speak to anyone. Was she still upset by what the king had said? Vor had been praised, while Vivi had lost ground. How unexpected. Vivi must feel crushed. Vor's thoughts turned to the aventurine. The audience couldn't have seen the green stone. So why did Vivi see it? It seemed odd that a spell on Vor would include Vivi, especially since no one else could see it. Vor couldn't wait until supper was over, so she could ask her mother these questions and more.

As she sat stewing over these things, out of the corner of her eye, she saw Gabriel smile over at her, and her scalp prickled. Then he gave the queen his full attention. At one point, when Vivi clammed up and chose not to respond to any more questions from the queen, Gabriel must have pinched her, because Vivi let out a surprised yelp.

As if her mother had read Vor's thoughts she leaned to her left and murmured into Vor's ear. "You performed no dark magic today, did you?"

Vor stared at her mother in surprise. "Of course not. Why do you ask? I wouldn't even know how to attempt such a thing..." She'd been about to refer to the aventurine in the box being the only unnatural element present that day, but quickly decided against it. She was determined to find these answers for herself.

Vor leaned over to pour water from a pitcher into her goblet and saw Luc and Atli slip in a side door, their hair damp, an indication they'd finished with the horses and hurried over to the castle after cleaning up.

As Vor looked down the long table at her father and brother, she wondered where the king kept the prize money. But more importantly, was it going to be enough to solve her family's financial problems?

Worry dampened her appetite and she set down her fork. The queen quickly took advantage of the lull in conversation and clinked her spoon against her goblet to get everyone's attention.

"Mademoiselle Vor, I've been meaning to ask—when did you start riding? I have a young daughter, Agnes, and for some reason, your tenacity reminds me of her when she wants to pursue something. She's already fascinated with horses. Is there a proper age when one should put one's child on a horse?"

Vor glanced at her father. "I honestly can't remember that far back, so I'll defer to my father on that question, your highness."

"It depends on the child, of course," offered Torleik. "Vor has always shown interest in Valhalla, my horse farm. She was three when she had her first official riding lesson." He glanced at Eilidh for confirmation, and she nodded, still chewing. "Tenacity is a good trait for a horsewoman. Your daughter may surprise you, your majesty. I know mine has."

Vor's cheeks felt like they were on fire as she saw Luc slide onto the bench. She ducked her head, but the queen appeared pleased with her father's response.

Vivi sat up straight in her chair and leaned in to grab a chunk of bread. "Of course, one needs talent and determination, as well, your majesty. Racing is not for the faint of heart."

A silence filled the great hall as everyone seemed to be waiting for the queen's response to that. Vivi turned her head and regarded Vor with a haughty expression.

"Of course, Mademoiselle Vivienne is correct," Vor added quickly, trying to restore the good cheer. "But then, the princess most likely doesn't plan on racing anytime soon. She'd probably rather ride in Bois de Boulogne at her leisure. Is that correct, your highness?"

Queen Adela looked from Vivi to Vor and smiled thinly. "*Oui*, you are correct, Mademoiselle Vor."

Finally feeling as if she could look away and not have to temper Vivi's conversation, Vor gazed over Vivi's shoulder and outside the windows, where the last of the sun's rays were visible. As much as she needed that prize money, she felt bad for Vivi, and could understand her embarrassment and anger.

Unfortunately, Vivi decided to drown her sorrows in potent wine, and soon began babbling incoherently and slurring her words. Soon, Gabriel enlisted Luc and another servant to escort Vivi home safely.

Vor felt the need to say something comforting in light of the king's questioning Vivi's skills and abilities, but it was clear she would have to speak to her later, when the girl was sober.

Once Vivi was gone, Vor felt her stomach relax. But then, she thought of Luc. Would she have a chance to see him, to say goodbye before he left? Surprisingly, the idea that she might never see him again made her sad.

It seemed very late at night, indeed, when the king waved a hand at a servant, who approached with several bags of silver. He set the bags on the cleared table. Vor felt butterflies in her belly, now that she was so close to having her problems solved. When she looked over at her parents and their obvious relief, she realized how much her parents' love meant to her.

"Vor Torleiksdottir, this is the reward promised to you. We thank you for your willingness to come so far from home for a horse race that has captured the imagination of a kingdom. Tonight, we celebrate your amazing accomplishment, and wish you well in your future endeavors. These bags are very heavy, so I've divided them up for now."

The king handed the first bag to Torleik, the second he gave to Atli, and the third bag, the smallest, to Vor, who experienced the tiniest letdown. She had wanted to hand the money over to her father herself. They thanked his majesty, and Torleik enlisted some of his seamen as guards, who'd made the trip for just this purpose, then headed for their temporary home at Lemon Garden Cottage.

Once she climbed under the covers later that evening, her dreams were pleasant and the monster contained.

After all that she'd been through these past months, Vor had learned her lesson regarding gossip, especially after what had happened with Gemma at the stable. She slept well that night, and was up early the next morning. As she slowly packed her belongings, she reminded herself that although she'd solved their immediate problem with the money, she still needed to discover the identity of the smugglers. Until then, her father would continue to be under suspicion, and if they couldn't keep up with the maintenance, the horse farm could fall to ruin, its stellar reputation a thing of the past.

And right when a newcomer had recently moved onto Meginland.

Atli had confided in her that sometime before their trip to Frankia, Torleik learned he had an island horse breeding competitor, a Ragnar Tollaksson. At first, Vor's father had played it down, according to Atli. But as they prepared to return home, she knew he was thinking about Ragnar, an ambitious young man fresh from Iceland, if what Atli learned was true. He'd settled on a property just outside *Kirkjuvagr*, and was said to be creating a training and breeding facility twice the size of Torleik's. Vor knew her father must be worried about that, but he must have known that it was bound to happen someday.

As she folded her gowns and placed them in a small trunk, she thought of home. Atli told her *The Sea Raven* was scheduled to return to the Orkneys the day after tomorrow, and her father had made sure his family would be aboard. Meanwhile, he promised to count the coins on their last night in Frankia, turning it into a celebration of sorts for the boys. Not that he wanted any of them growing into men who worshiped money, but more a celebration of the reward for Vor's hard work and dedication.

Vor felt the ice slowly melting around her father's heart and sighed in relief.

And now, due to her mother's organizational skills, Vor had that last morning free, with the midday meal scheduled for early afternoon at La Belle Rose, where the family enjoyed a midday meal of roast venison, spiced vegetables, sweet fresh fruit, and a lovely pastry. Vor and her family then said goodbye to Aila and Armand, who would officially start their lives as a married couple. Armand was already teaching Aila how to speak better Frankish, but Vor had made arrangements for a tutor for Aila, as well. No one was going to say her sister's language wasn't good enough to mingle with the upper echelons of society.

After the meal, Vor wandered outside to enjoy the garden for which the cottage was named. An entire section of the courtyard contained small lemon trees in bright blue ceramic pots, as well as more blue pots scattered strategically about, with bright yellow blossoms of all types. An abundance of fragrant petunias, lilies and roses graced the courtyard gardens, nestled between marigolds and yellow iris. Someone had put a lot of time and effort in planning an all-yellow garden.

Vor leaned down and inhaled a whiff of yellow jasmine. "Oh, I'm going to miss you, Lemon Garden." She moved along the path toward a large, ancient apple tree in another section with an inviting bench beneath it. To her surprise, Luc was seated there, a serene look on his face as he watched her approach.

"Luc! Why are you still here in Paris?"

"I have one more job I promised to do. When that's complete, I'm off."

"And what's that job?" Vor sat down next to him.

"You'll find out soon enough," he said with a grin.

"I'm glad you stopped by to say goodbye. We're leaving first thing in the morning."

"*Oui*. I am aware of that."

Vor felt awkward and didn't know how to respond, so instead she asked, "How's Vivi?"

Luc remained silent for a few moments. "Vivi's fine. She's tough."

"Gabriel must be angry with her."

He shrugged and gazed off in the distance. "You won the race. Let it go.

There's nothing you can do for her now."

Vor sensed a change in his demeanor, and rose, then glanced around for her mother. "I won't take any more of your time. I should finish packing."

She sensed a stiffness to his speech and actions, but was too tired to interpret his mysterious behavior. And yet it hurt after the pleasant moments they'd shared. "I guess this is goodbye. Good luck to you—wherever you end up."

"And you." He rose and stuck out his hand.

Vor stared at it, wishing he would have at least hugged her. She took his hand and shook it, then turned away.

As she followed the path back to the cottage, she wondered what Luc was really thinking. Had she done something wrong to offend him?

Her mind drifted back to those bags of silver coins. Perhaps Luc thought he deserved some kind of reward. Why hadn't she thought of it before?

Gabriel was a creature of the darkness. He didn't mind in the least not being the center of attention. He had Father Alceste to thank for that. His time and place would come. Soon. He crept through the public stable, the horses snorting and stomping, but otherwise, not sending up any alarms. Fortunately, they weren't afraid of him, despite the fact that he was dressed in a black cassock, his hood pulled up so that only a small portion of his face was visible.

Fate had delivered Vor and her father practically to his doorstep. Ruining Torleik's horse business and stealing it from him had become his only goal. But then, along came young Vor, who had tried to discredit his Vivi and make her doubt herself in front of the King and Queen of Frankia.

He didn't blame Vivi for getting drunk. She was no longer a fresh exotic flower who made people smile with her antics. No, this was a good time for Vivi to just disappear.

Earlier, he'd followed Luc and the servant as they escorted Vivi to her temporary home with Xavier and Jacqueline. Luc finally had to pick her up and carry her inside, she was so inebriated, while Jacqueline stood at the doorstep giving instructions. Also a guest of Xavier's, Gabriel entered a few moments later, as if he'd been with Luc and Vivi all along.

"What in the world did the king and queen give her to drink?" Jacqueline wanted to know.

Gabriel chuckled, leaning against the wall outside Vivi's door. "I suspect no one ever told Vivi not to mix her wine and mead. She was quite thirsty tonight and eager to toast the winner."

He'd watched Vor all evening. She looked as if she wanted to defend Vivi's actions, yet she never did. If the two were now "friends," and it would appear so, then no doubt, Vivi had told her things about him. Had shown her the bruises on her body from beatings. Gabriel knew people like Vor and her father. Thought they were better than everyone else because they'd moved up by their own efforts.

Jacqueline groused while he considered his next move. She left off with, "You should have paid closer attention. Poor thing. She can't hold that much liquor." She shot a dark look Gabriel's way, clearly upset with him.

Gabriel grinned and shrugged his shoulders. "She's a grown woman, *ma petite*. If that is what she wishes to do to drown her sorrows, who am I to stop her?"

Jacqueline shut the door in his face, muttering something that sounded distinctly like curse words.

Vor and Torleik would have their comeuppance ... very soon, if Gabriel had his say. Then all would be in balance once again. Good versus evil and all that stuff the Church taught the commoners. *Fie!*

Gabriel wandered outside, hands behind his back as he considered his resources to use against Torleik.

Where to start?

Chapter 26

As Vor and her family sat around the dining table after their midday meal at the Lemon Garden Cottage, her younger brothers gleefully repeated the number her father gave as they counted the prize money. Just to be sure, Vor wrote the final number in her journal so they'd have something to compare it to when they arrived back in Orkney.

Her mother got along well with Odette, the servant left behind by the owners of Lemon Garden Cottage who were currently visiting their first grandchild in Provence. They were cousins of Genevieve, so they had been glad to have someone watch over their home while they were away. Eilidh and Odette had been vigorously cleaning up the kitchen area until it glowed. After putting away the clean dishes and platters, Eilidh finally found a seat and put up her feet while Odette inventoried the pantry before the owners returned.

"So what's the total?" Vor's mother asked.

"Fifty thousand *livres*. Plus ten thousand *livres* as a bonus for coming all this way on such short notice." Torleik pulled out an extra stack of coins and grinned. "You made quite an impression on the king and queen, Vor. They threw in an extra five thousand *livres*. Grand total is sixty-five thousand *livres*." He tweaked her braid. "We're so proud of you."

"My little sister will go down in Frankish equestrian history," said Atli, who was breaking bags down into smaller units of twenty to make them more portable and to draw less attention.

Vor basked in their praise, knowing full well she couldn't have done it alone. "If we're invited to come back and do it again next year, perhaps we can round up a few female riders and their horses to make it a better competition. We'd need to train additional riders and start much sooner. What do you think?"

Eilidh chuckled and exchanged a look with Torleik. "That sounds very ambitious of you, dear, but a year is a long time from now."

"I could make myself available to train female riders." Atli raised an eyebrow and smiled his most charming smile, making Vor and her parents laugh.

"I think Vivi should train several riders, too. She may even be a better rider than me." A moment of silence followed, her words surprising those in the room. Vor glanced at the others, her shoulders inching up. "I'm serious. If you take that whip out of her hand, she's in the horse's head."

"Who's going to take that whip out of her hands... especially with Gabriel encouraging her?" Atli bent his head and tucked the last of the coin purses into a trunk that was bound for Orkney.

"He's got a point," Vor's father said. "Let's just focus on what you *can* influence."

Reluctantly, Vor nodded and finished writing notes in her journal. She'd never thought of riding in horse races as entertainment, so that gave her something new to consider. However, Vivi was more of an entertainer, so Vor would do well to study her actions. Crazy the woman might be, but the crowd loved her.

Vor turned her attention to the boys, who were easily distracted, once they'd finished eating. They hurried out to the garden to see the Mastiff puppies, where Izora and Trinette were bathing older pups in two huge tubs. As soon as Vor saw Izora and the girl close-up, she did a double-take, stunned. She recognized the two faces from the sandstone "mirror" she'd seen weeks ago in the Orkney caves. Her heart began to race. Something was starting to work its way under her skin and the goosebumps only confirmed it. She reached into the right pocket of her summer cloak and was surprised to find the small rock with the two faces. The faces that changed expressions. Today, they were smiling.

She was digesting that when Luc drove up in a wagon and carried a box containing five squiggling furry pups no more than a few weeks old. Vor couldn't hide her smile as she stepped outside and immediately crouched down to nuzzle the pups.

"They smell heavenly. Don't you think?" she cooed.

"Only if heaven is covered with dog poop," said a familiar voice.

"Vee-vee!" the boys called out in unison.

Surprised to see her rival, Vor rose, holding a brindle pup with huge feet. "Vivi, how unexpected." She saw Vivi test her shoulder and wince as if in pain. Vor quickly set the pup down. "You need to see my mother, if you're in that much pain. Let me go find her."

"No, it's not urgent. I just ... I just ... wanted to see if she had some salve."

Vivi winced again when Vor placed her hand atop her shoulder, so Vor knew the pain must be excruciating. "I'll be right back." She turned and disappeared inside. When she returned, her mother followed, bringing her medicine sack with her.

"Please, sit," Eilidh encouraged her, all business.

Vivi sat in the closest chair and sighed heavily.

"How long has this bothered you?"

"Since the end of the race. I think I pulled a muscle."

Vor's mother worked quietly as she reached in her sack for a specific salve and held it up. "This should ease the pain considerably. Use this twice a day for a week. Rub it in so the salve disappears. If you need more—"

"I'm sailing to Orkney with Gabriel for his new business, so I can find you there."

Eilidh nodded, showing no surprise at this announcement.

"Indeed. If you need to address the pain at night, try willow bark tea." She handed a small package of dried bark to Vivi. "Boil water and steep the bark until the water turns dark. If it's too bitter, you can add a dollop of honey."

Vivi inclined her head. "I don't know how to thank you. I only have a few deniers with me. I don't have any other money..."

Vor glanced quickly over her shoulder when she saw Vivi gazing at one of her storage trunks. Surely, Vivi wouldn't try anything with so many people around? Vivi had told her she received some kind of allowance from her prize winnings. Which had been lean lately, to be sure.

"Not to worry. Let's hope the next time I see you you're feeling much better."

Vivi nodded, for once at a loss for words. She put the container of salve and bark in her waist pouch and followed Vor outside.

"You're lucky. Your mother is very kind."

Vor saw her mother standing at the garden window, her hand over her mouth as she watched them walk away.

"That was no pulled muscle," Vor's mother said later that night, after Vivi and Luc had left. "I saw a distinct bruise shaped like a handprint. It almost made me weep. Someone is beating poor Vivienne."

Vor winced. "It has to be Gabriel. Can we do anything? Can't he be arrested for assault while his new 'business' in Orkney is being investigated?"

Torleik scratched his head and turned his gaze to his wife. "We could invite her to stay with us the last two nights."

"Aye, but what happens when she arrives in Orkney? I don't think Gabriel will release her until he's good and ready." Vor clasped her hands in front of her. "I don't like feeling helpless."

"The best thing you can do is be her friend. Invite her to stay overnight with you until we leave." Her mother wore a worried expression when, suddenly, Vor heard a knock at the door.

"I'll get that," said Torleik, who practically jumped up to answer the door rather than discuss "girl" problems. He returned several moments later with, of all people, Sister Marie Claudette, Genevieve, and Clotilde LaVelle, the latter two dressed in silk finery, a stark contrast to the nun's plain coarse wool.

"Welcome to Lemon Garden Cottage," Eilidh greeted them. "It's good to see you, Sister. Come in."

Sister Marie Claudette got right to work. "We know you're leaving Frankia the morning after tomorrow, but before you go... we have a business proposal."

Vor watched as Torleik blinked and looked from the nun to his wife and back. If Eilidh knew what was happening, she hid it well.

Eilidh began to make tea. "I'm intrigued. What's the subject?"

"Getting Gabriel de Maci out of our lives."

Vor had never heard the nun sound so strident, but she certainly could understand why.

"Vor, why don't you go outside and keep an eye on the boys. Atli, come with me." Eilidh turned her back and led the way to her father's temporary study.

Her mother's words weren't unreasonable, but Vor felt left out because of her age. Atli was seven years older, but for the first time, she resented him knowing more than she did. What was happening, and how could she find out more?

Chapter 27

Vor loved visiting Belle Rose, but something was definitely off that last day before they left Paris as she glanced around at her family members and other invited guests. Aila and Armand, sat stiffly in the salon with Genevieve, Clotilde, Luc and Atli, no one making eye contact. Noticeably absent were Vivi and Gabriel. At first, dread lodged in the pit of Vor's stomach. Had she done something wrong? But then Genevieve's companion, the ex-slave, Izora, entered wearing a fine wool, indigo blue gown, and gave Torleik a nod. From their reactions, Vor knew this was to be a different kind of conversation.

Torleik stood. "Now that I have most of the details, it's time I filled you in on the topic that resulted in my being questioned in Orkney... because I need your help." Torleik glanced meaningfully at each of his older children, then Eilidh. Now that he had their attention, he sank into a chair at the dining table and reached for a fresh mug of ale provided by the servant, Odette.

"As you know from your history lessons, the Normans invaded and conquered England in 1066. What you may not know is that the marauding Normans typically brought slaves from foreign countries via the slave trade. Under Gaelic custom, prisoners of war were routinely taken as slaves, either seized in raids or purchased from slave traders in Southern Alba. Slave families could be torn apart and sold to separate slave traders, so that many years might pass before they saw their loved ones again... if at all." He took a long sip of ale. "Unfortunately, Northern Alba and the Orkney Islands were some of the last areas to abolish slavery in Christian European areas."

Izora rose and her skirt swished as she crossed the room to stand beside Trinette, who sat alone on a sofa. Vor understood what she was hearing, but she'd yet to connect the news with her current circumstances. She glanced at Luc, wondering why he was there.

"I'll bring us to the present," said Izora, "so you understand our dilemma. I grew up in north *Ifriqiya* in a wealthy family. I was educated and lived a gentle, pleasant life until I was forcibly removed from my home by slave traders. Since then, I've lived in two locations on the Mediterranean Sea, as well as here in Frankia for six years." Izora seated herself and placed a protective arm around Trinette, who sat quietly beside her. "I miss my mother and father dearly, as well as my many siblings. Trinette, here, was abducted shortly after I arrived in Frankia. Since then, we have become good friends. She is like a little sister to me. We are fortunate that Genevieve LaVelle was willing to pay for our freedom. We are no longer slaves."

Odette appeared again and shyly held a tray containing two servings of fragrant chamomile tea. Izora nodded politely and handed one to the girl beside her and set one on a side table.

"If you wish to know where I was taken originally, you may ask me in private. It was not a pleasant experience." She sipped her tea.

Spellbound by what Izora was saying, it dawned on Vor, for the second time, that Izora and Trinette very much resembled the faces she'd seen in the sandstone mirror and water in the cave. How was that possible?

"I discovered something about myself while living here in Frankia."

Izora grinned at Luc, who stood in the doorway. Vor felt a quick stab of jealousy. She had always considered jealousy a useless emotion, but then, she'd never met anyone like Luc before. Izora had large, round brown eyes that sparkled when she was excited. And her voice was mesmerizing when she spoke. If she had any flaws, it may be that she needed to add a few pounds. Izora faced Genevieve once again.

"I love working with those dogs. That has been a delight, hasn't it?" she asked Trinette.

Trinette made a funny face. "I can't say I like shoveling dog poo, but the rest is alright."

Everyone laughed at that, and Vor noticed that Trini's skin was lighter than Izora's, more like warm coffee and milk, suggesting at least one of her parents was white. Izora pushed back a strand of her curls.

"Gabriel brought Trini here to ride Ivor beginning with the next race in the new year."

Vor exchanged quick glances with Luc. "What about Vivi?"

"Gabriel said not to worry about Vivi. She hasn't been well, but once she recovers and finds something else she can excel at, you needn't worry about her. And Trini will do just fine. She's a quick study."

While Vor wasn't exactly friends with Vivi, she felt a certain loyalty. They'd created a camaraderie in a sport that, for the most part, excluded women. She thought she'd have more time to build on that. She also wondered why Izora, a seemingly smart woman, would trust Gabriel with her young friend.

Luc had refused to take a seat, and still leaned in the doorway. His cool blue eyes scanned the room as he directed his question to Vor's father. "How does what you told us today bring us up to date with your situation?"

Torleik set aside his mug. "I've been told that Gabriel and Vivi will be on our ship to Orkney in the morning. If we're diligent, all we have to do is observe Gabriel until he makes a mistake. That's why I need your help watching him."

"What will happen to Vivi?" asked Atli.

"I imagine she'll be fine as long as she tells the truth when the time comes."

Vor wondered if the end was near.

Anxious to return to working in the stables, Luc leaned on the doorframe of the main salon and waited for Torlcik to finish talking. Although he was extremely curious to know what part of Izora's life she had refused to openly share, she seemed fine to answer all other questions.

At least it appeared that Izora was willing to leave the past in the past and move on—like Vor. In truth, although Torleik seemed to trust her, Luc hadn't made up his mind about Izora just yet. However, if she was truly wanting to imprison Gabriel for his mistreatment of women, then she must be alright.

At a slight lull in the conversation, the women glanced over at the puppies, their puppy-smell calming—something they all needed for the last part of the voyage. So instead of asking more questions, Luc kept his eyes on the squirming furry little bodies in shades of fawn, apricot and brindle.

One of the pups had wandered away from the mama dog and was chewing on Luc's boot lace. He reached down and scooped up the pup, then continued to listen.

When the discussion returned to horse racing, Luc switched his focus back to Trini. For a brief moment, he felt a jab to his pride. Would he be expected to mentor and train the new girl, Trinette? Vivi might treat him like dirt, but she was a familiar foe. He knew what to expect from her. He knew almost nothing about Trini, other than noting her horsemanship skills improved with each ride. He did wonder why Gabriel was bringing Vivi to Orkney if Trini would be taking over her main duties. No one had provided a word of explanation. Oh, Vivi would be fine in the long run. She was like a cat who always landed on her feet.

He stole a glance at Vor, wondering if she was still mad at him. What did she think of these changes? She was inspecting a fingernail at the moment, and he smiled when she narrowed her eyes in concentration to pull at a sliver with her lady's dagger. Did she have any idea how beautiful she was? None of the women in the room compared to Vor. She was like sunshine breaking through the clouds on a rainy day. Sometimes he had to remind himself she was only fifteen, two years younger than Luc. She liked to prove to the world how strong she was, but he liked her just fine as a sweet and sassy lass, with those lips that made him want to kiss her every time he saw her.

He placed the pup back at its mother's teat and stepped back to watch.

With the discussion ended, Vor crossed the room to stand next to Luc. "So you're going to sail with us tomorrow?" Vor asked after the others dispersed to other parts of the chateau.

He held his hat in his hands as he recalled why he was going. "*Oui*. Gabriel asked me to take care of Ivor."

She straightened her shoulders. "Why is Ivor sailing to Orkney? Does Vivi know?"

Luc shrugged and tried not to wince. "Gabriel has made arrangements to stud him out to a nearby farm with fillies. He wants a new foal in spring or summer. As to Vivi, I have no idea what she knows."

"Wouldn't you like to find out? It might help my father."

He ran a hand through his hair. "Do you know where she's staying?"

"At La Rivière. With Armand's father's family, I guess."

From out of nowhere, Atli appeared and frowned. "Vor, you're not going anywhere tonight. Father wants us alert when we sail tomorrow. Quit worrying about Vivi."

"But Gabriel is..." Vor started to protest.

Luc threw up his hands. "Atli's right. I think we should leave her alone. Vivi is not going to thank you for interfering, no matter what you say." He and Atli exchanged a look, and then Atli moved on to speak with his father.

Luc couldn't put his finger on it, but something about this whole slave situation seemed too neat and tidy. If Gabriel was still here in Frankia, leaving the slave ladies unguarded, why didn't they just run away?

The following morning, the anchor had already been raised when Vor heard a bustle of activity, followed by several deep barks. The gangplank had again been set down, and Vor and Torleik went to see what caused the delay. Armand struggled to lead a huge fawn-colored English Mastiff puppy up the gangplank. He had to finally give in and lift the not so little guy. Once he was on deck, he glanced around.

"Hey, Luc Frontier! Come get your new traveling companion!"

Vor's father had scheduled a ship due to take the fastest route to the coast this time, with no site-seeing built in. If all went well, they might make Le Havre before evening. Vor watched as he gauged the sun and let out an uncharacteristic sigh at another delay.

Luc's head popped up out of the cargo hold where he traveled with the horses. Vor couldn't help but laugh when she heard that deep bark, and saw the pup come bearing down on him, his mouth drooling and his tail wagging.

The ladies on board thought it tremendously funny, if their laughter were any indicator, but apparently, Luc did not. Armand handed him the leash, which was loosely attached to a big blue collar. Then he bowed politely. "My mother wants to thank you for the work you did around the kennels."

Luc took the leash and rubbed the dog's head. "What am I going to do with a dog at sea?"

Armand grinned and nodded toward Vor. "Stay on land and open your own kennel in Orkney. You'd do well."

Vor thrilled at the thought that Luc might stay in Orkney as she watched Armand make his way back down the gangplank. As soon as Armand was on the dock, the plank was lifted, and shouts for departure began in earnest.

Vor's insides fluttered at the thought of Luc living and working close to her home. Her parents would see him grow and become an expert, make a good living, even become a man of wealth, perhaps. Someone worthy of marrying the daughter of Torleik Sorensson. She could see it all now.

Vor smiled when her father stood across from Luc and admired the eighty-pound pup. "Looks like you'll have company from now on."

"I'll keep him with me in the cargo hold."

"Good thinking. Perhaps he'll keep Fillian and Ivor calm."

Vor saw that half-smile of Luc's, and knew he was still trying to figure out his future. She stood at the railing next to her mother and drank in the last of Paris as they started up The Seine. Vor pointed in the distance to the new cathedral still under construction, *Notre Dame*. She felt like she'd been in Frankia for years, rather than weeks. And she went out of her way to watch Gabriel, his arm around Vivi's shoulder, as they also said their goodbyes to Paris.

As the afternoon wore on, she could swear the pirate seamen kept walking by her cabin door, eyeing it. Since Aila wasn't there, and Vivi refused to share a tiny cabin, Vor shared the cabin with Eilidh, and made sure it was always locked when she or her mother went on deck. It had been a good idea to put the prize money in smaller bags throughout their belongings in case of theft, although the six men Torleik hired to avoid any theft until they reached home made for a good deterrent. However, when she glanced around the ship, Vor and Torleik sometimes had difficulty spotting them as they blended in so well with the pirates.

Luc had just fed and watered the pup that afternoon, and brought him up on deck for some fresh air when Vor spotted him. She was curious why Genevieve, who owned the kennel, would give such a valuable animal to a handsome young man like Luc. She'd thought about it ever since, and felt another twinge of jealousy. Consequently, she stopped to rub the pup's head as it settled in for a nap on an old blanket.

"Have you thought of a name yet?"

Luc scratched his head. "I look at him, and I think ... Pierre. I don't know why."

She nodded. "Pierre. That's Peter in French, and means 'stone' or 'rock'. Seems appropriate. How are you going to take care of him if you're out and about on different assignments?"

"I'm not sure yet. I want him with me. He's already good company."

"I can see that." She hesitated, then gave in to her curiosity. "Why do you think Genevieve gifted this valuable dog to you as a pet?"

He squatted down and scratched the pup's velvety head. "I did some repair work for her kennel facility. It's my guess she just wanted to repay me somehow." He regarded Vor from over his shoulder. "Why? Do you think Madame Genevieve has a crush on me? She's old enough to be my mother."

"I don't know her well. What do you think? Maybe she's still grieving since her husband left."

He let the dog sleep and rose. His distinct chuckle made her think of home. Of a kind and familiar man, such as her father or Atli, seated before a fire. "I had mentioned at one point that I was considering raising Mastiffs for hunting, as she's doing. Maybe that's what she was thinking by giving me a start with a quality animal."

"I thought you were committed to raising horses. Although, chances are this dog will grow up to be as big as a horse someday."

She found herself staring at Luc's mouth. Even though they had very little privacy with all sorts of people on board, including her parents, Vor had the sudden urge to plant her lips on his and see what his response would be.

Instead, she said, "I... I have to go. Good luck with Pierre."

"Thanks."

She started to leave but he stopped her as one of the pirates rolled a barrel of ale toward the kitchen. The barrel man paused to speak to another seaman, thereby blocking the view of her cabin. Pierre was up and sniffing at the barrel of ale when the barrel man slipped on the slick deck. Pierre barked and the man fell.

Luc pointed toward her cabin door. "Are those men guarding your cabin, by chance?"

Vor turned and discovered two men she didn't recognize wearing bright purple and yellow. They were using something for a pick to open the lock on her door.

"I don't know those men." She rushed over and pulled out her dagger. "Get away from that door!"

"Oh. There must be some kind of mistake, missy," said the first pirate. He eyed the sharp dagger. "My friend, here, was just—"

"I know exactly what your friend was doing. You're trying to get in so you can rob us. Get away from my cabin before I have you tossed overboard."

She opened the cabin door and stepped inside the empty cabin to see if anything had been disturbed. At the same time, a furry animal shot past her, brushing against her leg. The huge pup entered the cabin, barking ferociously, then turned on the pirates outside the door, teeth bared. The two men stood there, hands raised, their eyes huge.

"Go!" Vor warned them, angry that she couldn't do more.

They scuttled away, and Luc entered her room to try and chase down Pierre, who had slid out of his too-big collar. "Come here, boy," he said, picking the collar up off the floor. He pushed the door and reached for the dog. "I'm not letting you slide off the deck, you rascal."

Pierre moved fast for a dog his size, and managed to knock Vor on her back with Luc leaning over her.

Just then, Vor saw Vivi through the porthole. "Uh-oh!" she muttered when she saw Vivi's brows furrow.

Vivi pushed the door open and stepped inside. "What have we here?"

Chapter 28

Vivi shoved her way into the ship's cabin, startling Vor. Off-balance as she attempted to rise, Vor wind-milled her arms, then stumbled into Luc, who was trying to corral Pierre. Lucky for Vor, she landed on the bed. Pierre barked and everyone turned to look.

"Well, I knew you liked Monsieur Luc, Vor, but this is going too far—and in front of the dog." Vivi wore her best smirk.

Vor pulled herself up, feeling her whole body flush in humiliation. "You stop right there. This is not what it looks like."

"Did you just say Vor *likes* me?" Luc attached the dog collar and leash, and pulled Pierre closer to make more room.

Vivi heaved a huge sigh. "Pay attention. That's nothing new."

She walked slowly around the cabin, which was chaotic. Vor's belongings were strewn everywhere, including lingerie items. Vor grabbed them up and stuffed them under the bed covers. In all the commotion, the trunk lid had popped open as well, so she quickly slammed it shut.

"Now, what do you want, Vivi?"

"Does your mother know about you two?" Vivi ran her hands over the bedcovers, then the closest trunk. She glanced over her shoulder and smiled coyly.

"There's nothing to know. And if you can't recall why you came here, please leave."

Vor had never felt so embarrassed, and fortunately, Luc was obsessed with that dog and didn't appear to be listening.

Vivi shrugged and flounced toward the closed cabin door. "'I'll remember what I wanted to say... eventually." She opened the door and Luc and Vor shouted "No! Don't let the dog out!"

Too late. Pierre saw his chance to break free and lunged for the door, pulling Luc with him. The pup was strong. Afraid the dog would pull Luc over the side of the ship, Vor grabbed onto Luc's waist and held on. Pierre made it as far as middeck, when several pirates stopped him. Vor plopped on her backside and sat there, shocked. Out of the corner of her eye, she saw Vivi leave the cabin and sashay across the deck in her usual style. She made it as far as the bow, where Gabriel was conversing with the pirate captain, Drogo.

"Are you okay?" Luc held out his hand. "Pierre is in desperate need of obedience lessons, so I apologize for that."

"It's not your fault." Vor wiped off the dust and dirt from the skirt of her gown and glanced warily in the direction of her father. He and Atli were in a heated discussion, so she felt no compulsion to interrupt. It was a warm day for late June, so she pointed toward a shaded area. "It's actually nicer out here on deck. Why don't we sit out of the way and... um... catch up. You can tell me what you're doing for my father and about your next job."

For the next hour, they talked about their plans. Then, as luck would have it, her father must have been told about the commotion in her cabin because he assigned two of his seamen to stand guard over it, which made her feel better. Being the only person in the vicinity who knew what was in those trunks had made her more anxious than she would have expected. It was *her* prize money, after all. She would no doubt feel responsible until her father took charge and paid off his debts. Then she could relax.

On the day before they reached Orkney, Luc and Pierre bonded on deck while Vor relaxed outside her cabin, her back against the cabin wall, her long legs crossed at the ankles. She had been thinking about the first thing she'd do when she got back home. At the top of her list was paying off her father's creditors so things could get back to normal. At the same time, she needed to find the *Book of Delsiran* before Gabriel did. She may never know how he'd gotten his hands on the book, but according to Raven, who she'd managed to call upon the day they were leaving Frankia, Gabriel had the strange idea the book was meant to help women overcome men and rule the world.

"What's so funny?" Luc fed Pierre a piece of apple.

Vor hadn't realized she'd laughed out loud. She sat up and wondered how much she should tell Luc. "There's something I need to find once we're home. That's about all I can tell you now." She shook out her skirt and stood. "By the way, are you going to tell me about your next job? Or, why you're *really* going to Meginland?"

She sank down and leaned against the wall of her cabin next to Luc. In between the two, Pierre slept, his puppy legs taking him places in his dreams he'd yet to see in real life.

Luc narrowed his icy blue eyes and gazed off at the horizon. "I did have a job ready to go in Gascony, not far from my mother's home."

"Why did you come with us then? Did my father or Gabriel offer you more money?"

"Father Gabriel needed help with Ivor, so he offered a bit more. As you know, he stands to make a lot of money in stud fees and has a prospect near your village. That's why he brought Ivor along for the trip. Also, he's interested in purchasing a future champion from Valhalla Farms and needs help bringing it back to France. Does Fillian have any foals?"

Vor perked up and slid into sales mode. "We plan to have a foal by Fillian next summer. Meanwhile, we do have—"

"Gabriel wants a stallion."

Vor tamped down her enthusiasm. "I see. Well, we do have a one-year-old. He's dark brown and black. A part Arabian colt named Vidar. He'll be two next spring, and then there's Odin, who will be three." She reached out and stroked Pierre's wrinkled head between the ears.

Luc paused for a moment, pinching together his brows. "I heard your father may have a new rival on the island. I hope the man doesn't cause trouble for him."

Vor stiffened. "Who did you hear that from?"

"I overheard the pirates talking. Rumor has it the man came from Iceland, where he raised horses and made lots of money."

"Pure Icelandic horses can only be exported from Iceland. They can't return to the island because of possible diseases. It's the law." She rubbed her chin. "It makes me wonder what he thinks he can accomplish. Why he wants to outdo my father."

Luc's hand touched hers as he stroked the dog. Their eyes locked.

"Sorry. I didn't mean to do that."

Vor paused and lifted her hand, a slow smile forming on her lips. "No harm."

Luc reached down and scratched Pierre's tummy as the pup rolled over. "Let's see. Names for the horses. Vidar, Norse god of silence and revenge, or Odin, the All-Father, himself. Gabriel will like both those names."

"My father loves Norse mythological names, as well. But as to Gabriel offering stud service with a pure Icelandic pony, if he wants one of our horses, he will need to negotiate with my father."

She glanced up to gauge the sun's ascent. "I'm surprised Gabriel has that much money to purchase a new stallion, especially since he didn't win the prize money."

Luc shrugged. "I guess he has more than one plan in motion. Anyway, which horse do you think has the most potential to be a winner?"

Vor looked away. "I'd rather not say. I'm just a rider. Atli and my father are the experts on bloodlines. As for your purpose in the plan, perhaps Gabriel also wanted you around to keep an eye on Vivi while he continues to cause us problems," she said, only half joking.

Luc pulled a coin out of his pocket and rubbed it clean with his sleeve. "Vivi used to do whatever he asked of her, but she has started questioning him recently. If you ever get her alone, you might warn her to play dumb so she can learn what's what." Luc pocketed the coin before continuing. "No, I think he asked me to come for a darker purpose. I think he doesn't trust anyone and is looking for something on the island."

"In the caves, perhaps?"

"What?"

Vor leaned back on her hands and looked up at the screeching seagulls that had followed the ship for hundreds of miles. "I think what Gabriel is looking for is hidden in the caves. We need to get there ahead of him when we land."

"What's with this 'we' stuff?"

She regarded him for a moment, then heaved a sigh. "I could be wrong. But I think Gabriel has either removed from or hidden in the caves something extremely valuable to the Druids. I can't tell you what just yet, but ..."

He waved a hand. "I don't need to know. Will it get him arrested?"

"Perhaps. I think we'll find plenty of evidence once we get started. Oh, there's my mother." Vor stood and brushed off the dust and dirt once again. "I need to talk to her before we land."

Luc rose, and so did Pierre, his wrinkled furry brow making him appear worried. All at once, Luc looked unsure of himself, his hands clasped behind him. Then they shifted to the front, his eyes not meeting hers. "Before you go, I wanted you to know... "

"Yes?"

"I want to stay in touch with you. Is that all right?"

Vor tilted her head, surprised. "But... why? You'll be out seeing the world and meeting all kinds of gorgeous women."

"You're smart, and you're beautiful, and..."

Taken by surprise, Vor paused, her hand in the air.

Did he just call me beautiful?

No one had ever called her that before, and she hadn't a clue how to respond. Except to keep doing what needed doing. She patted his arm. "I mustn't keep my mother waiting. Look for me when we land. We'll talk later about... that other thing, alright?"

And here she'd doubted he even registered her existence, until now.

As her mother approached with a determined look on her face, Vor leapt to her feet.

"Well, hello, Luc... Pierre. He's such a handsome dog, don't you think? Vor, you look like you've seen a ghost."

"I'm fine, Mother. More than fine." She produced a high-pitched laugh, to which her mother gave her a peculiar look. It was just as well that Vor hadn't had a chance to speak more with Luc, because Vor's mind was still reeling from his last words.

Eilidh opened the cabin door and waved her daughter inside. "Come along, Vor. We have business to discuss before we land. Luc won't mind, right Luc?"

Vor paused as she passed by Luc. "We'll talk soon."

Luc's face lit up and Pierre barked to add an exclamation point to what she'd said.

Despite the talk that she knew would be forthcoming, Vor felt lighter as she followed her mother inside. In the meantime, she prayed her mother hadn't found someone else for her to marry. She knew Luc wasn't much of a prospect in the minds of her parents, but that didn't bother her. He was quiet, yet funny. He kept his temper in check around Vivi, which counted for a lot of points in his favor. Best of all, he loved horses and animals the same way she did. She could groom Fillian next to him in silence as he worked on Ivor, the two of them perfectly content not to speak out loud. Mostly, she liked the way his mind worked. He knew about things like architecture, for example. But perhaps the best part was the fact that he was a good listener. She sighed as she trailed her mother the short distance through the door to the cabin.

Once they were inside, Vor turned to Eilidh. "Mother," she said tentatively, "I need to talk to you about Luc."

But then her eyes darted to the closest trunk and her few belongings. The trunk had been closed... hadn't it? Just to be sure, she lifted the lid and looked inside, rummaging way down in the bottom corner, where Atli had tucked the small purse of money. Her heart sank.

It was gone.

Sometime later, after the purse was declared missing, Torleik appeared worried, as both he and Atli squeezed into Vor and her mother's cabin. He raked a hand through his hair and wouldn't look Vor in the eye, which bothered her terribly. As he and Atli checked each hiding spot, Vor felt that familiar sense of dread in the pit of her stomach that she'd failed her father all over again.

The good news was that only one purse was missing. The bad news was that the thief had to be right there, close to them, watching their every move.

"Twenty *livres* isn't the end of the world." Atli tidied up the top of the trunk and closed it. "That's why I broke the prize money down into so many smaller units."

Vor knew her father suspected Luc, so she lifted her chin. "I know you think Luc took it, but I don't see how he could have taken anything. We were seated outside talking. Anyone could have seen us. Besides, I trust him completely. He wouldn't do something like that."

"Was he ever alone in your cabin?" Atli inquired.

Vor tried to think, but the days all blurred together at sea. "I don't think so."

"Did Gabriel ever come by and talk to you?" Her mother sat on the bed, looking exhausted.

"I wouldn't call it talking. He said something and smirked, then kept walking."

"And what about Vivi? I thought you two were on friendly terms." Her father leaned his tall frame against a table used as a desk to hold maps.

"I can never tell with Vivi. It changes from day to day. When she came to see Mother the night before we left, she seemed glad for her help, and if not friendly, at least she wasn't hostile."

Vor's thoughts returned to that moment when Vivi had entered the cabin and found her and Luc practically in each other's arms. Could Vivi have stolen it then? Vor felt herself blush, too embarrassed to mention that incident. She could approach Vivi and fix this herself, if that's what happened.

"I think she was hurting, though." Vor looked from one family member to another, her thoughts turning to her brothers. It didn't seem fair to suspect everyone else when one of them could have just as easily taken it. "We have to ask ourselves about the boys. I think Erik understands how important the prize money is to our horse business, but I'm not sure Fionne and Graham would recognize the significance of losing so much money. Before we go blaming others, we should check with them."

"That's a good point," said her father. "I'll go talk to them now. When I open this door, nobody say a word. I don't want anyone to think we suspect them."

"Be sure to tell the boys to behave and remain calm when we turn them loose on the beach," Eilidh added, looking ahead. "I'll stay here. Vor had something she wanted to speak with me about."

Her father nodded and, in a low voice, said, "I'll see you both on deck later."

Vor had put off her talk about Luc with her mother as long as possible, and was actually relieved when the door closed and Eilidh came to her to discuss their return.

Her mother nodded to Vor. "Please sit, and tell me what's bothering you."

Despite her nerves, Vor tried to make herself comfortable on the bed. She'd originally wanted to discuss Luc. But when she opened her mouth, she surprised herself. "I have a bad feeling about why Gabriel is aboard ship."

"What do you mean?" Her mother frowned.

"I think he's after the *Book of Delsiran*."

Eilidh gasped. "How did he know about the book?"

Vor recounted everything that had happened leading up to her entrance into the caves and beyond.

"We must do something."

"As soon as we land, I'll go to the caves and secure the *Book of Delsiran* before Gabriel gets there. For all we know, he may try to sell it somewhere as a rare volume."

"It's also possible he plans on using it to blackmail rich men whose wives and daughters participated over the years in the Goddess Project," Eilidh said, her brow furrowing.

Vor proceeded slowly with her next question. "Can you remove the spell that holds it in place?"

Surprise settled on her mother's face. "I placed no spell on that book."

"Well, someone did. I saw Gabriel handling it, so it's either you or him."

For a moment, Eilidh appeared confused. She mumbled something and started pacing in the tiny passenger's cabin.

"Did something happen that caused you to discontinue using the book?"

Her mother stopped pacing and clasped her hands, her face pale.

Vor had never seen her mother appear so vulnerable or scared. Vor took her by the hands and sat her on the edge of the bed. "Tell me everything. I need to know."

"Aye, I'll tell you... what you must know." Eilidh grew quiet for a few moments, then folded a shawl on the bed. "It was winter. I was teaching a class of older women in the back of a sewing shop. There were five of us. One woman, Elisot, was a grandmother. Her daughter had died of a fever two years prior, and Elisot was raising her little granddaughter, Johanna. She would bring the girl to class because there was no one else to care for her. She was only three, but had a mind fast as lightning. I remember her because she had the most unusual pale green eyes. The father was a fisherman, so they didn't see him often. One day, the village priest dropped by.

The *Book of Delsiran* was on the table, since we didn't have time to put it away."

"And?" Vor encouraged her to continue.

Eilidh shook her head of the memories. "Johanna began speaking the Delsiran alphabet, which wasn't dangerous in and of itself. But when the priest picked up a page that had come loose, he was horrified that she had penned words on the side of the pages. He claimed Johanna must be possessed by a demon to be able to read and write at such a young age. The priest whisked her off and kept her in a cage until the father showed up to claim her.

"All because she read the *Book of Delsiran?*" Vor pulled up the bedcover on her side and smoothed it with her hand.

"The book wasn't the problem. It was the fact that the child could read. Still, the priest urged me to close down the school and promised that he would keep the matter private so that I wouldn't be caught up in the disaster that followed."

"What did you do?" Vor asked, wide-eyed.

"I took that book and was about to throw it in the sea when the Goddess intervened. She reminded me why Saraid created the language—so women and girls could learn in their own protective environment and not have to worry about those who disapproved of a woman improving her mind and widening her horizons."

"Knowledge is power," Vor whispered in Delsiran.

"Indeed," said Eilidh.

"So, how did the book end up in the tunnels?"

"I was ordered by the local priest to temporarily put the book where no one could find it until they decided what to do with it."

"So, that's when you placed a spell on it and put it in the tunnel?"

Her mother appeared fragile from the telling of the tale, and she shrugged her shoulders. "I suppose so. My darling Vor, I beg of you, don't ever repeat this tale of caution to anyone. Not to your father, not to Atli nor Aila or any of your brothers. It must remain our secret."

"What happened to the girl?"

"Johanna was taken by a spinster aunt to live in the Western Isles. No one's heard anything since that day over twenty years ago."

Vor stared at the floor and nodded. "I wonder how Gabriel found out about the book?"

"That's a good question."

Vor watched the sunset on the horizon through the small porthole and sighed.

"I know how important the Goddess Project is to you. Will anything bad happen to Aila because she refused to take on an assignment?"

Eilidh shrugged and ran a hand through her auburn hair, now tinged with patches of gray. "The Goddess is not one to punish arbitrarily. Despite the dire warnings in the instructions, I imagine she will wait to see how this all plays out in the end. Aila may wind up helping women in a completely different way."

"And me? I'm not a chosen one."

Eilidh reached out a hand and stroked Vor's face gently. "You are a very special young woman. If the Goddess doesn't see that, then I don't know why we're carrying on with her wishes. Be patient. I think your reward will come soon."

Vor hugged her mother, no longer jealous of Aila getting all the attention as the eldest, nor feeling sorry for herself for not bearing the spiral birthmark of those chosen by the Goddess. Then, she and her mother went topside to watch their return to Meginland.

Chapter 29

The last few hours of their journey had passed quickly, and Vor savored the intense joy of coming home. Her heart swelled with happiness at the smell of the familiar salty breeze while looking up at the manor on the promontory. Captain Drogo pulled up in the shallows that comprised Torleik's Landing, and row boats were immediately dispatched with the family's belongings.

"Long before you were born, we used to sail right up onto the sand and had no need of an anchor," Vor's father had said before departing. "That way, all we had to do was jump out, and we were on land."

But improvements had been made in the past twenty years, and more passenger comforts and cargo-sized boats necessitated a change to the hull pattern so the ships had to be anchored out in deeper water. Those extra touches made all the difference, as far as Vor was concerned. Especially the expanded cargo bay for large animals.

Right before Vor climbed into the first rowboat, she saw her parents waiting anxiously at the deck railing. Erik rode beside her with the trunk, his eyes carefully observing the activities of their impending homecoming. Luc had made himself scarce, as he left to help secure the ship. Even the seamen and French pirates' crew members were busy as they prepared for a landing.

As soon as her boat hit the sand, Vor jumped out and took off at a run to climb the footpath to the house. If she was to arrive at the caves ahead of Gabriel, she had to hurry. By the time she entered the house and ran up the stairs, she was huffing from the exertion. She quickly changed from one of her new Norse gowns to boys' clothes she could wear in the caves. Then she put on her sturdy old shoes, grabbed one of Atli's work coats and headed back downstairs before slipping through a side door that would take her to a path that led to the largest opening in the rock caves. She was nearly halfway there when she spotted Luc and paused as he caught up with her.

As he neared, he put his hands on his knees to catch his breath. "I couldn't yell. S-sorry. Why didn't you wait for me? I thought we were going together."

"What are you doing here? Mother said you were busy securing the ship so I should go inside the caves alone."

"Well, she must have changed her mind. She sent me here to keep an eye... I mean to help you."

She tapped a rhythm on her leg with her index finger. Should she believe him? But then again, she had no choice.

"We don't have much time, so I'm not going to argue."

He grinned and straightened up. "That'll be a first."

She ignored his comment. "Once we get inside, though, you have to do what I say."

He continued to smile. "That's what your mother said, too. I told her I can do that. Why do you think I let Vivi boss me around all the time? It was practice for dealing with the *real* princess."

"Huh." Vor offered the most disgusted expression she could manage. "Come on. You'll have to keep up."

She jumped over the "bridge" of rock and kept going. She didn't turn around, but heard Luc following at a slower pace.

They entered the tunnel and raced to where it divided into two pathways—one to the left, and one behind a closed and locked door to the right. Vor did a quick search of the left tunnel. Finding no *Book of Delsiran*, she grabbed Luc's hand and pulled him outside to stand before the locked door. Vor felt the first frisson of fear when she glimpsed the small scrap of vellum with her name on it.

"*Welcome home, Vor Torleiksdottir. Please enter.*"

Luc shifted his feet. "Why is your name on this door?"

"I don't know." More unnerved than she let on, she took her hand out of her coat pocket and rested it on the lock for a few moments.

The prickle along her scalp told her *he* was there... Gabriel. She stepped back and removed her hand. "Try the lock again."

Luc did as asked, and pushed carefully. To his show of surprise, the door opened easily. Several signs had been pulled down and he reached for one in Scots Gaelic. "What does this one say?"

"It's a warning to stay out of this tunnel. It floods when the high tide comes in. People have died here, according to my parents."

"And you will be next."

Gabriel.

Vor turned her head, a sense of dread settling in the pit of her stomach.

"You thought you could beat me here, didn't you?" Gabriel picked up the old signs and tossed them, leaving the vellum placards on the ground. "I made up my mind I would do away with the three of you now, so I don't have to worry about what you're up to anymore."

"You said 'three of you,'" Luc said, his expression neutral. "Who's the third person?"

Vor wondered how Luc could act so calm.

"That would be *me*." Vivi stepped from behind Gabriel and into the light that filtered in from outside. She wore a stylish French pale green wool gown, but it was rumpled and torn in places, causing it to appear shabby. Tears rolled down her pale cheeks at her predicament.

"You're right on time for high tide, my children," said Gabriel in a much too cheerful tone.

Vor had to admit that things looked grim, but she was determined not to let that stop her. She thought quickly. What could she do to distract him? "So, is now the time I ask why Vivi only took one purse with ten livres inside?"

The ex-priest laughed. "Go ahead and explain your actions, Vivienne."

She wet her lips and turned her gaze to Vor. "I didn't want to steal anything." She wiped the tears from her cheeks. "You earned that money, but Gabriel made me take your purse." She reached into the sac at her waist and pulled out the small bag of coins. I can give it back, though."

Gabriel swept his dark cape back over his shoulder and eyed the outside entrance. "That is but a pittance. You won't need coins where you're going. I hear the tide coming. Nature is so predictable, isn't it? I will leave you three to argue over the money or whatever. Meanwhile, I will steal the remainder of your winnings all for myself when no one is watching... because they'll be trying to save *you*." He laughed, sounding like a madman to Vor, and then headed out the door. A lock clicked from the other side.

Luc rushed to the door to check, then turned back. "It's locked, all right. Now what?"

Vor moved quickly over to Vivi and placed a reassuring hand on her arm. "At least we're not alone. Take courage, Vivi."

Once again, Vor felt the weight of her decisions press painfully on her shoulders. She did a quick inspection of the locked door, looking for screws they could loosen. She then turned to gaze in the direction of the rushing water.

"Do either of you know how to swim?"

Luc gazed down the tunnel to where the water was already pouring in. "Not well, but I can hold my own."

"No." Vivi shivered and held onto Luc.

Vor tried her best to focus on the crisis at hand, and not show how she really felt... jealous. She scolded herself for that useless emotion as the water surged through the tunnel so quickly that they had little time for preparation.

"Where does this tunnel empty?" Vor asked, shouting to be heard over the water.

Neither Luc nor Vivi were from the island, so they could only look at each other and shrug. Vor gazed at the end of the tunnel that opened into the sea, her heart pounding. Never before had she imagined she might die like this, in a violent manner. No, she'd imagined she'd go to sleep one night when she was a grandmother, and wake up in "The Other World," as her great-grandmother Marsaili called it.

"I'm not giving in!" she shouted above the noise. "Each of you, take my hand. We're going to ride this out. The water has to empty out into the sea not far from here."

"I can't hold my breath that long," said Vivi, her voice wavering. Again, she clung to Luc, and this time, Vor's heart remained strong.

Luc took Vivi's hand and put his mouth close to her ear. "You have to hold on to our hands, no matter what. You can't let go."

Vivi started crying in fresh sobs that sounded like hiccups. "I should have stayed in Frankia, where I belong." She grabbed Vor's arm. "It only got worse when you and that Devil horse came and showed us up. I know I should have won that race, but why is Gabriel always so angry with me?"

"Maybe you lied one time too many," Luc suggested, peering up at the top of the cave.

Vor was about to tell Luc to take it easy on Vivi, but she understood his anger.

Still, she was having trouble concentrating on the business at hand.

"Let's focus, you two. What if we climb up and put our heads above water? See? There's a water line where it stops." Vor pointed. "We don't have much time. Find some solid footholds."

Vivi began to wail. "I can't climb that wall."

Luc shot her a disgusted look, and kept climbing.

"Vivi, please quit crying and help us out of here."

Even though the water was surging in with great force, Vor took a moment to close her eyes and imagine footholds to the top of the cave. She didn't realize until later that she grasped the two heart stones in her pocket. In her mind's eye, she conjured up the third stone, a green crystal—the one that would save her family ... and maybe their lives. Luc and Vivi were like family now. She guided both up the rock wall, all the while focused on the green crystal that shone brighter and brighter in her mind as they reached the apex of the cave.

"Put your hands at the top. There's a ridge you can hold onto."

"Oh, oh. I'm going to die," cried Vivi.

"No, you're not," insisted Vor. "Hold onto that ridge with both hands. Put your nose where there's still air."

In the last few moments, the water level had risen above their knees. Vor looked to her right and saw Luc struggling with a secure hold. "Here. This one's steady," she said, moving to exchange places as the water reached her waist.

Luc hesitated. "I'm not taking your spot."

"Yes, you are. Don't argue. Remember what Mother said?"

"Your mother's not here."

Had there not been such noise from the rising waves, Vor's sigh would have been louder.

Don't give up. These two are counting on you.

"Is now a good time to talk? We may be running out of time." Luc's voice was thin, his eyes darting around the cave.

"Probably not."

"Vor, what if—"

"Please don't pledge your undying love for Vor right now." Vivi smacked her head on the cave ceiling and swore, appearing to be back in a typical foul mood.

Water climbed the walls. Filled the nooks and crannies of stone cut millions of years ago as ancient shorelines rose and fell, but all Vor cared about at this moment was the three inches of air left at the top of the chamber.

Vivi's teeth began to chatter. "I'm okay. How long before the water runs back out to sea?"

"I'm hoping it leaves as quickly as it came."

Now that they could secure a breath, Vor felt Luc's hand on her waist. "I meant what I said. I'm probably going to go away for a while and learn a trade, but when I return, I..."

"Look! The water's receding already!" Vivi shivered. "What I wouldn't give for a change of clothes right now. Something warm."

"I'd like a nice, juicy steak." Luc moved away from Vor, trying not to show his disappointment that she'd said nothing about his pledge.

"I'd like to ride Fillian."

Luc viewed her with surprise. "Fillian?"

"To keep me warm. He's my calm place. Today has been horrendous."

Slowly, they floated to the ground as the waves receded, and soon, their feet touched the bottom of the cave. Luc shook out his wet hair as Vivi hunted for a missing shoe.

Meanwhile, Vor sluiced water out of her gown and reached into her right coat pocket. Both heart stones were where they were supposed to be. Light pink rhodochrosite to symbolize love, deeper emotional connections and feelings of compassion. And red jasper to support her through times of stress and aid quick-thinking. She dried them off and replaced them in the right coat pocket, then reached into her left pocket, feeling something that hadn't been there before. The hairs stood up on the back of her neck, and a shiver ran down her spine.

To her surprise, her hand wrapped around a decent-sized, smooth stone that fit in her palm. When she pulled it out, a green crystalized stone appeared, about two inches high, its shape recognizable—a heart—with visible edges worn smooth by centuries of waves. Vor held her breath for a long moment.

"Oh, where did that come from? Is it worth a lot of money?" Vivi admired the stone.

"It's called Aventurine." For Luc's benefit, Vor didn't want to identify it as the stone they both saw at the end of the race. Nor did she want to debate the outcome of the race based on something no one else could see. "It governs prosperity and wealth, and can boost our chances in any situation. Just being near the stone can help an individual derive its benefits."

Vivi reached out a hand to touch it, but Vor pulled it away.

"I wasn't going to steal it."

"How do we know that?" Luc challenged Vivi. "You stole her prize money. Is that how you treat your friends?"

Now that the danger was over, he was in fighting form. Vor appreciated the support, but she didn't need it at this point. She pocketed the stone, elated that she'd finally found her own stone.

But what to do with it? And would it help her find the missing *Book of Delsiran*?

When Vor exited the caves sometime later, darkness had descended on the little cove that was a part of Torleik's Landing. Vor led the way back to the house so they could change into dry clothes. Vor's mother had been sick with worry when Vor didn't return right away. Not wanting to make things worse, Vor gave her a short version about being trapped in the cave, but not about Gabriel's murderous intentions. Not yet, anyway.

They sat in front of the fire, warm and dry, sated from their evening meal. Eilidh had offered guest rooms for both Vivi and Luc, but Vor wasn't surprised when Luc declined her offer. He was off to take care of business and to retrieve Pierre from Erik, who had been overjoyed to dog-sit while Luc helped Vor in the caves. As the house settled down for the night, Vor filled her mother in about her search for the *Book of Delsiran* while savoring her own bedchamber, at long last.

"So, Gabriel locked the three of you in that tunnel while it flooded? Didn't we warn you to stay out of that particular cave?" Her mother wrung her hands. "The coward. He's a demon!"

"Despite his earlier treatment of Vivi over the years, there's no love on her part for her guardian," Vor stated, her teeth beginning to chatter from the cold. "In fact, I think she's even more afraid of what Gabriel's capable of now." Vor picked up her damp gown and looked around for a place to put it. "I think he's run out of ways to use her."

"Which means she's vulnerable, especially if she's witnessed any of his crimes."

Vor sat in the chair by the window. "Which is exactly what I was thinking."

Eilidh took the damp gown out of Vor's hands. "Do you think Vivi knows enough to get Gabriel convicted for his crimes and for making your father appear the guilty party when it was actually Gabriel who was responsible?"

Vor started to undo the braid in her hair, then rubbed her scalp. "Father said we must wait for Gabriel to make his move. When he tries to transport the slaves from here to Castile, we'll catch him. Also, the details for sending the ladies home, or providing apprentice-like occupations to support themselves, will take time to put into place, so we'll need to hear from Izora and Sister Marie Claudette first. They promised to send the details by the end of this week. And if Gabriel appears before then and sees the three of us are still alive, I have no doubt he'll feel threatened."

Her mother bit her bottom lip. "I'm worried. How can I possibly protect you three with Gabriel nearby?"

Vor rose and hugged her. "We'll be okay. I promise. Besides, I finally have my own aventurine heart stone. It appeared in my pocket after the water in the cave receded. Maybe it will help me find the *Book of Delsiran* when I return to the caves."

"I don't think returning to search for the book is such a good idea. Gabriel could still be lurking around."

"That's unavoidable. The stone will protect me."

"Just promise me you'll stay away from the caves for now."

Vor's mother gave her a kiss on the forehead, then left. Vor eventually drifted off to sleep. She dreamed of that girl who had supposedly been possessed by a demon. The one with the pale green eyes. What was her name? Johanna. As if possession or obsession could be the only explanation for a young girl's voracious curiosity about reading.

The last thing Vor recalled was wondering what had become of Johanna Swan. She'd be twenty-three now. Was there a connection between her, Gabriel, and the slave girls he planned to transport to their destinations?

Chapter 30

Gabriel cursed the thick fog that enveloped the island, and although it was already a dark and gloomy day, he refused to use a torch to light his way. It wouldn't have helped, in any case. He stood back from the cliff edge and scanned the sea for the ship he'd hired. He'd schemed and planned for months now, but the weather was ruining everything. Now, he must wait for the ship's signal before he could leave, so he pulled out several pieces of vellum and held them close. He glanced at the writing, and smiled. Things couldn't have worked out better with the breeder from Iceland. Gabriel had made his acquaintance and had immediately seen the glimmer of desire to be the best breeder of elite horses in Orkney. Maybe the best in Alba. His pride and greed were so evident that it didn't take long for Gabriel to come up with the plan to ruin Torleik. Once the new breeder was established, Gabriel could use his new collaborator. And use him well.

"Father Gabriel, are you here? Blasted fog has me all turned around."

"Mister Tollaksson? Over here."

At last Gabriel was meeting the man face-to-face after considerable correspondence from Frankia to Iceland. From out of the fog, he saw that the man was a powerfully built Norseman with short red hair and a neatly trimmed beard. He was taller than

Torleik, and although he had on a fur cloak, Gabriel guessed his arms and legs were muscular and strong. He had the appearance of a man born on an island of volcanoes, used to forging his own path. The thought sent a shiver down Gabriel's spine. Consequently, he didn't waste any time on pleasantries, instead got right down to business.

"Do you have the manifests?"

Ragnar Tollaksson came into even greater focus as he moved closer. "*Ja*, I have them, just as you asked."

Gabriel took the ship's cargo manifest from the man and carefully read the entire page. When he got to the end, he nodded. "This should do nicely."

"This is all very organized and clean on your end. You seem to know your way around Frankish law regarding slavery."

"Don't worry about that. Where are the horses?"

Ragnar made a vague gesture toward the sea. "You may not see it now, but a ship is anchored offshore, and we can easily make the exchange right away. My ship will meet your galley as it heads south. Your part of the exchange will happen at sea before they dock at Bergen. My partner will have a ship anchored and waiting for you."

"And my split of the money for my cargo?"

After all the back and forth communications, Gabriel had expected to have to split his earnings from the sale of the slaves, but he hadn't expected that the shrewd negotiator would demand 60 percent of the proceeds from the slaves, and free stud service for the use of Ivor. In exchange, two pure Icelandic horses, a three year-old filly and a four year-old stallion, would be deposited on Torleik's land—just as the authorities appeared. Of course, Gabriel had made sure to have witnesses on hand who would claim Torleik's men stole those horses. And everyone knew horse theft was a serious offense. Once again, Torleik could end up in prison on new charges of theft. Gabriel would see to it that Ragnar assumed both Torleik's business and his reputation for the best horse flesh available in that part of Europe. Gabriel would then be free to run his slave operation on Ragnar's land unencumbered. As for the ladies, they would disappear in the cold fjords of *Nord Vegr* and Denmark, most likely. No one would be able to trace them back to Gabriel.

Gabriel chuckled, changing his mind about the weather. It was perfect for smuggling. Once he'd finished business with Ragnar, he shook hands, satisfied that he'd secretly hired an underling from his crew to accompany Ragnar to *Nord Vegr* to bring back Gabriel's cut of the money.

Alone once more, Gabriel sobered when he considered Vivi's betrayal. She'd packed up and moved into Torleik's home, claiming Gabriel was a monster. According to his sources, she hadn't been more specific than that, nor had she gone to the authorities, so he nurtured a soft spot inside his cold heart that maybe, just maybe, he wouldn't have to kill her. She'd been such an entertaining little thing, his Vivi. He would leave her with Torleik's family a bit longer, for surely Torleik would be arrested in the next day or so. She wouldn't even know Gabriel was behind the plan.

Vor shaded her eyes from the sun and scanned her father's property from the porch that wrapped around the entire manor. Winter was coming, though snow was rare in the Orkneys. The quiet morning was muffled by a fine mist, and everything appeared so peaceful that she had to remind herself that Gabriel had been seen around *Kirkjuvagr* so she must be on her guard. Ready to start her day, she ate a bowl of porridge and an apple, then headed out to the stable, alert for any sign of strangers.

As she performed her routine chores, she thought about how fond she'd grown of Sister Marie Claudette during their time together. The nun traveled through life with a ready smile and cheerful disposition, which Vor tried to emulate. Vor also had great respect for her knowledge and education, which she'd been allowed to pursue with the church's blessing. So when cold nights soon required warm blankets, Vor was happy with Sister Marie Claudette's unexpected arrival. It occurred to Vor that, seeing the sister dressed in her Carmelite nun's habit, an observer might think the clan was rededicating itself to the Church, or even better, preparing the remaining daughter to take her vows, which greatly amused Vor.

Eilidh had never run a particularly disciplined religious routine at home for the boys, consequently, Sister Marie Claudette decided their worship routine needed structure. And so, claiming she was concerned for their souls, the nun marched Vor and her family to the chapel. While the sister couldn't hear confession or participate in communion the way a priest could, she could make sure the boys took time out of each day to pray. When Graham complained about how cold and rough the stone floor felt, Sister Marie Claudette brought small rugs in bright colors and assigned one for each boy to kneel on.

"That's probably cheating, but if it makes you boys stay more than a few moments in the Lord's house, I think the good Lord would approve."

The nun also brought a welcome message from Aila and Armand in Frankia. Aila's note was filled with news of her life at the chateau, and as a favorite acquaintance of Queen Adela. Perhaps the most exciting disclosure, however, was that she was expecting a child.

Torleik and Eilidh were thrilled at the news of becoming grandparents for the first time. Equally thrilled, Vor sat down and wrote to Aila, telling her everything that had happened since she left. Much of the letter was about Luc and the horses, but she added bits and pieces about the new riding additions, Pogge, Agilina, and Elfleda. She also wrote about her dream of owning an all-female-run horse breeding facility and about their mother's new school.

When Sister Marie Claudette heard about Eilidh's school for girls, she took an immediate interest. She accompanied Vor's mother to and from the shed that had been converted into a small school room on the property, and offered advice based on her own experience. When she learned how the *Book of Delsiran* was once used as the foundation for the learning resource, she couldn't tear herself away. While a relatively patient woman, Eilidh discovered there were many questions she couldn't answer, the biggest question being where the book was currently located.

When Vor heard that part of the conversation, once again, she offered to search for the book. "I know you said not to enter the caves, but that's the last place I saw the *Book of Delsiran* ... in Gabriel's hands. Then again, maybe it's not even in the caves anymore."

Eilidh pondered Vor's suggestion, but said, "It's too soon to return to the caves, and even if I did give permission, I would send Torleik or Atli with you, to be safe."

So Vor fumed, but stayed busy. She enjoyed working with the four younger girls.

She showed them tricks and tips for working with horses. Only one girl, Elfleda, appeared afraid to approach the huge beasts. Vor proceeded carefully with her. The girls' demeanors and personalities were all very different, but none had the sharpness of Vivienne le Clerc, who might have won the previous race had she not been sidetracked by the stone placed in her path. Now the king was planning another competition. Vor gave a lot of thought to participating in a King's Race II the following June. She'd probably have Trini ready, since she'd had a head start, but she didn't know about the others.

The following day brought a heavy fog that enveloped everything above ground. It took Vor longer than normal to locate the stable, so she decided to mark the route with a rope, one tied at each end to make it quicker. Typically, she went stall by stall on down the corridor to do the cleaning, but that day, she opened the first empty stall and found a horse she didn't recognize. Stunned, she moved to the stall next-door, which also had a new face. Vor's hand went to her throat.

Both stalls should be empty.

She knew right away these were Icelandic horses. She felt a chill run down her back as she took stock of the horses with their typical long manes and tails. They were surprisingly small, but sturdy creatures, bred for extreme ice and cold. One was female, the other male. Hadn't Luc said that Gabriel was breeding Ivor with an Icelandic horse when they were aboard ship? She couldn't help wondering if the priest was trying to cause further trouble for her father, just when things were beginning to settle down.

Vor took a last look at the two newcomers, made sure they were fed, stood back and considered the possibilities. These were special horses, indeed. They could leave Iceland for international competitions, but could never return to their country of origin. Vor recalled reading about a ban on importing horses to Iceland due to genetics and diseases for which they were susceptible. Surely her father would have discussed all of this with her and Atli, if he had purchased these horses.

She ran a hand through the male's silky mane. These two wouldn't be returning to their homeland, but how did they get here so quietly? If indeed Gabriel was behind this, he had paid good money for the filly and the colt. He'd expect payment from her father, and she doubted they could afford these two. They couldn't return them, either. And if they were charged with horse rustling, it could mean banishment or worse, death. A chill ran through Vor. What a mess.

Vor reached out and lifted the long, shaggy mane of the female so she could scratch between her eyes. The filly stood patiently, grunting in satisfaction.

"I'm going to call you 'Skadi' for now. She was the goddess of winter and hunting. You like that?"

Skadi appeared content to chew on hay, so Vor ran her hands over her thick, light dappled gray coat, marveling at how she could have been transported over the ocean and deposited in their stall without anyone seeing anything. It had to have been by ship under cover of the dense fog. There wouldn't have been time to ride all the way from *Kirkjuvagr*, and the horses weren't wearing saddles, just halters and lead ropes.

She thought back to her time on the ship, trying to remember what Luc had told her. Or had Atli told her? Something about a new breeder in *Kirkjuvagr* who would compete with her father for breeding the best, most durable horses. Could that have been the competition Gabriel was referring to, and if so, what did that portend?

Unable to recall the new breeder's name, she again entered the second stall. The male was restive. He stamped his feet and snorted at Vor.

"You had quite the voyage, my friend. Welcome to your new home... for now. How about I call you 'Bragi?' That means god of 'eloquence'. Bragi nodded his head emphatically, and she couldn't help but laugh. Not yet ready to allow her to touch him, he stepped away and drank some water from the trough.

Just then, Vor heard someone enter the stable and boots scraping the stone floor. She peered outside the stall and saw Atli and Luc together.

"Do either of you know about these Icelandic breeding horses?"

Atli let go of his rake and marched inside. "What horses? What are you talking about?"

"I haven't heard anything," added Luc. "Just what I told you on board ship."

Vor paused in the doorway and pointed toward the two stalls. "Then who are these two newcomers?"

They crowded through the doorway of the first stall. Atli appeared speechless but he finally asked, "Where did these come from? How come we didn't see anybody deliver them?"

"There's a new horse breeder in *Kirkjuvagr* who specializes in Icelandic horses. His last name is Tollaksson. I'd suggest we start there." Luc's eyes flashed with anger as he reached for his saddle. "This is clearly a mistake... or a bad joke."

"What's a mistake?" Torleik strode through the entrance and came to a stop. He took one quick look at where Vor indicated. "Thor's bones! Where did these two come from?"

"They were both here, content and eating, when I came to work." Vor couldn't help wondering what went through her father's head.

Torleik rubbed the back of his neck, a perplexed frown in place. "This could spell trouble if we don't figure out who put them there soon. These horses didn't just appear magically, and they sure aren't without cost." He watched the colt rear up and whinny. "Maybe they were intended for someone else?"

Luc leaned down to scratch Pierre behind the ears. The dog followed him everywhere, and had shown himself to be entirely too curious. He sniffed at the colt in front of him. The colt must have found that offensive, because he reared up, scaring Pierre right out of the stall.

"Well then, I guess we ride to *Kirkjuvagr* today to see what we can find out." Torleik strode down the corridor and entered the stall of his everyday work horse, Justice. "Luc, can you stay here with the women?"

Luc gave Vor a wary glance. "Sure."

"We're not expecting trouble, are we?" Vor immediately felt anxious for the first time since Sister Marie Claudette's arrival.

"Not if I can help it."

Vor waited up for Torleik and Atli to return later that night. She met him at the door and plied him with questions.

"I've used up my resources in *Kirkjuvagr*," Torleik said, clearly exhausted. "No one has heard of this new breeder, Ragnar Tollaksson. It's like he's a ghost."

Vor hugged her robe tightly around her. She couldn't help but think it was another attempt by Gabriel to have her father arrested.

Chapter 31

As Vor waited on the rocks outside the caves, she marveled at everything that had happened in the past twenty-four hours. First, Gabriel and Ragnar had tried to frame her father, yet again. And now, with everything at stake, her father had decided it was time to help the slave women escape, before Gabriel and Ragnar got wind of it and tried to stop it. She just prayed that they could accomplish both tasks without anyone getting hurt, least of all her father.

Her eyes drifted to *The Sea Raven*, anchored close to shore, the mist burning off so that it was now visible and making the transition more dangerous. For the next few minutes, as the ladies boarded the ship, she offered cheerful waves and soothing encouragement that they would see their families soon. She knew there would be parents who considered their daughters "ruined" and unfit for advantageous marriages. Parents who would be unwilling to take them back into the family fold. For those, Vor wished she could promise an alternate life, one that was better than the one they'd left behind. But knowing Vivi's story, she wouldn't presume to offer them false hope.

Captain Drogo was in a very good mood when Torleik awarded him some of Vor's prize money to clean up his crew and escort the ladies back to their warmer, southern homelands in

Madrid and Portugal, and the mild green hills of northern England. Luc and Atli were to accompany the ladies and smooth out any difficult family communications. Any lady no longer wanted, was to be taken to Torleik's Farm. Vor had promised she would make room and find a way to help them.

Vor knew that to most, Meginland appeared to be a primitive island in terms of civilization. The majority of its inhabitants were men who originally came from the North countries, like the Danes and Norsemen. As a result, there was a shortage of females of childbearing age. Vor secretly hoped more of the female slaves would change their mind and settle on their island.

As the pirate ship raised anchor, a strong wind suddenly picked up the sails, and they were off to a good start. Vor didn't miss Luc standing at the rail, waving.

She waved back and whispered, "God speed."

Gabriel growled as he shaded his eyes and checked the sea. No ship in sight.

Where could the slaves have gone? He must have missed their departure by only moments.

He peered up at the sky and shook his fist. A storm was coming, and the birds and creatures of Orkney would be prepared for it, inside nests attached to the cliffs, where it was warm and dry. When he sniffed the air, he detected peat from fires the villagers used for heating, the smell of fresh-caught cod and herring, and the not-so-pleasant aroma of dead sea urchins and starfish that had washed up onshore overnight.

The sky grew darker by the moment, and the birds were already roosting. Gabriel could feel the cold blast right through his cloak. He briefly thought about returning to a warm fire in the village tavern, but first, he must dispose of a little fly on the wall.

Vivi.

The little liar had betrayed him and switched alliances. She must have been the one who told Vor of his forays into the caves with the slaves. He had to get her out of his way, but how, with all these people around?

Vivienne le Clerc must die.

The first flash of lightning lit the sky that was now completely dark. Shortly after, a crash of thunder spooked the sheep grazing in the open meadow, and they stampeded for a covered pen just as the rain came down. The wind picked up, and the waves below grew higher and higher, then crashed against the shoreline. When he crept near the manor house, he saw the candlelight in the windows.

It was dark enough that no one could see him as he took a quick peek. The great hall appeared to be filled with mostly women. He thought it odd that Atli and Luc were nowhere in sight, but then, he watched Torleik's wife take charge as she waved her arms and gave orders to Torleik and the others, most likely in preparation for the storm. He searched for Vivi, but didn't see her. Where could the little traitor have gone? Upstairs, hiding under the covers?

Another flash of light revealed the rope tied on a post at the front of the house that reached to the stable, probably put there because of the heavy fog that morning. That's when he saw a light in the barn. Perhaps his little turncoat was there, hiding amongst the horses. Maybe she'd even discovered the new horses already. That fool Icelander had simply put them in stalls, like they belonged there.

He gripped the rope and followed it to the stable. The door was open a few inches, and he slipped inside, seeking the shadows so he could get the lay of the land. To his surprise and delight, he saw Vivi murmuring as she brushed and combed the colt in his stall. Gabriel's first thought was that it would be easy to overcome her. On the other hand, she could be a handful. A loud, foul-mouthed handful. He couldn't hear what she was saying, but every now and then, she'd look up at the roof as if it might crash down on their heads with the sounds of thunder and lightning pounding overhead.

Gabriel crept closer.

"I guess I don't need to worry about you two getting cold tonight," she said. "I hear Icelandic horses can handle just about anything."

The colt shifted and snorted.

"Well, it's time I got back to the house. You've got your food and water, and straw to make your bed. I'll see you in the morning, Bragi. And you, too, Skadi."

Gabriel clasped his hands and smiled into the darkness. This was going to be easier than he'd anticipated. He stepped out and pulled his knife. "I wouldn't count on that, my Vivi. You have a date with the Devil."

By the time she'd turned around, he'd pulled a potion from the sleeve of his cassock and waved it under her nose. Vivi dropped to the floor, never having a chance to open her big mouth.

Chapter 32

Vor had searched everywhere for Vivi but found no sign of her. After scouring the house, she headed outdoors. She found the rope strung up between the house and barn, and recalled how heavy the fog had been earlier. Her father had told her they used that method to keep track of stock and people during major snowstorms in *Nord Vegr* and other countries where snow was heavy in winter. Vor felt grateful they didn't have to deal with snow at that moment. The fog was enough to make her nervous, coming and going as if the pagan god of weather was playing a joke on them.

When she entered the barn, she decided to do a thorough search of each stall. Perhaps Vivi had checked on the horses to make sure none of the horses was sick and required observation. There were times when Vivi's compassion surprised Vor, just as there were times when she lacked it completely. She counted the stalls as she went, and when she entered the seventh stall, she noticed a comb Vivi had used on the young Icelandic filly's mane. Still no sign of Vivi. Leaving the mystery for now, she found the new colt in the next stall as well—the other Icelandic pony. They were easy to spot in comparison to her father's horses. They sported the famous long mane and tail and were a bit smaller, but sturdy.

"Well, Mister, I don't suppose you can tell me where Vivi is?"

The colt was not as shy as the female, and leaned against Vor while she talked for a few moments.

Still confused about the presence of these horses, but confident that Vivi had been there recently, Vor decided to inspect the stall further. She found nothing of interest, but noted a strange herbal aroma that permeated the air, perhaps from the salve her mother used on Vivi's sore shoulder. Vor opened the stable doors wide to air it out, and then checked the rest of the stalls. She called Vivi's name several times, but received no answer. Vor's stomach clenched, making her grimace even more. She had to find Vivi, or she wouldn't rest.

Vor closed the barn doors and headed out. The only plausible place left to look was in the hills or the meadow near the cliffs. Or the caves.

She didn't think Vivi would head for the caves, since it only reminded them of their near-death experience in the flooded tunnel. Vor stopped for a moment to give her heart time to slow down. She wished Atli or Luc were there with her. And while her father was in the house, she wouldn't be able to live with herself if she knowingly put his life in danger again after all he'd endured.

Vivi didn't remember being carried by Gabriel across the meadow, which was a good thing. When she'd been a child, she recalled cuddling up to him on cold rainy days—this man who was her guardian. After all the nightmares and memories of late, his touch made her ill. She couldn't figure him out. Had he always wanted to kill her to make sure no witnesses lived to tell the tale?

He opened the door to the shepherd's hut and dumped her on the floor, which woke her up to this new horror. Gabriel made quick work of tying her hands and ankles, and gagging her so she couldn't ask questions.

Gabriel did all the talking, which was agony to Vivi, since she couldn't respond.

"Where is my ship, and where are my slaves?"

She shrugged and rolled her eyes.

"You really don't know?"

She shook her head vehemently.

He cursed and removed the gag. "Why did you move into Torleik's house?"

"Vor wanted to keep me safe. And I do feel safe there."

"So she's your new best friend? After all we worked on and prepared for?"

"The King's Race. Yes, that was a lot of work. But if you'd told me about the box in the road ahead of time, I might have won the race. Did you ever think of that?"

"Don't you dare talk down to me!" He yanked her to a standing position. "I wash my hands of you, Vivienne le Clerc."

"But I..."

He opened the door and shoved her out ahead of him. They continued through the meadow, walking and walking until she feared her legs would give out. At last, they stopped at the cliff where he untied her hands and ankles. She'd lost her shoes somewhere along the way, and the dead grass tore at her feet, making them bleed.

While crossing the meadow, Vor spied the shepherd's hut in the far distance, where the herdsmen took cover in bad weather. As she approached, she could see the door was open an inch or two, which she found odd. She wasn't aware it had been used recently. Rains had been sudden, but so had sunshine when it popped out.

She carefully pushed open the door and stuck her head in. "Vivi! Are you in there?"

When there was no answer, she stepped inside. The small hut smelled like wet sheep. But Vor also detected the faint aroma of the perfume Vivi liked to wear. And when she saw an old rag lying on the floor near the wall, she picked it up with one hand and shoved her other hand into her pocket to see if the stones reacted.

She hadn't expected the flash of light that brought her to her knees. Her hands shook, as her vision quickly adjusted to the sight of Vivi previously tied up, then being forced to march across the meadow... to the cliff.

Poor Vivi. She was almost out of time. Vor's heart raced and she was having trouble seeing through fresh tears that threatened to blind her. Although she hated to admit it, Vivi had become a true friend over the past few weeks, and had shown a different side of herself with Vor's brothers, always playful and patient. If anything happened to her, Vor would never forgive herself. She raced across the meadow, hoping the fog would lift. Just as she thought the mysterious fog would never give way, her wish was finally granted when she spotted Gabriel towering over the petite Vivi, his face contorted with rage.

She was about to lunge forward and grab Vivi, when Raven appeared at her side and whispered, "*You must wait. Not the time.*"

"I have to help Vivi!" she whispered back.

"*You will. But not until I give the word. The word!*"

"Why did you stop winning for me?" Gabriel demanded of Vivi.

Vivi's eyes grew large as he took a step closer. She sank to the ground and inhaled a deep breath. "I started remembering things. Horrible things. *You* were the Executioner for the King of Frankia. You chopped off people's heads." Tears ran down her cheeks. "You chopped off *my father's* head. That makes you a monster. And I was afraid of ending up just like you. *That's* what you did."

"Oh, Vivi. You do embellish, don't you? Well, you won't be telling those tales to anyone else from here on."

Vor didn't need magic to read the cruelty in Gabriel's soulless black eyes. Why had she never seen it before? His hatred and contempt spilled over, curling his lips as he pointed at Vivi.

"You are a broken puppet!"

"Wha-what do you mean?"

When Gabriel yanked her to her feet, she began to struggle.

Vor attempted to grab Vivi, but Raven once again warned her. *"You must wait longer. You will know when the time is right."*

Gabriel continued his ranting, still unaware of Vor's presence a few feet away.

"Where is my ship, Vivi? I had a dozen women and girls ready to go on that ship. Did it just disappear?" Though he spoke the words calmly, his face had turned purple.

"I don't know. I wasn't here."

The mist had returned, the fog thicker than before. Vivi ducked her head as it quickly turned to heavy rain.

Vor had the uncanny feeling someone was manipulating the weather, and it spooked her to wonder who. A playful god she wasn't supposed to believe in? And why was she listening to a bird regarding when to make a move, anyway?

"I think I spoiled you with all those clothes I bought you." He yanked on her arm, clearly expecting her to respond. "You needed more incentive, didn't you?" He tied a rope around her middle.

Vivi glanced around her, her confusion growing. "Where are we? What are you doing with that rope?" Tears flowed down her cheeks. "Why did you poison me? You were my guardian and supposed to make sure nothing bad happened to me."

Vor looked down and saw Vivi's bare toes on the edge of the cliff. Vivi yanked on the rope he was holding and screamed her loudest. Unfortunately, the sound was muffled in the dense fog.

"Tsk, tsk. You really are a nuisance, Vivi, you know that?" He stopped walking.

"This is far enough. Now, you're going to answer *my* questions. Is that clear? Simple questions and answers."

Raven nudged Vor's cheek with his beak. "*Now, you speak, Miss Vor. You do!*"

"Nothing is simple with you, Gabriel." Vor's voice came from out of the mist.

"Vor? Is that you?" Vivi's voice came out small and threaded with fear.

Vor felt a sick dread in her core at the thought that Vivi's young life could end if she went over that cliff edge. Vivi, so full of spunk and zest for life. So angry at the world she'd been exposed to.

"Ah, your new friend and ally, Miss Vor." Gabriel's words were meant as a slight, but Vor caught the edge of anger. She needed to be patient, and she needed to play it smart. She could only do that with Raven's presence.

"Raven, make the world light, bring *Fitheach* to this fight."

The fog disappeared, and much to her surprise, the family sword suddenly appeared in her hand, the raven in flight on the hilt glowing with power—something Vor had never seen before.

Gabriel raised his hands, his eyes questioning what had just happened. "I should have known all along *you* were the one with all the power. The sorceress. You're more powerful than your healer-mother. Don't you agree?"

Vor held the sword in front of her with both hands. "You leave my mother out of this. I'm going to take Vivi, and you're not going to follow. You will never bother her or my family ever again." She hoped he didn't notice her hands shaking.

He bristled at that. "Vivienne is my adopted daughter. *I* control what she does, so you stay out of it."

Vivi drew herself up and stared at Gabriel through slitted eyes at the word, "control".

"Save your energy, Vivi. He's not worth it." Vor motioned Vivi closer to her side.

"You've tried to turn Vivi against me, but I can't allow that to happen." Gabriel reached inside his cloak and pulled something out. Vor didn't see what it was until he snapped his wrist to reveal a long whip—much longer than the one Vivi had used on Ivor.

"N-no!" Vivi cried out, holding her hands out for defense.

But it was too late. With a sharp crack, Vivi screamed in agony as the whip laid bare her left cheek.

"That will teach you not to go about discussing our personal business, Vivienne."

Determined to allow no further attacks, Vor glanced at her sword, then the whip. But how would she handle something so different from the type of combat she was trained to do? She did have her short lady's dagger in her boot, but she wasn't as confident using it as she was the sword.

Vivi's pain must be agonizing. She cupped her cheek and lay on the grass, groaning.

In the end, Vor decided to talk him down. "She's telling the truth. You killed her father. That tragedy caused her mother to take her own life. You can't deny that." Vor bent down and gently helped Vivi stand.

Gabriel put a hand to his mouth, as if thinking. After a few moments, he turned his gaze to her sword and chuckled. An evil sound.

Now that she had Vivi more or less safe, Vor recalled her last obligation. She straightened her shoulders. "We're looking for a large book written on vellum. I believe you've stolen it and hidden it somewhere. It belongs to the MacAoidh women. It's called the *Book of Delsiran*. We want it... now."

"Oh, how tedious." He rubbed his hands together. "I tell you what. You tell me where my slaves are, and I'll tell you where the book is... and remove the spell."

The only thing Vor knew was that his slaves were headed for Spain. But she didn't want him to know that. "I don't know where the slaves are."

"You're a foolish girl. But I'm not without heart. I'll let you in on a hint: I already told you where you can find the book. When the rare primrose is born, you'll know where they reside."

Rare primrose? Born, not a flower that blooms?

What nonsense was he talking about? Vor's head hurt. She would have placed hands on either side and pressed her temples with her fingers, but she knew better than to lower her sword or set it aside.

She barely had time for those thoughts when Gabriel lunged for Vivi, pulling her back to the edge. Vivi screamed, blood gushing down her face from the lash wound. Vor aimed *Fitheach* at Gabriel's throat. They stared at each other—a stalemate. Gabriel smiled and took a step to the side.

Terror rolled off Vivi's body in waves as she cringed next to Vor. "You're not going to use that... whip again, are you?"

"I'll ask one more time. Where are my slaves? Whoever answers first gets to die second, and watch the other."

Vor didn't know much about devils and demons in this world, but when she saw Gabriel's eyes change from dark brown to black, then shiny red, like a rat in the dark, she knew he was not quite human. Again, she pressed her blade against his throat and was satisfied to see the trickle of blood it caused.

"You're going to release her, Gabriel. *Now*." She took a careful step sideways. When Gabriel eased up on his grip, Vor untied the rope around Vivi's middle and tossed it in the grass. "I won't let him hurt you, Vivi. I promise."

Vivi squeezed her hand in return.

Gabriel wore a thin smile as he started to look away. Then, once again he lunged and grabbed his ward by the arm, pulling her to the edge. Before he could push her over, Vor made a counter move, grabbing Vivi's other arm. In doing that, the much stronger priest's black aura was visible in the glowing daylight, and it sent pain lancing through Vor's heart. Her parents had always taught her to treat others with respect, no matter what their station in life, and her own inner drive insisted she approach adversity as a challenge or new opportunity. But Vor had never experienced anything like Gabriel de Maci before. His heart and soul shone black as volcanic ash turned to cold hard obsidian. Evil lurked there. There would be no turning back after this day.

She straightened her shoulders just as he laughed and cracked the whip. This time, it didn't hit anyone, but the force of it almost sent Vivi over the cliff. She cringed and closed her eyes.

Vor glanced around, hoping to see her father's hired men about the property, but saw no one close enough to help her out. She rolled up the sleeve on her sword arm and pushed Vivi away from the cliff's edge.

"Gabriel, I beg you to let Vivi stay with me—where she will be safe."

"How much will you pay me for her work?"

Vor's mouth dropped open, even as her temper climbed. "What pittance did you give her as purse money before?"

Vivi started to say something, but seemed to think better of it. She crouched close to the ground, as if to disappear.

Gabriel cracked the whip against a large boulder that had probably graced that spot on Meginland since the glaciers melted. "I want you to come with me, Vivi. We will be a family. Don't listen to Vor. She's been feeding you lies and practicing bad magic. She's influencing your decisions. You don't need that in your life. All you need is me, my dear."

Vor glanced at Vivi and saw her eyes grow heavy-lidded. Gabriel had somehow learned to use his voice as a tool to put others into a kind of trance, and Vivi was most susceptible. She wasn't fully under his influence just yet, but Vor worried he would order her to do something to her. And there was no way she would allow Vivi to live the rest of her life knowing she'd killed her only friend.

"Vivi! Don't listen to him!"

While making this new discovery of Gabriel's abilities, he'd crept closer, and she could smell something sweet, yet foul, emanating from his heated body, making it hard for her to breathe.

To her amazement, he opened his mouth wide and howled like a wolf, then cracked his whip so that it caught the toe of Vor's boot. She lunged and thrust her sword at his ribcage. He backed up, rage taking over once again. Several more times, he released the whip so that it inched closer and closer to Vivi. Vor lunged at him with the sword, confident *Fitheach* would take care of her and help her make the right moves. She was completely unprepared when the whip wrapped around her hand and knocked the sword away. She watched in horror as the blade hit the nearby boulder, then bounced over the edge of the cliff.

"*Fitheach*!" she cried, hoping the sword would return to her at the sound of her voice. She was shocked to find how helpless she felt without the sword in her hands. Could she retrieve it somehow?

She couldn't bring herself to peek over the cliff edge, but she could hear the steel blade hit other rocks on its descent. She turned to Gabriel, oblivious to the pain in her foot from the whip's edge. "What have you done?" she screamed. "That sword was commissioned by the Goddess of the Moon for my great-grandmother Marsaili, who was a Druid!"

Gabriel leaned a hand on the boulder and raised his chin. "You've been using that sword to do your dirty work, haven't you? Well, it's *gone*. You can only rely on yourself now. And you're just a pitiful, whining girl, Vor Torleiksdottir."

Vor focused on thoughts of her sister, Aila. She was the epitome of calm—usually. As hard as she tried to regain her composure, she felt the anger rising from her stomach, to her chest, to her cheeks, the heat flowing unchecked. Though mad at herself for somehow letting go of the sword, she also felt like she'd let Vivi down.

"Vivi, stand up."

"No! Don't listen to him, Vivi!"

When Gabriel cracked the whip again, Vivi flinched, but stood as ordered, her eyes dull and unfocused.

Out of the corner of her eye, Vor could see Torleik and the sheriff's men racing around the meadow, just out of Gabriel's line of vision. Vor worried about her sword, not that she expected anyone to steal it. But then, she worried more about Vivi. She really hoped she was faking the trance, but had no way of knowing.

"I've decided to make you watch your new friend die first. Then I'll be able to focus on you, my dear," Gabriel informed his ward.

"Just get it over with, you maniac." Vor didn't mince words.

"Names don't become you, Miss Vor."

Gabriel's mild-mannered speech was almost worse than his threats. Venom dripped from his voice. Vor broke into a sweat. She had nothing to attack with, her sword likely dashed on the rocks and useless...other than a not-so-sharp dagger hidden in her boot.

"*Fitheach*, I don't care if you're dented and broken. Come to me."

She knew it was worth a try, but wasn't surprised when the sword didn't respond. She gave a moment's thought to her spirit guide, Raven, but didn't expect there was anything he could do, either.

Vor kept her eyes on Gabriel, ready to attack with her bare hands if he made a move toward Vivi. It was at that moment Vivi hiccupped and lurched to her right just as Gabriel pulled her to the edge.

"Noooo!" she cried, trying to grab onto anything to break her fall.

Vor reached out to pull Vivi away from the cliff edge and had managed to pull her from the brink of disaster, when suddenly, Gabriel grabbed her by the arm and yanked her toward him.

Vivi called out, trying to break free. "Let me go, you monster!"

"I'm getting a bit tired of that word, Vivienne. Now, behave yourself." He shook her hard, his grip like iron. "I was going to let you live, but now I see I'm being too soft-hearted." Once again, he dragged her to the cliff edge.

Vor stood closest to them and pulled the dagger from her boot. It might not slice skin as nicely as the sword's blade, but it could do enough damage. "If you harm a hair on her head, you filth, I will..." She tried to recall Atli's words that day Gabriel had slapped her. "I will put this dagger through your heart and kill you, Gabriel." She took a stance, ready to do just that.

He laughed.

Vor advanced, preparing to be hurled over the cliff edge.

Chapter 33

Vor shifted her feet, using her toes to hold onto solid ground. She kept her back to the sea as Gabriel circled around her, trying to make her face him. The dagger felt useless in her hand, but it was all she had.

"I'll admit, you surprise me, young lady," said Gabriel with a nod. "I thought you would have shown some sense and given up by now. It looks like I was wrong."

Vor intentionally didn't look Vivi's way to see what she was doing. She hoped she'd know enough to try and escape and bring help, but one never knew about Vivienne le Clerc.

As they continued their dance, Gabriel appeared to be tiring, but she couldn't count on that to save her and Vivi. When did the Devil ever take time out?

That pause gave Vor time to think, to come up with a plan.

"Gabriel, there's one thing I want to know."

"Only one?"

"Where did you find the other local horse breeder? And why use him to ruin my father's business?"

Gabriel smoothed the sleeve on his cassock, never taking his eyes off of her. "I heard talk in *Kirkjuvagr* last autumn that he was coming. I discovered that Ragnar was the perfect partner." He gave a self-satisfied smile. "Greedy, dishonest, proud. He was ripe for the plucking."

Vor digested that information as she listened to the plaintive cry of the kittiwakes above.

"He won't get away. Once the sheriff learns you are behind this, his men will be crawling all over his property. It won't be long until they come to capture you, too."

"You think I'll allow that?" He smirked, as if superior to not only her, but to the sheriff's authorities, as well.

Vor wondered why the sheriff's men hadn't come to her aid. Were they waiting for something? A confession perhaps? Maybe they recognized that Gabriel's over-confidence would be his downfall. She had to trust their judgment.

With her back to the meadow, she realized she'd manipulated his position while she made small talk. Now his back was to the ocean, just as she'd hoped. With one last glance at Vivi, who hadn't gone for help, and instead remained frozen to the spot, Vor could see she would have to be accurate. She couldn't let Gabriel squeak out of this situation if they were to survive.

Her heart hammered in her chest, as she steeled herself to thrust her dagger and jab it into his stomach.

"Vivi!" Gabriel called out to get her attention.

Before Vor could get close enough to use the dagger, he surprised her by making a side lunge for Vivi. However, his long cassock had wrapped around one leg. As he stepped forward, it twisted around the other leg and he started to fall backwards. Before Vor could do anything to stop it, he let out a shout. His arms whirled around him in an attempt to balance, but with only air beneath him, he had no place to gain a foothold. For several seconds, she watched in horror, as his legs pumped the air, as if he could fly, but he kept falling. Vivi screamed and came to stand by

Vor as, in grim resignation, they watched him plunge to the rocky shore below.

Relief washed over Vor. He'd been an unforgiving, arrogant, evil man, and deserved tears from no one. On the other hand, Vor wasn't sure any man deserved to die in such a manner.

As she peered over the cliff's edge, she saw that he'd landed on a sharp rock. It must have punctured a lung or artery, the blood seeping out while his face stared up at the sky, his expression one of horror.

Vor stood there for some time, coming to terms with what had happened. Then, suddenly, she was distracted by a glint of sun on steel, and she knew that it was *Fitheach*. She didn't know what shape her beloved sword would be in, but it appeared to be in one piece.

Vivi grabbed Vor's arm. "Is he really dead?"

Vor would have answered right away, but felt her stomach burning, and then she quickly stepped away from the cliff, leaned over and lost her midday meal. When she'd emptied everything she could, she wiped her mouth, but just as she stepped back, to her surprise, the sheriff's men came scrambling through the bushes and grass. Several had taken the path to the shore below, to verify that Gabriel was indeed dead.

The only thing Vor cared about at that point was the arrival of her parents, who came running from out of the mist. She felt like a little girl of five once more, enveloped in her father's big, strong arms, his long hair tickling her face.

Vivi sat whimpering in the grass, and when Vor looked, she saw her friend holding her hand over the wound on her cheek that had been all but forgotten in the melee. When she lifted her hand for Eilidh to take a look, Vor could see where Gabriel's whip had caught her, causing a diagonal slash across her left cheek. Vor tried not to wince and scare Vivi.

"It's not so bad. My mother will fix you up in no time."

Torleik put an arm around Vor's shoulder. "Let's all go back to the house now, so your mother can treat Vivi. It's time you and I had a long talk, as well, Vor." Torleik placed an arm around Vor's shoulder while Eilidh did the same for Vivi, and the four headed back to the manor house.

After all that had happened, Vor felt relieved to be surrounded by family once again, and for a short while, she forgot all about finding the *Book of Delsiran* or anything else for that matter.

In the months that followed, Vor learned that Aila and Armand were coming for a quick visit, which gave her something to look forward to. She missed her older sister, and had so much to tell her. Consequently, she was terribly disappointed when she learned from Armand that Aila had to stay put in Frankia until the baby was born. Vor would have to make do with Armand.

However, her brother-in-law came mostly to settle matters regarding the smuggling charges, and to explain to the authorities and Torleik that he was simply trying to gather enough evidence to put Gabriel and Ragnar away for life, without compromising Izora's escape route for slaves through Frankia and Britain.

Based on his initial observations, Armand had at first only suspected Gabriel, but over time, he felt certain someone else was involved. When he learned the new breeder's name and that he sold Icelandic horses, all the parts fell into place. Vor had never met Ragnar, but she felt relieved that he'd finally been arrested and would stand trial for passing off stolen goods—those poor horses.

Now, as Armand appeared in the stable with a new female English Mastiff puppy for Vor as a thank you for being a good companion to Aila during a stressful wedding event, Vor could scarcely contain her excitement as she saw the fawn and black colored pup. She immediately fell in love.

"Genevieve thought you and Luc might want to open your own kennel for hunting dogs. Is that something that might interest you?" Armand asked Vor later that afternoon in late spring as they sat in Saraid's Garden on the side of the house.

Vor glanced at the blue ceramic pots she'd been collecting for her own lemon garden. She smiled and imagined Luc helping her find the best-smelling yellow flowers for the pots, which he'd agreed to do as soon as he finished reinforcing training facilities and expanding fences for Torleik. Influenced by the size of Ragnar Tollaksson's outfit, her father had made it his top priority.

Armand brought all kinds of news from Frankia. Aila was growing big with child, and the baby was due in September. According to Armand, Grandmère Genevieve was ecstatic, and so was Tante Clotilde. Vor had the feeling her niece—for she felt certain it would be a girl—would be spoiled with all that attention.

Vor and Vivi, who was still nursing her scar beneath a sheer dark scarf, followed Atli and Luc to the stable, where things had been in an uproar months earlier after discovering that Aila's horse, Primrose, was carrying a foal.

Vivi thought it wonderfully exciting as she ran her hands over Primrose's belly. "How far along do you think she is?" she asked Vor.

"Well, Bragi was the only horse loose here in early November, and we haven't bred her with any other horse." Vor counted on her fingers. "I'd say she's going to foal sometime in September of this year." She glanced at Atli. "Does she look about five or six months along?"

"That sounds about right." He pulled out a bag and poured fresh oats into it. The gentle mare waited patiently as Vor followed Vivi's example and ran her hands over Primrose's belly.

Some time after supper, Vor was surprised when her father asked to speak privately with her. Armand sat at the long table with Atli and Luc drinking ale and telling stories that made the men laugh.

Vor and her father sat in front of the crackling fire. Vor arranged her gown so she could sit on the floor with the pup she'd named Pansy. Luc's pup wasn't normally allowed in the house, which she considered unfair, but Pansy was such a good little girl that she'd been allowed in. Pierre was well over a hundred pounds, and not exactly the most obedient animal. He could easily crush or break any one of Eilidh's prize dishes she'd collected.

When her father didn't speak right away, Vor jumped in. She'd never admit it, but she wanted to spend more time with Luc and get to know him. She had no intention of ending up unhappy in an arranged marriage.

"I'm so glad everything turned out alright with your business," she started hesitantly. "I don't know what I would have done if you'd had to sell the horses."

"Fortunately, it didn't come to that. Mostly because of you and your efforts to right a sinking ship. Vor, I hope you can forgive me for some of the things I said to you before."

She glanced at him, thinking he had more white hairs mixed in with the blond these days. He was still handsome at forty-two, and she liked how her mother sometimes gazed at him with a smile on her face when he wasn't looking.

"Of course, I forgive you, *Fadir*."

He smiled at her use of the Norse word and gave her a big hug.

Vor rested her head against his shoulder. "I did the paperwork to turn Fillian over to Atli. I think he was secretly relieved and very happy to have his name on the registration."

"*Ja*. That horse means the world to Atli. That was a kind thing you did for him. Do you have any plans for this next year?"

Her father gave Vor such a look of tenderness, it startled her. She smiled back at him. "I think for now, anyway, I'll focus on the yearlings. I'll train the ladies to ride them, and work with Vivi and Trini for the King's Race next June. Don't you think it would be worth our while to take as many horses and riders as we can handle to Frankia? At least three of us can ride them already. The more, the better, right?"

Torleik chuckled and looked into the fire. "Ah, my little ray of sunshine, you don't want to bite off more than you can chew. You'll have your hands full... with your new business."

"Wha-what business?"

He squeezed her shoulder as she sat there, mouth agape, then reached into the pocket of his work tunic and pulled out a piece of vellum. "This is thanks from your mother and I for all you did to help us regain what was ours to begin with. This is the deed for the land just beyond Torleik's Hill to the south. It's now in your name and is yours to do whatever you like. Breed and train horses. A hunting dog kennel. Taking in women who need help in this world. Whatever makes you happy. You risked a lot, and you deserve some autonomy. Thank you." He leaned over and kissed her forehead.

Vor gazed at him in shock. "I don't know what to say." She tried to hug her squirming puppy, so patted her on the head instead. "Thank you?"

"It will be hard work, but I have faith in you. Armand says you did well in your dealings with Aila."

Vor sipped her cup of chamomile tea and gazed at the fire. "I think I was hard on Armand in the beginning. I was just so worried about Aila."

"Aila is doing fine. Armand said she's starting to really embrace her role as a future mother. And her Frankish is coming along, too." He leaned back and scratched Pansy between the ears. "How's Vivi doing?"

Vor picked up Pansy and deposited her on her lap. "She's having a hard time. She's very self-conscious about her scar. But she likes working with the horses. I'm encouraging her to offer riding lessons for any lady who wants to learn. She can easily do that on the side. I want her to have her own money to manage."

"You're a good friend, Vor."

She smiled and puffed out her cheeks. "It was a rough beginning, but we made it." She glanced out the window to judge the time. "I'm going to see Andrei the blacksmith tomorrow morning. He said he could shine up my sword and make it as good as new."

"I'm glad to hear that. That sword has had a real workout between you, your mother, and your great-grandmother."

Vor laughed and jumped up. "It sure has. Well, I'm exhausted, so I should get some rest. Good night." She motioned for Pansy to follow her upstairs.

She stopped on the staircase and for a moment, thought about all that had happened and how things had turned out. She picked up Pansy and held her like a baby. "I hope it's alright with you if I have Pansy sleep beside my bed. I've been having nightmares about Gabriel."

Torleik waved a hand. "That dog should give you great comfort. I'm glad Armand thought to bring her on this trip. Goodnight, my love. Sleep well."

Vor climbed the stairs and entered her bedchamber, hugging a squirmy bundle of fur. She put her on the bed and played with her until the moon came out and the sky remained bright as midsummer grew closer.

After preparing for bed, she leaned her chin on her arm and gazed out at the garden, her world turned right-side up once more.

"Pansy, I'm thinking of having a lemon garden like the one in Frankia. Do you think that's a good idea? It smelled so wonderful, and those blue pots..."

Pansy gently woofed, as if she knew playtime was over for her mistress.

Chapter 34

Vor sat on the floor of Primrose's stall, waiting to jump into action at any moment. The mare behaved almost as calmly as her mistress, Aila, who was far away now, also experiencing labor at any time. Vor imagined her older sister was apprehensive, but with Armand there, along with Genevieve, Clotilde and Izora, she most definitely was not alone.

Vor even went so far as to ask her mother to train the mild-mannered Elfleda to become a midwife to horses. The way Vor saw it, they lived in an isolated location with a nearby village that boasted of only one midwife, who was not always available, and not willing to learn about horse midwifery. Problem solved.

She'd been up all night, and as Vor dozed, her mind played various scenarios for her of her first time seeing her niece. Whether a girl or boy, it would be a beautiful baby with either Armand's dark curls or Aila's straight, silky strawberry-blonde locks. Vor suspected a girl, so that was how she'd been referring to it. She would be intelligent and wise behind those intense baby eyes. But would she have the MacAoidh greenish-blue eyes of her mother?

Vor sighed, realizing her niece would be almost one year old by the time she saw her. That is, *if* she could afford to enter the King's Race.

Vor's eyes popped open when Primrose made a sound she hadn't made before, more of a squeal than a grunt. Vor had insisted Eilidh be there as well, because her midwifery skills were more extensive in case anything went wrong. It bothered her terribly that she still hadn't found the *Book of Delsiran*, but she had no idea how to fix it. Her mother was sure Vor would find it, once she relaxed from all the projects she was working on. Vor wasn't so sure.

Primrose rose to her feet awkwardly and stood near the wall, swishing her tail.

"Do you think it may be a breech birth?" Elfleda asked.

Vor took a few moments to feel the mare's stomach, trying to find where the new foal was located. She stood back and patted Primrose's sweaty back.

"I don't think it's a breech birth. But the foal is taking its time. What do you think, Mother?"

"I think you're right. Any moment."

A moment stretched into several. Several moments stretched into an hour.

Primrose was clearly uncomfortable, and no longer a young mare, so her fatigue began to show.

Vor and Eilidh got her to lie down in fresh hay, and sure enough, her water broke. After that, the foal came quickly, and it tried to stand on spindly legs. Vor had Elfleda clean off the afterbirth and fluids.

"A girl!" exclaimed Vivi, as she entered the stall with Trini and Agilina, who'd just finished their training.

"Oh, she's so tiny. And her coat is so pretty." Agilina squatted, but didn't touch the foal as she searched for her mother's teat.

"I've never seen a coat like that before. It reminds me of a pearl that glows in the night." Vivi hunkered down next to Vor, looking on in awe, for a change.

Pearl...like the ones I saw at the caves those many months ago.

Vor didn't respond, because all of a sudden, she knew what Gabriel meant. She covered her ears and closed her eyes. The *Book of Delsiran*. It wasn't lost at all. It was right where it had been these past few years. Where she'd first come across the rare cave pearl. On the very same ledge where she'd last seen it.

The rare primrose had arrived. The book awaited.

Vor was inundated with feelings of good will and contentment now that the riddle was solved, when suddenly, Graham came running into the stable, followed by Erik and Fionne. Graham didn't even look at the new foal. His eyes were huge as he started to lean down and touch Vor's shoulder. Seeing the blood and gore, he backed off.

"What is it, Graham? Is something wrong?"

He tore his eyes away from the blood. "*Fadir* says he will blow up the caves tomorrow morning! Isn't that exciting?"

Vor's moment of clarity evaporated and she felt an ache in the back of her throat, her fingertips tingling. She turned to her mother. "What about the *Book of Delsiran*? If Father blows up the caves, won't this destroy the book as well?"

Her mother drew her away from the stall where they could be alone. "I haven't said anything because your father doesn't know about the book. This may be dangerous to ask of you, but..."

"You want me to go before dawn tomorrow and locate the book and bring it to you for safekeeping?"

Eilidh hugged her daughter, looking vulnerable for the first time that Vor could remember.

"I'll take Luc, so he'll be there if anything goes wrong."

"You must be careful. Promise me."

Vor's thoughts flitted by. In the blink of an eye, she saw everything that went wrong this past year, ending with Gabriel's death. "I promise to be extra careful. Thank you for having faith in me."

Eilidh gulped and hugged her second daughter.

Vor had trouble sleeping that night, afraid she would awaken past dawn. She'd spoken to Luc, but he wasn't too keen on the mission. But then, she couldn't explain how important the book was, nor what it contained that might feel threatening to certain men of power. Luc had to take this on faith, and he wasn't as open to spontaneous acts as she might be.

She dressed in Erik's clothes and pulled on an old cloak to keep her warm. She and Luc proceeded quietly across the meadow and past the spot where Gabriel had plunged to his death. She refused to look in that direction, instead, heading down the footpath as the sun began its slow ascent. They had just enough time, so she didn't waste any of it in conversation on the way down. When they reached the sand and shoreline, she led the way.

As Luc eyed the cliffs that might be affected, his face grew pale.

When they stood in front of the large cavern opening, Vor hesitated to catch her breath.

"Are you sure about this?" he wanted to know.

She made a quick visual scan of the area. "I don't see any of my father's men here yet, so I'd say we have plenty of time."

He looked down and shook his head. "Let's just be quick and get this behind us." Before she crossed the bridge boulder, he put a hand on her shoulder. "Should one of us stay behind to watch for your father's men?"

"That might not be a bad idea."

He nodded, satisfied. "I'll..."

"You wait here. This may require a bit of magic, so it has to be me. You give a shout inside if the men appear."

Luc didn't look pleased. But he must have guessed by now that when Vor wanted to do something, she did it, because he nodded. "As soon as you come out, we take the footpath and get to higher ground. Agreed?"

"Good plan. I'm going in now."

"Vor..."

She turned around, starting to feel impatient.

Before she could utter a word, he pulled her toward him and kissed her soundly. "Just in case you forget who's waiting for you on the outside."

Her face relaxed as a grin appeared. "I could never forget that face." She kissed him back, accepted a lit torch to light her way, then took off over the bridge and into the large cavern. She couldn't help questioning if leaving Luc outside the cave had been the right thing to do. But she had no more time to waste.

She'd remembered to bring *Fitheach* in its scabbard, and had hidden it beneath her cloak. "Good as new," she muttered, her eyes adjusting to the dark.

She walked briskly uphill to where the two tunnels split off. As she looked up, she could see where her father's men had explosives ready to collapse the tunnel and undermine the wall.

Focus, Vor!

She dashed down the left tunnel, then shoved a large piece of driftwood into place before the shelves. Stepping on it, she reached her hand as far as it would go. Nothing.

Her hands began to shake. It had to be there. The prophecy had said that "By oak and ash and thorn, may the Goddess Book be gone... until the rare primrose is born." *Think, Vor!*

She pushed the piece of driftwood as close to the shelf as possible. Standing on tip-toe, she reached all the way to the back right corner. No book. Back left corner. No book.

"Raven, help me out here. I must find the key to the riddle."

He appeared on her right shoulder. *"You have the key. You do, you do!"*

"What key?" Vor glanced all about her and saw no key, in the traditional sense.

She thought for a moment, realizing time was running out. "Well, Aila's filly, the daughter of *Primrose*... She has white, shiny fur, kind of like pearls. But I already knew that. That's why I'm here in the first place."

Raven hopped up and down on her shoulder. "Dig! Dig! Pearl can mean many things."

"And how am I supposed to know which meaning is correct?"

Raven "tsk-tsked" three times.

All of a sudden, it dawned on Vor. "The rare primrose doesn't just hint at the location, as I originally thought? Do you think the birth of the horse *removed* the spell as well?"

Excited now, she reached up toward the center of the ledge as far on her tiptoes as she could reach. At last, her hand touched something solid. The book! Very carefully, she pulled it down. It crackled in her hands. Little round pieces of something that had been on the shelf came with the book. They fell between her fingers and landed at her feet.

"What are those, Raven?"

"They're cave pearls. They are, they are!" Raven cackled.

Cave pearls. An allusion to the horse's beautiful coat. That's what Gabriel had been trying to tell her all along. The book crackled in Vor's hands, but the temperature remained the same. As she slid the book and its many loose pages into her sack, some of the rare cave "pearls" came free from the shelf and deposited in her sack as well.

She turned to thank Raven, but he was gone. She gave a pointed nod of respect and hurried out of the cave. When she found Luc right where she left him, her heart resumed its normal beat.

He reached for the sack. "You got it?"

"Yes. I had to solve a riddle of sorts..." She'd started to add that her Spirit Guide had helped her, but re-thought that. She'd never talked to Luc about spirit guides and the Old Ways. Now was probably not the time.

"We can talk about your riddle later," he said. "In the meantime, we need to get out of here before the caves start to collapse." He gave a nod toward Torleik's men as they neared the cave with torches.

"Right you are."

When Luc held out a hand, she smiled and took it as they crossed the sand and entered the cliff path, where they had to walk single file.

"I saw the explosions set and ready to light. Do you think it will be dangerous using this cliff path?" she asked, glancing around for another exit.

"Let's race to the top, where we'll be safe."

Climbing the path was more difficult now, but better with Luc carrying her travel sack. She repeatedly offered to carry it, but she suspected his pride wouldn't allow for that. At one point, she stopped to catch her breath, and when she turned to look in the direction of the caves, she could distinguish her father among several men with torches near the cave entrance. When her father disappeared inside, she grabbed Luc by the edge of his cloak and hurried him up to the top. It felt like mere seconds before she felt the ground beneath their feet begin to shake.

"Let's stand away from the edge. If the blast is strong enough, this cliff could collapse." Vor had barely said the words and stepped back when two more explosions sent dirt and sand into the air, like spouts on a whale. "Nothing like smuggling slaves or illegal goods can ever happen here again." She gave him a watery smile. "*Never* again."

Luc smiled and set down the travel sack so he could use both hands to squeeze hers. He kissed them for good measure.

"Vor, you're sixteen now. Would you..."

"Yes!" She didn't bother waiting, and threw her arms around him as the last set of explosives sent water into the air. Vor kissed him like she'd always wanted to, but hadn't known how until now. "I want to marry you, Luc."

"I'm glad. We don't have to have a long engagement, unless you want to?"

"I want to move into my own home now. I'm ready."

He hugged her as she sighed into his neck.

"I'm going to remember where you proposed to me... forever."

"You proposed to me." He grinned.

"Right again."

When she was finally alone that night in her bedchamber, she opened her sack and discovered what appeared to be little cave pearls rolling around among her papers.

They were the exact colors of Primrose's new filly: white on sparkly white. She'd read that the pearl represented innocence and modesty, and was a metaphor for rare, fine, admirable, and valuable. *Valuable*: just like the women they'd helped save from a life of slavery—Vivi, Trini, Izora. And all the others.

"Gem of the Sea." Another meaning for pearl.

Vor decided then and there that she would name her filly Perla.

Great-great-grandmother Saraid would have approved.

Vor smiled, secretly pleased.

EPILOGUE

1 Year Later

Vor raised her glass as her father proposed a toast. It had become a new family tradition to gather in the great room of her parents' home each summer before the final harvest, to give thanks for the blessings of the past year. It served as a somewhat public way to acknowledge personal contributions, if nothing else.

"Congratulations to our Vivi, who won the King's Race 2 in Paris, Kingdom of Frankia, aboard Ivor, which we now own!" Torleik held up his mug, a smile lighting his handsome face.

Vor was happy that Vivi had won the prize this year. She had worked hard, without Gabriel's cruel punishments as incentive, and she deserved to win. Besides, with Gabriel dead, it made sense in a way that Vor's family should purchase the beautiful cream-colored racer from Xavier, Armand's father, the remaining co-owner. Vor noticed Vivi raise a hand to trace the scar across her cheek made by Gabriel's whip. She'd sworn she would never use a whip on an animal again, and she had kept her word, the physical scar a reminder.

Vor looked around the table and beamed. She'd been shocked to receive a generous gift of land from her father, just south of Torleik's Hill. He'd given it to her in gratitude for her performance at the first King's Race, and for her part in solving the mystery of the caves. Her training facility was new and modern for the day, and was transitioning into a useful facility for horse breeding. She'd grown to love those young ladies who worked so hard with her, Dalla, and Vivi to care for the horses at Primrose Farms, and prepare them for horse racing.

Torleik also built a modest home for Vor, which she had yet to take advantage of, feeling oddly comfortable at her parents' home. As their workforce grew, Torleik also built a few huts for married workers, similar to those on his land. In the meantime, Vor and Luc had opened a kennel to raise hunting dogs. Pierre and Pansy loved to roll and play with the stray dogs from all over Alba that they took in, but for the most part, English Mastiffs ruled the day.

As Torleik's speech wound down, Vivi waved and grinned, as if in a parade. Always happy to be the center of attention, she was in her element on this day. She sat next to Vor and clutched her arm.

"I wouldn't be here if it weren't for you."

"May the future hold only good times for you, Vivienne le Clerc," Vor whispered.

"Belated congratulations to Aila and Armand on the birth of their son, Dominic, and to Dominic's over-the-moon grandparents." Eilidh grinned and sipped a cold cider. Everyone clapped at that, with joyful laughter added in.

Vivi leaned over and whispered to Vor. "You said it was going to be a girl. You *swore*."

Vor tossed her loose hair over her shoulders and grunted. "I was wrong. I admit it. That's the first time, and it won't happen again."

"Congratulations to Vor after one year's operation of Primrose Farms and Kennels. I'm proud of you, little sister." Atli raised his mug, and clapping all around made her glow inside.

Vor grinned. "Thank you to everyone who pitched in.

Torleik held up his mug once more. "To my clever wife, Eilidh, for graduating her first class of female readers and teachers, and for sending them off to pay it forward." The women clapped and whistled, and Vor's eyes met her mother's. Vor waited to see if her father would mention the use of *The Book of Delsiran*. He didn't, which appeared to be fine by the set of her mother's shoulders. This project meant the world to Eilidh, and no one could ever take that from her. She'd do anything to make ends meet so she could devote time to that. Vor glanced at Luc and smiled. She'd done some research with Druid doctors and healers and learned more about learning disorders having to do with how the brain and eyes interpreted words, but Luc was learning how to deal with that, much to Vor's appreciation.

On this special occasion set aside to celebrate those present, it also included Aila, Armand and their son, Dominic, who had come for their first visit as a family.

To Vor's right, Vivi leaned over and whispered, "Doesn't Dominic look like a miniature Armand? He even has that cleft in his chin."

Vor smiled and reached for the bread. "I did, indeed, notice that. They're almost identical. I'll have to ask Aila how she feels about that."

As her eyes lit momentarily on each guest, she realized Sister Marie Claudette

had invited Gemma, who sat to the nun's right, at the bottom of the table. Gemma had been collecting information for the nun about the slave movements. Vor conceded she may have judged Gemma too hastily.

Luc, who sat to Vor's left, kept a close eye on Pierre and Pansy, who drooled excessively, an unfortunate characteristic of the breed. Last, but not least, she spied Atli, Erik, Fionne and Graham, along with cousin Dalla and her parents, Gregor and Ashilde. Along with them came Dalla's siblings, her twin, Cameron, and the younger Linnea. Gowan, Graham's best friend, rounded out the lineup. Thank goodness they had such a large table.

Food and drink soon disappeared, and Vor's father stood up to make one last announcement. Once again, he held up his mug of ale, but this time his face took on a somber expression.

"The past two years have been difficult for the family, trying to get Valhalla Farms back in business and creditors satisfied. As you're probably aware, this was due to miscommunication and rumors regarding a slave smuggling operation in the sea caves on our land. That situation has been cleared up and all evidence removed. As of tomorrow morning, just after dawn, I and some of my men will be setting explosives inside the caves to close the tunnels that have taken lives going back several generations. This is a warning to avoid the caves tomorrow, please. The process shouldn't take long. If you have questions beforehand, please ask. By this time tomorrow, slave smuggling on my property will be a thing of the past. Thank you."

Rather than clapping, voices rose in animated conversation.

Vor felt the ache in the back of her throat, her fingertips tingling. She turned to her mother. "What about the *Book of Delsiran*? Won't this destroy the book as well?"

Her mother drew her away from the table. "I haven't said anything—in case that is intended. This may be dangerous to ask of you, but ..."

"You want me to go before dawn tomorrow and locate the book and bring it to you for safekeeping?"

Eilidh hugged her daughter, looking vulnerable for the first time that Vor could remember.

"I'll take Luc, so he'll be there if anything goes wrong."

"You must be careful. Promise me."

Vor's thoughts flitted by. In the blink of an eye, she saw everything that went wrong this past year, ending with Gabriel's death. "I promise to be extra careful. Thank you for having faith in me."

Eilidh gulped and hugged her second daughter.

Vor had trouble sleeping, afraid she would awaken past dawn. She'd spoken to Luc the night before, and he wasn't too keen on the mission. But then, she couldn't explain how important the book was, nor what it contained that might feel threatening to certain men of power. Luc had to take this on faith, as well, and he wasn't as open to spontaneous acts as she might be.

She dressed in Erik's clothes and pulled on an old cloak to keep her warm. She and Luc proceeded quietly across the meadow and past the spot where Gabriel had plunged to his death. She refused to look in that direction, instead, heading down the footpath as the sun began its slow ascent. They had just enough time, so she didn't waste any of it in conversation on the way down. When they reached the sand and shoreline, she led the way.

Luc eyed the cliffs that might be affected, and his face grew pale.

When they stood in front of the large cavern opening, Vor hesitated to catch her breath.

"Are you sure about this?" he wanted to know.

She made a quick visual scan of the area. "I don't see any of my father's men here yet, so I'd say we have plenty of time."

He looked down and shook his head. "Let's just be quick and get this behind us." Before she crossed the bridge boulder, he put a hand on her shoulder. "Should one of us stay behind to watch for your father's men?"

"That might not be a bad idea."

He nodded, satisfied. "I'll ..."

"You wait here. This may require a bit of magic, so it has to be me. You give a shout inside if the men appear."

Luc didn't look pleased. But he already knew by now that when Vor wanted to do something, she did it. He nodded. "As soon as you come out, we take the footpath and get to higher ground."

"Good plan. I'm going in now."

"Vor ..."

She turned around, starting to feel impatient.

Before she could utter a word, he pulled her toward him and kissed her soundly. "Just in case you forget who's waiting for you on the outside."

Her face relaxed as a grin appeared. "I could never forget that face." She kissed him back, accepted a lit torch to light her way, then took off over the bridge and into the large cavern. She couldn't help questioning if leaving Luc outside the cave had been the right thing to do. But she had no more time to waste.

She'd remembered to bring *Fitheach* in its scabbard, and had hidden it beneath her cloak. "Good as new," she muttered, her eyes adjusting to the dark. She lit the torch from a small fire her father had kept going and walked briskly uphill to where the two tunnels split off. As she looked up, she could see the special wooden shoring where they would set a fire that would burn out the shoring and allow the tunnel to collapse and undermine the wall.

Focus, Vor!

She dashed down the left tunnel, counted to fifty, and stood before the shelf that had held the book previously. She'd lifted a piece of driftwood into place, and she lifted that out of her travel sack and put it before the shelves. Stepping on the stone, she reached her hand as far as it would go. Nothing.

Her hands began to shake. It had to be there. The prophecy said so. Her mother said so. Gabriel had said so—not that he could be trusted. *Think, Vor!*

She pushed the stepping stone the piece of driftwood as close to the shelf as possible. Standing on tip-toe, she reached all the way to the back right corner. No book. Back left corner. No book. And finally found the book. What had Gabriel said? *When the rare primrose is born.*

"Raven, help me out here. I must find the key to this riddle." He appeared on her right shoulder. *"You have the key. You do, you do!"*

"What key?" Vor glanced all about her and saw no key, in the traditional sense.

"Who *is the rare primrose?*"

She thought for a moment, realizing time was running out. "Well, Aila's filly, the daughter of ... *Primrose*. She has white, shiny fur, kind of like pearls. But I already knew that. That's why I'm here in the first place."

Raven hopped up and down on her shoulder. "Dig! Dig! Pearl can mean many things."

"And how am I supposed to know which meaning is correct?"

Raven "tsk-tsked" three times.

All of a sudden, it dawned on Vor. "The rare primrose *removed* the spell? Makes the book appear where it's been all this time?"

She reached up towards the center of the ledge and slowly pulled the book down. It crackled in her hands. Little round pieces of something that had been on the shelf came with the book. So tiny were some of them, they fell between her fingers and landed at her feet.

"And so you have them: cave pearls."

As she slid the book and its many loose pages into her sack, some of the rare cave "pearls" came free from the shelf and deposited in her sack as well.

She turned to thank Raven, but he was gone. She gave a pointed nod of respect and hurried out of the cave. When she found Luc right where she left him, her heart resumed its normal beat.

He reached for the sack. "You got it?"

"Yes. I had to solve a riddle of sorts ..." She'd started to add that her Spirit Guide had helped her, but re-thought that. She'd never talked to Luc about spirit guides and the Old Ways, and probably should stay mum on that. Too much room for misunderstanding.

Luc took Vor's hand and pulled her across the sand, keeping up a brutal pace until they reached the path leading up the cliff.

"I saw the explosions set and ready to light. Do you think it will be dangerous using this cliff path?" she thought to ask and glanced around for another exit.

"Let's race to the top, where we'll be safe."

Climbing the path was more difficult now, especially with Luc carrying her travel sack. She repeatedly offered to carry it, but his pride wouldn't allow for that. At one point, she stopped to catch her breath, and when she turned to look in the direction of the caves, she could distinguish her father among several men with torches near the cave entrance. When her father disappeared inside, she grabbed Luc by the edge of his cloak and hurried him up to the top. It felt like mere seconds when she felt the ground beneath their feet begin to shake.

"Let's stand away from the edge. If the blast is strong enough, this cliff could collapse." Vor had barely said the words and stepped back when two more explosions sent dirt and sand into the air, like spouts on a whale. She swept a tear away. "Nothing like smuggling slaves or illegal goods can ever happen here again. I just realized that. *Never* again."

Luc smiled and set down the travel sack so he could use both hands to squeeze hers. He kissed them for good measure.

"Vor, you're seventeen now. Would you..."

"Yes!" She didn't bother waiting, and threw her arms around him as the last set of explosives sent water into the air. Vor kissed him like she'd always wanted to, but didn't know how. "I want to marry you, Luc.

"I'm glad. We don't have to have a long engagement, unless you want to?"

"I want to move into my own home now. I'm ready."

He hugged her until she sighed into his neck.

When she was finally alone that night in her bedchamber, she opened her sack and discovered what appeared to be little cave pearls rolling around among her papers. They were the exact colors of Primrose's new filly: white on sparkly white. She'd read that Pearl represented innocence and modesty, and was a metaphor for rare, fine, admirable, and valuable. "Gem of the Sea." It was perfect.

Vor decided then and there that she would name her Perla.

Great-great-grandmother Saraid would have approved.

Vor smiled, secretly pleased.

Acknowledgments

I want to thank my amazing editor, Carol Craig, of The Editing Gallery, for keeping me on the straight and narrow for the plot. I could not do this without her guidance and suggestions. I admit there are times when this Aries girl gets the spark of an idea, and then Carol has to tell me when I'm over halfway through that it's no longer the same story!

A very special thanks to my brother, David, for his never-ending patience in trying to help me figure out the technical details in a digital age. I almost miss the old days of libraries with paper card catalogs and the smell of old books, and mailing paper manuscripts to an agent or publisher in a box big enough to hold them. Everything can be so much faster now, so that's all good. Meanwhile, if anyone has come up with a digital naming system to keep track of the many "final" versions of your manuscript, drop me a line: lainestambaugh@gmail.com. :)

Thank you, readers, for your enthusiasm and passion for historical fiction. I can't wait to see where we visit next in time and place.

(LS 12-09-24)

Author Bio

LAINE STAMBAUGH is a life-long learner of languages and interested in cultures around the world. She earned a bachelor's degree in Russian, and worked for several years in a community college library very close to what came to be called Little Saigon in southern California. Fascinated by differences in how people spoke, she pursued a master's degree in Linguistics, followed by a master's degree in library science. Her love of language and culture led her to a long career in academic libraries. Now retired, she writes full-time from her home in the Pacific Northwest, under the watchful eye of her tuxedo kitty, Minka. *The Sea Raven* is her third published novel, and is Book 3 of *The Heart Stone Trilogy*.